## THE PEOPLE INVOLVED

ranged from a dedicated Russian submarine commander and a ruthless political commissar to a beautiful woman whose body was at the service of her country, and a pair of half-Chinese agents who spoke perfect Russian and worked for the West . . . to mention but a few of the bizarre cast of characters . . .

## THE WEAPONS

extended from sexual seduction to drug-induced brain-washing . . . from the most sophisticated electronic snooping to the most brutal physical violence . . .

## THE WINNER

would be the side with the most savage swiftness and the fewest humane scruples—as a crippled giant of the deep became the prize of the most unforgettable undercover war of them all . . .

## THE ZHUKOV BRIEFING

*Don't even try to guess the shattering climax!*

"Highly-charged drama . . . nerve-wracking suspense!"
—*Josten's Reviews*

# THE ZHUKOV BRIEFING

## BY ANTONY TREW

POPULAR LIBRARY • NEW YORK

All POPULAR LIBRARY books are carefully selected by the POPULAR LIBRARY Editorial Board and represent titles by the world's greatest authors.

POPULAR LIBRARY EDITION
May, 1977

Copyright © 1975 by Antony Trew

Library of Congress Catalog Card Number: 74-83584

Published by arrangement with St. Martin's Press, Inc.

ISBN 0-445-08602-5

"There has been nothing in the past 20 years which has upset the balance of power so violently and so fundamentally as the emergence of the Soviet Union as the second largest naval power in the world, with a navy nearly twice as numerous as the combined navies of Britain, France, West Germany, Italy and Japan. This navy has become a force able to take part in any kind of war Russia desires, from an all-out nuclear conflict, to gun-running on behalf of local communist parties or their friends anywhere in the world."

David Woodward,
in *The Listener*, 7th November, 1974

# PROLOGUE

Entry in the movements log of the Flag Officer Commanding New Construction, USSR Baltic Fleet, Leningrad Naval Base:

*1st October, 1974—BMS Zhukov*

2035   *Zhukov* cleared submarine pens.

2102   *Zhukov* completed passage Morskoy Kanal.

2117   Forts Pavel and Pyotr report *Zhukov* crossing anti-submarine defence loop 47g.

2215   ASD, sonar and radar stations at Karavalday and Flotskiy report *Zhukov* crossing anti-submarine defence loop 23e.

2229   Guardship *Tolstoi* reports *Zhukov* clear of inner defences.

       *Note:* Refer signal log for message C-in-C, Baltic Fleet, repeated C-in-C Northern Fleet, reporting departure of *Zhukov* on familiarization patrol en route to

Office of the Commodore (Intelligence), Ministry of Defence (Navy), Whitehall:

Entry dated 4th October, 1974, in Top Secret file BMS/USSR/Delta Two/2713a: "Agent *Clematis* reports sailing of first operational Delta Two ballistic missile submarine *Zhukov* from Leningrad Naval Base during the night of October 1st. Believed bound Polyarnyo to join Seventh BMS Squadron, Northern Fleet. *Clematis* confirms structural and equipment defects revealed on summer sea trials now made good in *Zhukov* at Zhdanov Yard but work on *Timoshenko* unlikely to complete before end November. Principal defects in both apparently due technical problems welding new type alloys in pressure hull. *Clematis* regrets unable to obtain information on structure abaft bridge fin, twin blisters forward of tailfin, and missile warheads as directed last briefing and considers success unlikely in view exceptionally high security classification.

C-in-C Fleet, Northwood, informed 0917/4/—R/BMS/OPS."

# THE FIRST DAY

## *One*

Soon after midnight Krasnov's voice came through on the speaker: "Sonar bearing zero-two seven. Range eighteen kilometres. Classified single screw diesel. Bearing moving left."

In the dim red light of the control-room Sergei Yenev, captain of the *Zhukov*, transferred his attention from the systems console to the sonar screen repeater. With trained eyes he scanned the abstract patterns of light acquired by the submarine's transducers as they probed the sea ahead. To starboard the cluster of the Vesteralen Islands showed in a glowing broken line; an isolated neon speck fine on the bow was Vrakoy, the outermost of them all. In the few minutes since he'd last viewed the screen the only changes were those of relative movement. There were still five ships to starboard, two to port, and some smaller pips which had been classified as fishing boats.

Yenev watched the darting neon strobe which drew attention to the new contact: a pinpoint of light, glowing and fading like a firefly as it emerged from behind Vrakoy. *Zhukov*'s sonar range was sixty kilometres; but the contact, masked by the island, had been picked up at only eighteen.

The buzzer on the receiver bleeped. "Contact now zero-three-five, range sixteen kilometres, single screw diesel," announced a disembodied voice. "Check sound signature," ordered Yenev.

In the sonar room Ivan Krasnov's sensitive face broke into a grimace. Of course he'd check the sound signature. He was already doing it. Why did Yenev always order what was routine procedure as if he'd suddenly come up with an inspired idea? The young lieutenant's elegant fingers punched away at the computer keys with the ease and grace of a concert pianist. Seconds later he pulled the flexible neck of the mike closer and read aloud from the print-out. "Target's course and speed two-seven-three . . . speed seventeen knots . . . computer comparison with sound signatures of Soviet and NATO fleet auxiliaries negative repeat negative. Classification large single screw commercial tanker."

In the control-room Yeven acknowledged the report with a terse, "Good. Disregard. Resume normal scanning."

"Resume normal scanning," echoed Krasnov, jerking his chin outwards and upwards as if exercising his neck muscles.

Yenev decided to speak to Krasnov about the report later. The lieutenant should have given the sound signature first. That was what Yenev had ordered. It was top priority. Target data should have followed. Yenev respected Krasnov's ability. He was a good sonar and torpedo officer, but like many graduate entries his manner suggested that academic skills placed him in a category above the seamen officers who'd qualified in the naval academies. And so at times, among other things, he disregarded well tried naval procedures. What the captain didn't know was that Krasnov was unhappy in the navy. The young man wished fervently he'd taken a degree in arts and not physics. He was an intellectual, by nature a philosopher. But his father, a retired naval petty officer with understandable ambitions for his son, had more or less pushed him into physics and the navy.

Yenev scratched his sandy *en brosse* hair and shifted his attention to the plotting table. The head scratching was a familiar gesture. Because of it the crew called him "old dandruff", in spite of his thirty-five years and the conspicuous absence of dandruff from the blue collar of his uniform jacket.

A chart of the Norwegian Sea showed under the glass on the plotting table. An electronic trace-arm, fed by SINS, the ship's inertial navigating system, moved slowly ahead leaving a spidery line representing the submarine's track. It showed that *Zhukov* was keeping to seaward of the two hundred metre line as she moved up the Norwegian coast.

Sergei Yenev was a conscientious captain and though he knew that SINS with its fail-safe and back-up systems showed the exact geographical position of the submarine at any moment, when close to land he often double and treble checked the position by sonar, radar, and visual bearings at periscope depth.

The clock above the plotting table showed 0010. Next check at 0020, he reminded himself as he watched the flickering figures on the ocean-depth-recorder and compared them with those on the chart: 1440 ... 1500 ... 1620 ... metres.

"Good," he muttered. Yenev had the submariner's instinctive liking for deep water. *Zhukov* was on a northerly course, running parallel to the Vesteralen Islands which led on from the Lofoten Wall. Average distance of the land to starboard was 30 kilometres. They would pass within 15 kilometres of Vrakoy. Quite close enough, he decided. He was never happy near the land although they'd be in almost 1000 metres of water off Vrakoy. But it was important that the crew should have every opportunity of becoming familiar with *Zhukov*'s complex electronic systems and that was one reason why he was inshore. There was another, a more important one. Soviet Naval Intelligence believed there was an anti-submarine

11

minefield between Vrakoy and the island of Andoy to the west. *Zhukov*'s sonar could prove or disprove this if she came close enough inshore. Norwegian territorial waters extended 20 kilometres to seaward and, by taking his submarine within 15 kilometres of Vrakoy, Yenev would be infringing Norwegian territorial rights. Norway was highly sensitive about these but that was not Yenev's concern. He had his orders and would carry them out.

He went to the systems-state board and consulted the formidable array of gauges, dials and tell-tales, concentrating his attention on the flooding and pumping gauges, the flow meters and ballast tank readings. What he saw pleased him. During sea trials *Zhukov* had developed leaks in the pressure hull due to weld failures. Much time had been devoted to rectifying these at the Zhdanov Yard in Leningrad but despite the assurances of the base constructors and engineers, recollection of the defects still nagged at Yenev. A hull failure at depth was every submariner's nightmare.

"All well, comrade Yenev?"

The high-pitched voice at his shoulder caused him to stiffen involuntarily. It was Boris Milovych, the commissar and missile control officer. Though subordinate to Yenev in command, he was the most important man on board. Not only did he control the firing of the submarine's ballistic missiles but as *Zhukov*'s political commissar he represented the Party.

Yenev, very much the naval officer and a man with little time for politicians, resented the duality of command imposed by the system. Yet he had to make the best of it. Superficially the two men got on well enough, but each was resentful of the other's authority. Their inner tensions and frustrations had not yet boiled over but had somehow communicated themselves to the crew. This did not make for a happy ship. *Zhukov* was newly commissioned. Yenev wondered how their relationship would fare in the months ahead.

He nodded towards the instruments. "There is no evidence of leakage, comrade Milovych." What nonsense, he thought, having to call him "comrade". The man's rank was commander. Why not use it?

Milovych was plump and pink with deepset eyes. Pig's eyes, Yenev had long since decided. Milovych as it happened disliked Yenev's pale grey eyes. They conveyed no emotion, he would complain to himself; one never knew what the man was thinking.

"The dockyard's done a good job, then?" Milovych smiled enquiringly. He always smiled. It meant nothing. He could smile when speaking to a man whose career he'd just ruined with a confidential report.

"Yes. But ..." Yenev's reply was interrupted by a series of bleeps followed by a deep voice. "Control-room, torpedo compartment here. Request permission withdraw torpedo from number three tube for examination." It was Borchoi, the chief torpedo technician.

"What's the trouble, chief?"

"Routine maintenance, Captain."

"Very good. Shut all watertight doors and vents. Check bowcap. Reload without delay." Yenev knew that Borchoi would do these things anyway, but naval procedure demanded that the orders be given and Yenev was a stickler for naval procedure.

"Aye, aye, Captain."

Milovych smiled. He, too, knew that Borchoi would have done those things anyway. "You were saying comrade Yenev?"

Borchoi, a big bearlike man, looked round the torpedo compartment, past the torpedoes in their racks to the ram loading gear, on to the tube doors and instruments grouped above them on the forward bulkhead, then back to the men around him..

"Where's Somolov?"

"Gone to the heads, chief," said the leading torpedo technician. "Taken short."

"He's always taken short when there's work to be done. He's just come on watch. Why doesn't he do it in his watch below? Lazy little bastard." Borchoi sighed. "You'd better take over the loader, Gregorowski. Somolov can

13

mop up that oil under the maintenance cradle. Teach him not to piss off when there's work to be done."

Gregorowski moved into the loader seat, checked the hydraulic controls. "Ready, chief."

Borchoi looked over his shoulder. "Watertight doors and vents shut?"

"All watertight doors and vents shut, chief."

"Number three tube. Check bowcap. Test drain cock."

"Number three tube. Drain cock tested, bowcap shut, chief."

"Right," said Borchoi. "Number three tube. Withdraw torpedo."

Gregorowski repeated the order. The door to the tube space was opened. The hydraulic loader moved forward.

"Smell that?" challenged Borchoi, holding up a warning hand. Gregorowski stopped the loader.

The crewman sniffed in the direction of number three tube. "Hydrogen peroxide," said one of them.

"Leak from the pressure tank," said Borchoi.

"Or from Somolov," suggested a young crewman. There was a snigger.

"Can't be him," said another. "He's in the shithouse."

"Pack that in," Borchoi growled. "Let's get on with the job."

Gregorowski pulled the control lever. With a subdued hum the loader moved forward. The empty cradle rose level with number three tube. A torpedoman secured the extractor to the tail of the torpedo. "Extractor secured, chief," he reported.

"Carry on."

There was a thin whistle of compressed air. The torpedo slid slowly out of the tube on to the cradle which was lowered and drawn aft. The withdrawn torpedo was transferred to the maintenance cradle, and another loaded into number three tube. When this had been done Borchoi reported to the control-room, "Number three tube reloaded."

The report was acknowledged. Borchoi and his men set to work on the torpedo. With skilled hands he loosened the holding screws on the inspection plates before remov-

14

ing them from the motor and fuel compartments. To examine the valves on the fuel lines he had to lean forward. He suspected the cause of the gas leak would be found in the valve recess. The torpedo, the latest in use in the Soviet Navy, was propelled by a piston-type swashplate engine powered by high pressure gas driving a pump jet propeller. He had an instinctive dislike for the system. "Give me the old electric motors," he used to growl. "Can't beat them."

The compartment was well lit but Borchoi could not see clearly into the recess. "Inspection lamp," he called without looking up. A torpedoman took a wire-guarded lamp from its bracket, pulled at the spring-loaded lead and switched on the lamp. He moved across to Borchoi. "Lamp, chief."

Still leaning over the torpedo, head down as he peered into it, Borchoi lifted an arm to take the lamp. The torpedoman pushed it against the outstretched hand and believing it to be held let go. The lamp fell. There was a tinkle of broken glass. It was the last sound they were to hear for a thin ripple of flame was followed by a flash of yellow light and the roar of an explosion.

## Two

As Milovych went through the watertight door to the missile control centre, Yenev moved to the sonar screen. He was turning the scale to short range when the control-room shook violently, the lights went out and there was the subdued roar of an explosion. Yenev, thrown forward against the sonar screen, at first thought *Zhukov* had struck a mine.

The control-room reverberated with the sounds of disaster. The rattle of broken glass, the tinkle of metallic chips, the hiss of ruptured hydraulic and air pressure lines, the snap and crackle of electric circuits shorting, all mingled with the startled cries of men. The emergency lighting came on. Yenev and others who had fallen staggered to their feet. Crewmen, dazed by the shock, groped drunkenly for support and blood flowed from lacerated hands and faces.

Through a haze of smoke the deck could be seen to be littered with fragments of broken glass, metal and plastics from instrument panels, and paint flakes lay scattered like thin snow. Over this scene of chaos hung an invisible pall: the smell of burnt oil and smouldering rubber.

Within seconds of the explosion Yenev ordered, "Blow all main and trim tanks. Planes to hard-arise." From long habit he noted the time. It was eighteen minutes past midnight.

Feodotik, the chief technician at the diving systems console, repeated the order as he flicked switches with one hand and blood from his face with the other.

Stefan Lomov, the executive officer and second-in-command, came rushing into the control-room. The seated fore- and after-planesmen had their joy-sticks pulled fully back for hard-arise. Lomov, standing behind them, watched the depth, rate-of-rise, and trim gauges with intense concentration. The depth was decreasing: 140 metres . . . 127 . . . 105 . . . but it was doing so too slowly. The trim level showed *Zhukov* had not assumed anything like the bows-up angle she should have.

"Depth decreasing, Captain, but the response is slow. She's bow heavy."

Yenev said, "As long as she's rising all's well." His voice was steady and in the dim light he looked calm. He felt anything but that. There were many decisions to be made, many problems to be resolved. If the explosion had damaged the pressure hull he could reduce speed. But if he reduced speed the hydroplanes upon which so much

16

now depended would become less effective. And he still did not know the cause of the explosion or where it was, except that it appeared to be somewhere forward.

From the diving systems console Feodotik reported, "All tanks blown, Captain."

Yenev looked at the bilge alarm lights on the warning panel. The three red lights glowing among the line of green struck him between the eyes like a clenched fist. The bilges in three compartments were flooding: the torpedo, the air-conditioning and emergency generating spaces. The last two were on the lower deck, immediately forward of the watertight bulkhead to the missile compartment, well aft of the torpedo-compartment. So the damage was not localized. The force of the explosion had, he realized, generated a shock wave through the submarine the passage of which had been marked by whipping and straining of the hull. Immediately he thought of the welding defects revealed on sea trials.

He picked up the action mike. "Torpedo-compartment—Captain here." He repeated the call several times but there was no reply. He tested the circuit. It was alive. Instinctively, he knew that the explosion had taken place there. The torpedomen must have been killed or so severely injured that they could not answer.

Krasnov, his pale face drawn with fear, appeared at the captain's elbow. Yenev shouted at him. "There's been an explosion in the torpedo-compartment. It's flooding." He pointed to the lights on the warning panel. "Put an armed sentry on the watertight doors and shut all vents. Even if tapping is heard from the compartment the W.T. doors and air-conditioning vents must be kept shut." As Krasnov moved away Yenev added, "When we've surfaced we may be able to do something for them. If they're alive."

It went through his mind that he might well have said *if* we surface. It depended now on the rate of flooding and the extent to which *Zhukov*'s powerful pumps could cope with the inflow of water.

A stream of damage reports was coming into the control-room; some of them delayed by shorts, thrown

17

switches and other failures in communication circuits. The missile compartment, reactor, boiler and engine-rooms were intact but for damaged instruments and electrical and hydraulic failures caused by shock waves.

The main communications centre immediately abaft and one deck above the torpedo-compartment had been seriously damaged by a leak in the pressure hull, the throwing of various switches and circuit breakers and electrical fires. The carbon-dioxide extinguishers had operated automatically and the now gas-filled compartment had been evacuated. The communications officer and some of his men were preparing to re-enter with respirators but a number of tests and precautionary measures had first to be taken.

There were severe leaks through cable and pipe glands in the pressure hull in the air-conditioning room and in the emergency generating centre alongside it, though the two compartments were separated by a fore-and-aft watertight bulkhead. Chloride fumes were leaking from the storage batteries beneath the seamen's bunk-deck, and a confused report of damage in the emergency communications room on the main deck, abaft the missile control compartment, had just come in. Yenev decided to sort these out later. For the moment all his faculties were concentrated on getting *Zhukov* to the surface.

He picked up the telephone to the engine-room. Vladimir Ilyitch, the senior engineer officer, answered. Yenev said, "Captain here. Concentrate all pumping power on the torpedo-compartment. We're losing buoyancy forward. Difficulty in keeping the bows up."

"I'll harness everything we've got, Captain. She'll have to be taking a lot of water if that doesn't cope with it."

"She is taking a lot of water," said Yenev quietly.

He knew that if the pumps could discharge more water from the torpedo-compartment than it was receiving he'd get the submarine back to the surface. It would be time enough then to consider the other problems. In the meantime officers and technicians in various compartments would be doing all that could be done. They were well drilled in damage control. He only hoped they would come up to scratch now that they were faced with the real thing.

These thoughts fed into Yenev's mind like the input of a computer, just as the damage reports had registered there, been evaluated and the necessary decisions taken. Yenev had spent fifteen years in submarines and survived two disasters. He was as frightened now as any intelligent man would be, but that did not upset his judgement. To the men in the control-room he seemed a model of calm and resolution.

Still more reports were coming in. The shock of the explosion and the electrical failures it had caused had thrown the master gyros out of phase. This in turn had upset the running of the SINS, the navigational plot, the compasses and much other equipment fed by the gyros. Kulchev, the navigating officer, had already up-dated the submarine's position by dead-reckoning. When Yenev joined the young lieutenant at the chart-table he saw this. "You have done well, Kulchev," he said.

Yenev noted that Vrakoy, almost abeam, now bore 135 degrees, distant 15 kilometres. At once he ordered an alteration of course to starboard, towards the island. That meant making for shallower water while the fight to get Zhukov to the surface went on.

Boris Milovych, flabby face agitated, appeared in the control-room. He made for Yenev at the systems console. "What do you make of it, Yenev?" he mumbled, forgetting in his distress the "comrade". For once he was not smiling. There was nothing like the imminence of death to clear the commissar's mind. Here was a situation which was not in the least amusing and certainly one which no amount of political expertise was likely to clarify.

It was Yenev's moment and he knew it. "There's been an explosion in the torpedo-compartment. We are having difficulty in controlling the flooding."

Milovych's eyes bulged. "You mean . . . ?"

"I mean there have been failures in the pressure hull. Not only in the torpedo-compartment. Water is entering the main communications centre, the air-conditioning and emergency generating centres and the battery spaces."

19

"But what . . . I mean how has all this happened, comrade?"

"The explosion. The shock wave has shaken the whole ship. The welding must have failed in several places, probably around pipe and cable glands in the pressure hull. Maybe in the plating also. Where the shock was most severe."

"God help us." Milovych blanched, kneading his hands together. The reference to "God" caused Krasnov, who had just returned to the control-room, some surprise, worried and frightened as he was. It was not the Party line to invoke the aid of the Almighty. Krasnov liked neither the commissar nor the Party.

"What can we do?" In his distress Milovych again omitted the "comrade".

"I'm already doing it," said Yenev tersely. "But I'm too busy to explain." He swung away from the commissar. "How's the trim now, Lomov?"

The executive officer's eyes never left the instruments on the panel in front of the planesmen. The depth-gauge needles seemed to exert a hypnotic influence. "Depth 103 metres, Captain. We have some positive buoyancy. She's coming up slowly but . . ." he hesitated, ". . . the rate of rise is also decreasing slowly." They both knew what that meant. *Zhukov* was losing positive buoyancy.

Yenev picked up the telephone to the machinery control platform. "Machinery control, Captain here."

"Ilyitch here," came the senior engineer officer's voice.

"We are losing positive buoyancy. Are you pumping to full capacity yet?"

"About eighty per cent, Captain."

"What's the delay?"

"We're rigging and testing emergency power cables and pumping lines. It takes time, Captain."

"How much time?"

"Another five, ten minutes, maybe."

"We might get away with five. We won't with ten."

"We'll do our best, Captain." There was a note of desperation in Vladimir Ilyitch's voice. He and his team were working like men possessed. It was impossible to do more.

Yenev knew that too, but the urgency had to be driven home. The additional pumping power, once it was harnessed, could mean the difference between losing *Zhukov* and saving her. It was typical of Yenev that he thought of the disaster in terms of the ship rather than those in her.

He went across to Lomov. "We should have full pumping capacity soon. When we do we'll flood aft and see if we can't get the bows up a little."

He called Feodotik, "How are things looking now, chief?"

"Almost holding the water level in the torpedo-compartment, Captain. But we'll have to switch some pumping capacity soon. The air-conditioning and emergency generating centres are taking water. The battery spaces too."

"Much?"

"Nothing like the torpedo-compartment, Captain. But enough to be serious."

"Soon we'll have full capacity, chief. Then you can do something about them. Top priority now is the torpedo-compartment. We've got to get more water out than's coming in if we're to get the bows up. If we don't, we won't make the surface."

Feodotik nodded. "Yes, Captain." In the red light he looked as if he'd seen a ghost.

The bleep on the captain's phone sounded. He lifted the handset from its rack. "Captain speaking."

"Gallinin here, Captain. Radiation level in emergency communications room rising." Gallinin was the officer in charge of the atmospheric and radiation control centre. It was on *Zhukov*'s middle deck, immediately abaft the control-room. The console there contained a complex of systems relating to radiation and air-conditioning. Instruments fed by geiger counters and other devices recorded radiation in the seas through which the submarine travelled and measured radiation levels, temperatures, humidities and air pollution in all compartments.

21

Yenev shivered involuntarily. There was much about the new generation of ballistic missile submarines he liked and admired but not their radiation potential. It was a new hazard in an already hazardous environment. He tried to recall details of the confused report which had reached him earlier about damage to the emergency communications room. Something about an electrical fire?

"Any idea what's causing the trouble, Gallinin?"

"The emergency communications room is one deck above the reactor, Captain. The reactor screening is on the same deck."

"But there are watertight bulkheads between these compartments."

"Possibly the shock of the explosion has invalidated their integrity." It was like Gallinin to report in such formal jargon. He, too, was a graduate entry.

Yenev said, "Do what you can, Gallinin. Once we've surfaced things'll be easier."

"Yes, Captain."

Yenev swore as he hung up the phone. As if he hadn't enough problems without rising radiation levels.

## Three

In the minutes that followed much happened on board *Zhukov*. Some of it could be chronicled for it was seen, but much was anonymous: the struggle of small groups of men, hidden away in watertight compartments, to repair damaged circuits, fractured pressure lines and electronic systems which had gone off stream.

The efforts of Ilyitch and his team had resulted in the application of full pumping capacity to the torpedo-compartment less than four minutes after Yenev's order. As the level of the water fell the after trim tanks were flooded and the bow-heavy trim of the submarine corrected. For a time positive buoyancy had been lost and *Zhukov* had begun a slow descent. But full pumping power gradually checked that and at 0031 by the chart-table clock came Lomov's long awaited report. "Periscope depth, Captain."

"Hold her there," said Yenev.

A sigh of relief like the sound of a small wave breaking came from the men in the control-room. Faces which had been drawn with fear relaxed into smiles and knowing nods as if the men were saying, "I told you he'd get us back to the surface."

Yenev's sharp, "Up periscope," broke the euphoric spell.

As the big instrument rose from its well he snapped down the training handles and looked into the eyepiece.

Despite every attempt by technicians to repair the damage done by the shock wave, the sonar, radar and SINS systems were still unserviceable. To bring a submarine almost the size of a cruiser to the surface without them, made the operation a particularly hazardous one in busy waters. Yenev, well aware of this, carried in his mind a picture of what had appeared on the sonar screen before it failed: to the eastward the long line of the Vesteralen Islands; Vrakoy, the island outpost; the five ships to starboard and two to port; the scatter of fishing vessels. But there had been relative movement since then, including *Zhukov*'s turn of seventy degrees to starboard, and he wondered what the periscope might reveal.

It stood high above the water and he was able in a quick sweep to cover the sea around the submarine to a range of at least thirty kilometres. It was a dark moonless night but the powerful lenses showed many lights. Mostly these were land lights from the islands, but some were those of ships and fishing boats.

Yenev said, "Plot these lighthouse bearings as I call them."

From the chart-table Kulchev replied, "Ready, Captain."

Yenev trained the periscope, steadied it on a flashing light. "Distant light—flashing white and red—fifteen second intervals—bears that . . ."

"One-eight-three," called the seaman on the bearing indicator.

There was a moment's pause before Kulchev reported from the chart-table. "That's Frugga on Langoy, Captain."

"Distant light occulting white, red and green, bears that . . ."

"One-four-seven," said the seaman.

Kulchev laid the bearing off on the chart. "That's Anda, Captain."

"Medium range—light flashing white—ten second intervals."

"That's the Fyrbergnes light on Vrakoy, Captain."

"Give me a position," demanded Yenev.

Kulchev ran the parallel rulers across to the compass rose, plotted the last of the three bearings, drew a neat circle round their point of intersection and noted it against the time. "Position, Captain. Three-two-zero Fyrberg light, distant twelve kilometres."

"Depth of water?"

"One-zero-eight-five metres."

Yenev executed a final sweep with the periscope. "Surface, Lomov. Bring her up."

A tremor of excitement swept through the control-room. It was reflected in the executive officer's voice as he repeated the order they'd waited for so long. Soon afterwards he called, "Surfaced, Captain. Bridge is clear," adding quickly, "The trim's still not right. She remains bow heavy."

"Steer one-one-zero. Twelve knots." Yenev betrayed no emotion but he experienced profound relief. The prototype of the USSR's new Delta Two class ballistic missile submarine, technically well in advance of its US rival, with a crew of one hundred and twenty highly skilled men, a battery of nuclear missiles capable of taking out sixteen of the world's largest cities, had been brought to the surface after a brief but epic struggle. That she was just commissioned with a fresh crew confronted with the intricacies of new and complex systems made the achievement all the more remarkable. Yenev was too much of a realist to believe the struggle was over. *Zhukov*'s situation remained precarious. To battle for survival on the surface was, however, infinitely better than to do so hundreds of metres beneath it.

On Yenev's orders the lower-hatch was opened and he began the long climb up the steel ladders inside the tower. When he reached the upper-hatch he withdrew the safety bolts, unfastened the clips and opened it. Steadying himself against the rush of warm air from below as pressure inside *Zhukov* was released, he stepped on to the small bridge at the fore end of the conning-tower or "fin" as it was known in the submarine service. Two-way berthing radio, a voice-pipe and telephone on running leads were brought to him by the chief signalman, the bridge navigation lights were switched on, and Kulchev joined him.

To the three men on the bridge the night air had never seemed sweeter, more exhilarating, more welcome—and the scatter and twinkle of lights ahead, the evidence of communities, of normality, of a warm safe world, was reassuring beyond belief. They no longer felt helpless and alone.

The submarine rolled slowly in the swell which came in from the north-west, and a chill breeze ruffled the sea. Ahead of the fin, many metres below them, the steel casing lost itself in foam which creamed and tumbled as the whale-like bow thrust through the sea.

To counter the heaviness forward, Yenev had ordered twelve knots, and hydroplanes to hard-arise. He had done so reluctantly because the greater the speed the more likely it was that external damage to the pressure hull could be increased. But he had no option for it had already become essential to divert some pumping power

25

from the torpedo-compartment to the bilges farther aft where water was rising to unacceptable levels.

The beam of light showed no external damage other than a slight, scarcely-visible fracture in a weld some distance along the casing forward of the huge fin which dominated the superstructure.

Yenev said, "See that? Above the main communications centre?" But the real damage, that which promised the greatest danger was, he knew, in the torpedo-compartment. It could not be seen because the bows were almost submerged.

## Four

Shortly after surfacing Yenev handed over the bridge-watch to Lomov. Back in the control-room he summoned a conference of key officers. To it came Vladimir Ilyitch, the senior engineer officer; Krasnov, the torpedo and sonar officer; Yusof, the missile systems officer; Uskhan, the communications officer; Gallinin, the atmospheric control officer; Feodotik, the chief diving systems technician. And, of course, Boris Milovych, the commissar.

Yenev was brief and to the point. "There is little time. First a quick summary of the damage state. Commissar?"

The muscles in Milovych's face twitched. "My staff tell me there is no serious damage in the missile-compartments and systems. There are certain electrical and hydraulic failures which they are working on and some damaged instruments. You have no real cause for worry on account of my department."

Smug bastard, thought Yenev. Everyone in the subma-

26

rine knew that the real responsibility and technical know-how for the ship's missilry came under Yusof and his assistant, Vatutin. Yenev turned to Krasnov. "Your department?"

"The torpedo-compartment remains sealed off, Captain. There is no evidence of life there. We still do not know what caused the explosion. It was not a warhead."

"Obviously," said Yenev dryly. "We wouldn't be here if it was. Continue."

Krasnov jerked his chin nervously. He was only doing his duty. The captain's comment was surely unnecessary. "Using eighty-five per cent capacity, the pumps are just containing the inflow of water. The remaining fifteen per cent has been diverted to other bilges. The sonar systems are still unserviceable. The transducers have suffered severe shock. They are close to the torpedo-compartment."

Yenev's mouth shut in a tight line. He nodded towards the senior engineer officer. "You, Ilyitch?"

"The main motor rooms, the turbo generators, secondary propulsion units, the boiler and reactor rooms, hydraulic power plants and auxiliary machinery spaces are in reasonably good shape. Various circuit and pressure line failures, of course—damaged switchgear and blown fuses. Also some minor leaks from glands in the pressure hull. But there is serious damage in the air-conditioning and emergency generating centres on the lower deck forward of the missile-compartment."

"Briefly, what's the trouble?"

"A big inflow of water. Must have been a failure in the pressure hull welding under both compartments. At first I thought it came from leaks through cable and pipe glands. But it's more than that. Whatever it is, the inflow is increasing. The fracture is probably extending."

"Has it been possible to make any sort of detailed examination?"

Ilyitch shook his head. "Impossible. The break is in the bilges themselves. Possibly between frames. But there is another complication."

"For Christ's sake, what's that?"

27

The commissar made a mental note of Yenev's blasphemy. The Party didn't like that sort of thing. A bad example to the men. Effete religious habits asserting themselves in times of crisis.

Yenev's pale eyes held Ilyitch's. "Go on," he said.

"Chloride fumes from the battery spaces are leaking into the air-conditioning and emergency generating compartments. Also into the seamen's bunk-deck. We have evacuated those compartments, but for men with respirators who are checking the extent of the damage."

"Any idea of that extent?"

"Not really. We've had to shut down the air-conditioning plant and emergency generators."

"Can you get them going again?"

"Not without dockyard or other outside assistance."

"So," said Yenev grimly. "Nothing but disaster. Has no one a favourable report? What about communications, Uskhan?"

The dim red light of the control-room emphasized the communications officer's Mongolian features. "The situation in my department is very serious, Captain. There is a leak in the pressure hull over the main communications centre. Water flooding in and the shock of the explosion started numerous electrical fires. The carbon-dioxide cylinders operated automatically. The compartment was then evacuated and sealed off. Later I went in with my senior technician. We had respirators. The damage is considerable. There is no possibility of on-board repair of the transmitters. There will have to be complete stripping and overhaul of the entire system."

"And the emergency communications aft?"

Uskhan shook his head. "No better, Captain. There was a bad electrical fire there. The shock of the explosion, you know. It broke circuits, threw switches, blew fuses and . . ."

"I know." Yenev held up a hand. "What's the damage?" He asked the question calmly but they all knew what he was thinking.

"Again, the carbon-dioxide extinguishers functioned at once. The watchkeeper had to evacuate and seal off the

28

compartment. Now there is a serious radiation leak there. From the reactor room."

Yenev switched to the atmospheric control officer. "What's the situation there, Gillinin?"

"Bad, Captain. The radiation level is rising steadily. I sent a man in. Fully protected, of course. Apart from the radiation problem, he reports extensive fire damage. I understand a lot of the equipment has melted from excessive heat. He says it's a shambles."

"Why did you not go in yourself, comrade Gallinin?" Milovych smiled as he put the question.

"Because he is not allowed to," snapped Yenev.

"Why not, comrade Yenev?" The fat man's parted lips revealed uneven yellow teeth.

"Because the radiation control officer is the only man in *Zhukov* who knows everything worth knowing about controlling radiation. We can't *afford* to lose him."

"This is something we may have to look into." Milovych rubbed his hands together slowly. "I would imagine . . ."

"By all means do so, commissar. In the meantime I would remind you that every second counts." He turned to the communications officer. "So we have no means of communication, Uskhan?"

The Mongolian's long fingers clenched and unclenched. He was a clever nervous young man and feared the captain. He felt somehow that the extent of damage in his department might reflect upon his professional competence. "No means at present, Captain. But for the submarine indicator buoys." These were the emergency buoys which *Zhukov* could release if she were trapped on the bottom. They would surface and transmit SOS signals automatically. Surface vessels and land stations receiving them would take radio bearings and locate the sunken submarine.

"They're no good," snapped Yenev. "We've got thirty minutes, perhaps. Our need is to talk at once to Naval HQ in Leningrad or Murmansk—or at least with other Soviet warships at sea. Not to send out SOSs."

"What about the radio berthing sets?" suggested Milovych.

"Useless," said Yenev. "Their range is about twenty kilometres."

Vladimir Ilyitch had been talking in undertones with Feodotik. He broke in. "Chief Feodotik has just been examining the bilge and tank gauges and flow meters. Using our full pumping capacity—where it is most needed and switching as necessary—we can do no more than keep *Zhukov* afloat for between thirty and forty minutes. Forty at best. Thirty at worst. That is our belief."

Yenev focused his pale eyes on Milovych. "Commissar, we must now, at once, make a decision. The alternatives are simple. Either we make for deep water, set the charges, abandon *Zhukov* and blow her up . . ." He paused to let the words sink in. "Or . . ."

"Or . . . ?" Milovych's mouth twitched like a child on the verge of tears. There were no smiles now. He was already wondering what his political masters might think of any decisions he made. It was unfair, he reflected. He should be able to consult with them. Outline the facts. Let them make the decision. There must be gross inefficiency on board. How could both communication systems have been destroyed? How was it that the most modern, the most powerful ballistic missile submarine in the world was without means of communication of any sort?

"Or . . . ?" he again demanded.

"Or we make for the nearest land—that's the island of Vrakoy—with the chance of grounding *Zhukov* there." Yenev's eyes challenged the commissar.

"What? On Norwegian territory? NATO territory?" The commissar swept his arm round the control-room in a dramatic gesture. "This submarine. With its new weapons, new electronics. Secrets our enemies would give anything . . . I mean *anything* . . . to obtain. You don't know what you're saying, comrade Yenev."

Yenev continued to stare at the commissar. "Well, perhaps while we sink you'd like to think up alternatives." His mouth tightened in the hard line the crew were getting to know. "Let me assure you, however, there are none.

Now listen. If we destroy *Zhukov* we not only deprive the USSR of the Soviet Navy's most powerful warwhip ... the prototype of a new class of eighteen ... but we destroy the evidence of the hull failures and we destroy the possibility of ascertaining the cause of the explosion. Evidence which is vital to our designers and constructors. Do you understand the implications?" He looked at the commissar as if he'd like to throttle him, which happened to be how he felt. He added, "Also, though I agree it is of little importance, if we destroy *Zhukov* and take to inflatable life-rafts ... well these sudden October gales ... you know ... get caught in one of them and you can say goodbye to life or anything else important to you." Yenev thought it likely that argument might impress the commissar.

"But if we ground the ship on Vrakoy ... on Norwegian territory ... that is to say on NATO territory ... What then? Think of the security risks."

"Yes," agreed Yenev. "They exist. But let's examine them objectively. Norway is anxious to maintain good relations with her powerful neighbour. That's us—the Soviet Union. Norway's a member of NATO but on qualified terms. She will not, for example, permit NATO troops or NATO nuclear weapons on Norwegian soil. There is, and long has been, mutual respect between the Russian and Norwegian peoples. Particularly in the north, in Finnmark, where there has been inter-marriage."

"True," said Milovych looking mollified. "Very true."

"And," Yenev continued, "the Norwegians have never forgotten that it was Soviet arms which liberated them from German occupation in the Second World War."

"So ..." Milovych challenged, once again showing the authority appropriate to his position.

Yenev looked at him with contempt. He could read the man like a book. "You should understand the political implications better than I, comrade commissar." Yenev emphasized the "comrade". "But let me deal with the practical aspects. When we have grounded *Zhukov*—that is to say, if we succeed in doing so—we will at once inform Leningrad of the situation."

31

"How?"

"Through our embassy in Oslo. Using Norwegian channels of communication. I've no doubt our Navy will at once deploy massive assistance. I'm equally certain that the Soviet Government will, as its first priority, request the Norwegian Government to assist and protect us in every way." Yenev paused. "But I must apologize. I'm trespassing on your area of authority. The political problem. I deal only with the naval one. Now ..." Yenev's voice hardened and the pale eyes narrowed. "What do we do?"

Boris Milovych pulled at his cheeks with the thumb and forefinger of one hand, drawing down the skin until the lower eyelids revealed the pink membraneous tissue. This was for him a signal of extreme distress. "I wonder," he mumbled. "I wonder what is best?"

"You mean you wonder what the Kremlin will think?" suggested Yenev.

"No. No. Not at all. I am balancing the advantages and disadvantages of the actions open to us, comrade."

"Well, you'll have to do it pretty quickly, commissar. This submarine is sinking. The Kremlin won't thank you for that."

Boris Milovych smiled. I'll get the bastard for that, he thought. I'll get him sooner than he thinks. But he said, "Comrade Yenev. What do *you* feel we should do?"

Yenev said, "Neither course is easy. But I believe it is our duty to make every attempt to save *Zhukov*. The only chance of doing that is make for Vrakoy."

Vladimir Ilyitch's deep voice broke into the sudden silence. "Captain. We have now only twenty-five to thirty-five minutes in which we can remain afloat."

Yenev looked at the clock over the chart-table, then back at Ilyitch. "You are right. Now. Tell me. Can we safely increase to fifteen knots? If so it will assist in two ways. First, it will help to keep the bows up. Second, it will cut down the time taken to reach Vrakoy."

Ilyitch thought for a moment. "I cannot say whether it will be safe, Captain. We do not know the nature or location of the damage. It may be dangerous. It may make

32

little difference. Why not try fifteen knots? We can always reduce."

Yenev touched the engineer officer's shoulder. "Well said, Vladimir." They were old friends. He went to the chart-table, looked at the large scale chart of the Vesteralen Islands, and consulted the Soviet Navy's *Pilotage Guide to the Norwegian Sea*. He saw that Vrakoy, a mountainous island rising steeply from the sea, was shaped like a prawn. Strangely twisted about its long east-west axis, it was ten kilometres in length with an average width of two. The southern side was heavily indented by the bay at Uklarvik, and by Kolfjord. At the head of Kolfjord, recorded the *Pilotage Guide*, would be found the fishing harbour and village of Kolhamn which supported the local community. The principal activity was fishing. It occurred to Yenev that Vrakoy—Wreck Island— was well named. How many wrecks, he wondered, had this craggy islet claimed?

Abandoning those thoughts, he checked the features of the western end of the island, that which lay closest to the *Zhukov*. It was dominated by a mountain, Fyrberg, of which the highest peak was Bodvag. The mountain's south-westerly slopes led down to the lighthouse at Fyrbergnes, the north-westerly to a line of rocks off Knausnes. The safest course, he decided, would be to get *Zhukov* into the bay at Uklarvik. Ground her at its head where the water shoaled in a small inlet. But to get there would add ten kilometres to the distance. There wasn't time for that. Yenev decided to make for the light at Fyrbergnes. In that way he would keep his options open. With luck they might just succeed in rounding Fyrbergnes and making the shelter of Uklarvik. If they couldn't, he'd have to head for the rocks off Knausnes. The large scale chart showed a long rockshelf to the south and west of these with water of a more-or-less even depth over it. An indentation at its north-east corner bit into the foot of the cliffs. It was an unpleasant alternative for the rocks were exposed to the north-westerly gales which blew at that time of year. But beggars couldn't be choosers.

The decision made, Yenev laid a course for Fyrbergnes.

"Steer one-five-zero," he ordered. "Revolutions for fifteen knots."

The coxswain was repeating the order when Boris Milovych's high-pitched voice interrupted. "I must request, comrade Yenev, that the decision to make for Vrakoy be recorded in the log-book as yours. Taken after I had drawn attention to the grave security risk involved in grounding on the territory of a NATO power. It must also be recorded, please, that I withdrew my opposition solely on account of your professional advice."

"By all means," said Yenev. "Record it yourself. Anything you like. Important to keep one's yard-arm clear."

"My yard-arm," Milovych smiled uneasily. "What has that to do with it, comrade Yenev?"

"Nothing," snapped Yenev irritably. "Nothing you'd understand." Turning to the navigating officer he said, "Bring up the chart and pilotage guide, Kulchev. We go now to the bridge." Yenev looked at his watch. It was 0027.

## Five

Much to Yenev's concern *Zhukov* was not able to maintain fifteen knots. The submarine had covered no more than three kilometres when Ilyitch reported the inflow of water to be increasing. Yenev at once reduced to twelve knots. Even that proved too much. Soon afterwards he ordered ten.

He and Kulchev stood shoulder to shoulder on the small bridge, the easterly wind cold in their faces. The darkness of the night intensified by a cloud-covered sky, was relieved by the lights of ships and the wink and glitter of those of the Vesteralen Islands. On second thoughts Yenev ordered the *Zhukov*'s steaming lights to be switched off. There was no point in advertising the presence of the submarine. It was upon the flashing lights of Langoy, Anda, Fyrberg and Andness that the two men concentrated. The navigating officer, head and shoulders in the chart recess beneath the bridge screen, plotted the position of the submarine as Yenev called the compass bearings.

Normally this would have been done in the control-room. Now, with so much equipment damaged, Yenev had decided the bridge would be better. To assist the task of pilotage, a leading seaman in the control-room sent up a steady stream of readings from the ocean depth-recorder.

"Position, Kulchev?" Yenev asked for the fourth time in as many minutes.

"One-six-seven Fyrberg light, distant seven kilometres, Captain."

"Distance to Uklarvik?"

"Eleven point four kilometres, Captain."

Yenev looked at the luminous dial of his wristwatch and did some mental arithmetic. The bridge phone bleeped. "Lomov here, Captain. We continue to lose buoyancy. I believe we have at most twenty minutes left." The executive officer's voice, normally calm, betrayed anxiety.

"Very well," Yenev sighed with resignation. "We shall make for Knausnes." He turned to Kulchev. "Alter course for Knausnes. Make allowance for the north-going stream. It's close to high water." Thank God for that, he thought. It would at least help to get *Zhukov* on to the rockshelf. Kulchev acknowledged the order. Yenev spoke again to Lomov. "Have the inflatable skimmer made ready for launching. Two seamen to stand by to man her. Give them a radio berthing set, a battery-powered signal lamp and a hand lead-line. Kulchev will take charge. As we approach the shoal water near the rocks, Kulchev will station the skimmer five hundred metres ahead, report sound-

35

ings on the rockshelf and lead us in. It may not help much but it will be better than nothing."

"Yes, Captain," said Lomov. "I'll organize that at once."

For a moment the captain's thoughts ran away with him. The situation was a nightmarish one. The huge submarine lumbering through the dark northern night, rolling slowly to the incoming swell, her buoyancy and with it her life ebbing away with each minute that passed; ahead the rocky shelf on to which he was conning his command in a desperate effort to save her. Would he wake to find it was no more than a horrific dream brought on by indigestion? His thoughts were interrupted by the bridge lookout's urgent, "White light bearing red-four-zero. Close."

Yenev trained his night glasses to port. A swinging white light had appeared on the port bow. Soon, faint green and red side-lights showed up and he heard the throb of a diesel engine. It was a small fishing boat which had just come clear of the rocky headland at Knausnes. The light at Fyrbergnes was an automatic one, unattended; there were no witnesses there. But this fishing boat was an unwelcome complication.

It came closer and a voice hailed them from the darkness. Yenev at once ordered Krasnov who spoke fluent Norwegian to come to the bridge with a loud-hailer. "Ask him what he wants," said Yenev.

Krasnov shouted the message through the loud-hailer and a reply came rumbling across the water.

"What's he saying, Krasnov?"

"Warning us that we're making for the rocks off Knausnes. Only a few kilometres ahead."

"Tell him to keep clear. Say we know what we are doing."

Krasnov relayed the message. Again a shouted reply drifted over the water.

Krasnov said, "He says we must be mad, Captain."

Yenev swore softly. "Don't blame him. But tell him to keep clear. Say we are full of explosives. That'll frighten him off."

It did. The fishing boat passed astern, chugged away

into the dark night. Yenev saw that it was making for Fyrbergnes. He said, "Returning to Kolfjord, I expect." He knew that the story of a giant submarine without navigation lights heading for the rocks off Knausnes would soon be out. But there was nothing he could do about that. More urgent matters demanded attention.

When Kulchev reported the rockshelf to be only three and a half kilometres ahead, Yenev ordered, "Stop main engines. Keep her steady on one-four-zero."

In the control-room the coxswain repeated the orders and the rhythmic hum of the turbines ceased. The sound of breakers ahead could be heard clearly on the bridge. From the chart recess Kulchev called, "Two and a half kilometres to go, Captain."

Yenev said, "Carry on in the skimmer, Kulchev. You know what to do."

The navigating officer' left the bridge. Yenev ordered the signalman to train an Aldis lamp along the fore-casing. Although he'd expected it, he was alarmed at the extent to which the submarine was down by the bows. The forward hydroplanes were no longer visible and sea swirled around the foot of the huge sail-like fin.

If confirmation were needed that the submarine was sinking there it was.

When Kulchev reached the after-casing he found it almost awash. Most of the crew had mustered there. Huddled in a long line in the darkness, they were holding on to a wire which had been rigged from the tail stabilizing fin to the after end of the conning-tower. It was evident to Kulchev that *Zhukov* was unlikely to remain afloat much longer.

The leading hand reported that the skimmer was ready for launching. Kulchev informed the bridge by radio berthing set. Yenev ordered, "Slow astern together." When way was almost off the submarine, the skimmer was lowered over the side. Kulchev and two seamen boarded her. With a sound like a buzz-saw the outboard engine came alive and the skimmer passed quickly up the side of *Zhukov* to take station ahead. From the submarine's bridge nothing could be seen but the glow of the small craft's stern light.

Yenev increased revolutions until *Zhukov* was moving through the water at three knots. He was talking to Kulchev by voice-radio when the bridge phone bleeped. It was Lomov. "We can't keep her afloat much longer, Captain. We have perhaps only a few minutes."

Yenev acknowledged, swore with anxiety and concentrated on the bobbing stern light ahead.

In the skimmer Kulchev switched on the Aldis lamp and searched the darkness with its powerful beam. The effect was dramatic. A chain of jagged rocks seemed suddenly to leap from the sea ahead and to port.

Yenev did not know that Vrakoy's fishermen knew them as the Dragetennene—the Dragon's teeth. Beyond them loomed the rocky cliffs of Knausnes. Around and to the south and west of the Dragetennene, the sea swirled and foamed on an invisible rockshelf. Kulchev steered for that part of it which lay in the lee of the rocks. There the sea was least disturbed.

*Zhukov* was now so deep in the water that she needed at least fourteen or fifteen metres under her keel if she were not to touch bottom before grounding. Using the signal lamp as a probe Kulchev edged the skimmer forward while providing Yenev with a running commentary by radio. "The leadsman has not found bottom yet," he reported. "But it won't be long now. We're coming to shoal water in the lee of the big rocks. I see what looks like a small cove between two lines of shallow rocks and am heading for it. Steer about ten degrees to starboard."

Soon afterwards the seaman on the leadline called out, "Twenty-five metres, Lieutenant." Kulchev reported the sounding to Yenev. They had left the deep water and were now over the shelf. The broken shoal water shook and buffeted the skimmer, whirls and eddies making steering difficult. But Kulchev clung to the tiller, making for the centre of the cove. The leadsman, kneeling to steady himself, kept the lead going. The soundings he called revealed that the depths over the rockshelf had become fairly constant. The tallow in the heel of the lead kept showing sand. Because Kulchev knew that was of enormous importance, his voice rose when he reported, "We are in the cove now, Captain. The bottom is sand, repeat sand. We have already traversed half its length and so far the bottom is sand."

Quickly Yenev asked, "How many metres is that, Kulchev?"

"About two hundred, Captain. Depths over the first fifty metres were between twenty and twenty-five metres. After that between fifteen and sixteen meters. Still shoaling."

"Right," came the reply. "It'll have to do. Stay in position over the point where you think our bows should ground."

"Will do, Captain."

Moments later a beam of light from *Zhukov*'s bridge pierced the darkness, picked up the skimmer and held it.

To Yenev on the bridge the light revealed not only the skimmer but the chain of jagged rocks reaching out dark and sinister from Knausnes. Beyond them steep cliffs towered over the submarine as she edged her way in.

*Zhukov* was still in deep water, wallowing more than rolling in the north-westerly swell. Yenev steadied the bows on the skimmer's white light and ordered, "Stop main engines." Then, "Slow astern." He waited in a sweat of anxiety as the shallow rocks lining the cove came slowly towards them. Several times he gave wheel and engine orders to keep the submarine heading up the centre of the cove. Much depended, he realized, upon the sand Kulchev had reported. Was it a thin layer over a rocky bottom, or was it something more? A really sandy bottom, perhaps. That would be the only good fortune which had come *Zhukov*'s way that night.

"The water is shoaling rapidly now, Captain," came Kulchev's urgent report. "We have covered about one hundred and fifty metres of the cove. I am stopping."

Yenev acknowledged, stopped engines and waited, helpless. The *Zhukov* was committed. There was nothing more he could do. Soon she seemed almost to have stopped but the illusion was dispelled when the sunken bow lifted and she lurched, rumbled and shuddered along the bottom she'd touched sooner than expected. The bow-down trim and the swell had done that. The impact was softened by the sand but each incoming swell lifted the huge hull and pushed it forward, and with each onward lurch the submarine trembled as if in the grip of a giant hand. From the control-room beneath the bridge came the clatter and rattle of loose gear being thrown about.

To Yenev it seemed that the *Zhukov* would never come to rest. In fact less than two minutes elapsed between the first impact and the final grounding.

Having ordered Kulchev to take soundings round the submarine, Yenev went down to the control-room. The crew on the after-casing had returned to their normal stations and reports of damage state were coming in from various compartments. It was evident that the hull forward had suffered, but not as much as Yenev had feared. He concluded that the strength of the pressure hull and the apparent smoothness of the rockbed under the sand had combined to minimize the damage on impact.

He recorded in the log-book that the submarine had been stranded in a cove south of Knausnes at 0047 in accordance with the decision taken earlier. "The stern, for a distance of approximately twenty metres, is overhanging the edge of the rockshelf at the entrance to the cove," he wrote. "But she is not working unduly in the prevailing weather. It is now within a few minutes of high water."

As the tide fell she would, he knew, settle more firmly.

The only satisfaction he could derive from an otherwise disastrous situation was that wind and sea were moderate, and the rocks off Knausnes provided more of a lee than he'd expected. But *Zhukov* still shook and trembled as the swell, its main force broken by the Dragetennene, surged into the cove.

Yenev called his officers together in the control-room. There a lengthy discussion took place on the problems associated with maintaining the submarine, her machinery,

40

equipment and living conditions in reasonable shape until assistance arrived.

Later, to decide how best to get that assistance, he asked Boris Milovych to his cabin.

It was several hours after midnight before they concluded their discussions. These ranged over a wide field: the overriding need to communicate with Soviet naval bases in Leningrad or Murmansk; the security arrangements to protect the submarine and her secrets; the extent of the damage suffered and possibilities of salvage. If salvage were not possible, all classified equipment and radio-active material would have to be removed or destroyed, and the submarine blown up. Ultimately these would be matters for naval headquarters and the Soviet salvage experts to decide. There was the highly complicating factor that *Zhukov* was stranded on Norwegian soil. That, they knew, was a matter the USSR and Norway would have to settle on a government-to-government basis. And there was the NATO involvement.

Throughout the remaining hours of darkness *Zhukov*'s men were busy surveying the damage, carrying out emergency repairs and restoring interrupted services. Pumping was maintained at full capacity, but with positive buoyancy now gone the submarine had settled firmly on the bottom of the cove. Nevertheless, it was still vital to control flooding as far as possible, particularly in view of the high tides which would be experienced. Skin divers went down to the flooded bilges and compartments to examine and report on damage, and Ilyitch and his technicians considered ways and means of checking the inrush of water by temporary patching.

On Yenev's orders the watertight doors and vents to the torpedo-compartment were kept shut since the bows had been further damaged by grounding and the flooding in that compartment could no longer be contained. Armed sentries were posted on the bridge and on the casing at the foot of the fin. Sonic buoys were lowered to port and starboard, a listening watch instituted and two armed scuba divers maintained a continuous anti-swimmer under water patrol around the hull of the submarine.

Yenev intended to make things difficult for underwater snoopers.

## Six

Shortly before first light the skimmer left the *Zhukov* and set off for Kolhamn on the south-eastern side of the island.

It was manned by two seamen with a sub-lieutenant in charge, and had as passengers Boris Milovych and Ivan Krasnov. Krasnov had been selected for his fluent Norwegian, high level of intelligence and known reliability. With the torpedo and sonar systems out of action and beyond shipboard repair, there was little point in keeping him on board.

It had been agreed with Yenev that Milovych would contact the local authority in Kolhamn and through him transmit to Soviet Naval HQ the message which the captain and the commissar had prepared. It was in code and contained details of the stranding, a non-committal account of the damage suffered, and an urgent request for assistance. They had agreed that the name of the *Zhukov* should under no circumstances be disclosed to the Norwegians. The Russians who went ashore were to stress that she was one of the first generation of nuclear boats, no longer suitable for operational work, now only used for training purposes. She had been, they were to say, on a training cruise when the stranding had taken place. No reasons for that occurrence were to be given.

The skimmer rounded Fyrbergnes keeping close inshore and under the powerful beam from the lighthouse which swept a wide arc of the sea every ten seconds. Once round the point the sub-lieutenant steered for the light on Kolnoy, the small islet on the southern side of the mouth of Kolfjord. Travelling fast the small craft bounced over the undulations of the sea, spray sweeping over its occupants, increasing their discomfort on this dark cold October morning north of the Arctic Circle.

When the light of Kolnoy was close ahead, the skimmer swung round into the fjord and ran in on the red transit beacons. It passed two fishing boats making towards the open sea. The lights of the small town at the head of the fjord grew steadily brighter and soon the skimmer entered the harbour, the high note of the engine dropped and the small craft went alongside a fishing boat lying at a rough quay standing on wooden stilts. Milovych, Krasnov and the sub-lieutenant clambered across the fishing boat and climbed a ladder on to the quay. Krasnov saluted a small knot of men who stood there talking. "Please direct us to your burgomaster," he said.

A bearded man in oilskins asked, "Who are you?"

"We are officers of the Soviet Navy."

"What brings you here?"

"Our ship is outside." Krasnov extended an arm vaguely in the direction of the sea. "We must at once see your burgomaster."

A deep Norwegian voice said, "So you're from the big submarine. Did you manage to ram the Dragetennene?" He laughed in the darkness. The others watched the Russians closely, wondering what their reaction would be.

Krasnov said, "Please. It is urgent. Take us to your burgomaster."

"We don't have one," said the bearded man. "But follow me. I'll take you to the home of Hjalmar Nordsen. He's our *Ordforer*. That's much the same thing, I suppose."

43

# Seven

At eight-thirty in the morning the telephone rang in the back office of an insurance, travel and press agency in Lonsdahl Street, Bodo. Gunnar Olufsen, head of the small business which bore his name, answered it. The staff of two girls did not arrive until nine o'clock.

"Gunnar Olufsen here."

"Hullo, Gunnar."

Olufsen's leathery face relaxed. He pulled up the chair and leant forward. "Hullo, Inga." Breaking into English he added, "How's the body?" Her name was Inga Bodde. It was an old joke.

"Fine," she said. "But missing you."

"Not my fault." He spoke in Norwegian again.

"Listen, Gunnar. Here's an important press item."

"Good." He grabbed a ballpoint. "Go ahead."

"A Soviet submarine ran aground off Knausnes about midnight. It's still there. In a cove on the rockshelf."

He whistled. "Any more?"

"Some Russian officers from the submarine came into Kolhamn early this morning. In a skimmer. They went to the house of Hjalmar Nordsen."

"Anything happened since?"

"Yes. Two messages by teleprinter. A coded one from the Russians to the Soviet Embassy in Oslo."

"The other?"

"From Nordsen. He has reported the happening to the *Fylkesman* in Bodo."

Good, thought Olufsen. That'll mean delay. So much

44

for red tape. The report would have to go to Norway's Northern Command Headquarters in Bodo. But the *Ordforer* of a small island like Vrakoy had to submit his reports to his county authorities. They would pass it to the military.

"Anything else, Inga?"

"One of our fishing boats saw it heading for the rocks. Very slowly. Our skipper tried to warn them. They told him to keep away. Said they knew what they were doing."

"Glad I'm not the Russian captain. Any idea what class of submarine?"

"No. It was a dark night and it had no lights. They say it was very big."

"Good girl. This is a marvellous news item. I'll get it off right away. How's your father?"

"Not so good."

"I'm sorry."

"Are you really, Gunnar?"

"That's unkind, Inga."

"Well. You know the way things are."

Gunnar Olufsen's seamed face set hard. "I do," he said. "Only too well."

"Cheer up. It's not the end of the world."

He laughed without humour. "Anyway, thanks for the story. More news of it will be welcome."

"Okay, Gunnar, I'll do my best. Look after yourself."

"You too. Maybe I'll be coming over soon."

"That'll be great. Time you did."

"Bye now."

"Bye, Gunnar."

For a moment he sat thinking about Inga Bodde. As Vrakoy's only telephone and teleprinter operator she was for him an invaluable source of information. Vrakoy, the most westerly of the islands off the Norwegian coast, had a considerable fishing fleet. The men who manned it often brought news of naval units, both Soviet and NATO, operating in the Norwegian and Barents Seas. To Gunnar Olufsen, professional gatherer of information and accredited stringer for news agencies in Oslo and London, this was important. Inga didn't expect payment. They were in

45

love. It was a long-standing affair. Too long, he decided, as he thought of her. He'd lost his wife many years earlier in a car accident. There were no children. He was forty-five, Inga ten years younger. Devoted to an invalid widowed father who would not leave Vrakoy, she'd not married. Marriage to Gunnar Olufsen was only practical if he moved to Vrakoy but that was not on. He had often explained to Inga that he had no intention of becoming a fisherman, the only occupation open to him on the island, while there was much to do in Bodo.

One hundred and fifteen miles south of Vrakoy, this port was a thriving trade, traffic and tourist centre. With its busy harbour at the mouth of Saltenfjord, the Nordland railway terminal and large airport, it lay on the west coast between Narvik in the north and Trondheim in the south. It happened also to be the military headquarters of Norway's Northern Command.

Shrugging away his thoughts, Olufsen wrote a brief account on Inga Bodde's news and punched it on to teleprinter tapes. When it was ready he fed the tape for the London agency into the teleprinter. That for the Oslo agency he delayed for an hour.


In a sleazy upstairs office in a newsagency tucked away in Essex Street off the Strand, a girl read the message from Bodo as the flicking keys of the teleprinter typed it. When they stopped she tore the sheet against the cutter bar and took it to the long-haired young man with dark glasses who sat at the desk behind her.

"From Bodo," she said. "It's got a Y."

The young man read the message as he bit into a hot-dog. The time of dispatch concluded with the letter Y. He took another mouthful and reread the message.

"Better get on with it, hadn't you?" she said.

He pushed back the chair and stood up. "Okay, love."

"It's immediate for them, isn't it?"

"They're going to get it immediate, aren't they?"

He went through the back door to a small sound-proofed room, unlocked the door, turned on the light, shut and locked the door, picked up the telephone handset, set the scrambler and dialled a number.

A girl answered. "You are?"

He swallowed the last of the hot-dog. "Frank-seven-two-zed-four-seven."

"Go ahead, Frank."

"Plain language Y teleprint from Gunnar Olufsen, Bodo."

He read the message slowly, careful not to slur the words, knowing it was being tape-recorded at her end. He did this very efficiently.

"That's all," he said.

"Thanks, Frank," she said.

She sounds okay, he thought. Wonder if she's a dish? He reset the scrambler, hung up the handset, turned off the light, shut the door, locked it and went back into the office. He stopped behind the girl, put the teleprinter message in his pocket, slipped his hands over her shoulders and felt her breasts. "Know why you've got two?"

She shook him away. "Take your filthy hands off me, you sex maniac."

"Okay. No need to get your knickers in a twist. You know you like it."

"I do," she agreed. "That's the trouble."

"No trouble, love." He kissed the back of her neck. "Now shake it up and get on with your work."

"You're a bastard," she said.


In an office in the Ministry of Defence in Whitehall Commodore Oliver Rathouse, a small man with a puck-like face and peppery manners, looked at the lieutenant-commander who'd just come in. "What is it, Briggs?"

"Message from Bodo, sir. From *Daffodil*."

"What's he been up to?"

"Rather interesting, sir."

The commodore took the message. When he'd finished reading he said, "It's not only interesting, Briggs. It's extremely important." He picked up one of several phones and dialled an internal MOD number. It was quickly answered. "Lewis here."

"Hullo, Freddie. Ratters here."

"Hullo, Ratters. What's the trouble? One of your lot sinking?"

"Not this time. There's a big Soviet submarine aground on the rocks off Knausnes on Vrakoy. That's the most westerly of the Vesteralen Islands."

"Yes. I know. Our geography's rather good. We fly over the maps."

"She went on about midnight last night. Probably a ballistic missile job. Listen. She might be the *Zhukov*."

"Christ. How bloody marvellous."

"Would be if she were. Remember *Clematis* reported her sailing from Leningrad on October first. Bound for Polyarnyo."

"Yes, I do. I'll get on to 120 Squadron at Kinloss right away. We'll push a Nimrod up there. Should have photos within a few hours."

"Splendid. Watch out for Norwegian air-space, mate. They're sensitive."

"Not to worry. We have good friends there."

"By the way, NATO is not in on this. Not yet, anyway. We'll keep it that way for the moment."

"Okay. I'm with you."

"Many thanks, old boy." He put down the phone. "Get me that BMS/USSR file, Briggs. I'd like another look at the *Clematis* report."

His short title in Whitehall was VCNS—Vice-Chief of the Naval Staff. He was a dark lithe man with a strong face that fitted the title.

"I see they were taken within minutes of 1100 this morning," he said, examining a set of aerial photographs. High altitude shots, some oblique, others vertical. The commodore (Intelligence) slid sections cut from the large photos into a stereoscope. "Look at them now, sir. The photo enlargement of these cut-outs is a factor of six. The stereoscope enlarges them again by a factor of ten. So you're looking at the thing enlarged sixty times."

The VCNS put his eyes to the stereoscope. What had been a minute object, no more than a tiny scratch close to a line of rocks, became a submarine, its whole length visible but for the submerged bows. The details of its hull could be seen quite clearly.

"Taken at high water," said the commodore. "There was a good deal of cloud. The Nimrod had problems."

"So you think it's the *Zhukov*, Rathouse?"

"Pretty certain, sir. One—it's a class we've never seen before. Two—the hull configuration resembles closely reports we've had on the Delta Twos. Three—there's only one at sea, the prototype. That's the *Zhukov*. Four—we know from the *Clematis* report that she sailed from Leningrad on the first of October, bound for Polyarnyo to join a BMS Squadron. Today is the sixth. So the time and place of her grounding are consistent with those movements."

"Sounds pretty conclusive. Now. What are these unusual features?"

"Well sir," the commodore (Intelligence) seemed uncertain where to start. "Well—our boffins have looked these over and found certain things." He leant over the admiral's shoulder. "Those parallel lineal shadows along the after-casing for example," he indicated them with a pencil, ". . . are fairings over the missile tubes. There wouldn't be shadows unless they stood well proud of the casing. That suggests a longer missile than the Sawflys used in the Y class."

"That means . . . ?"

"Greater range for a start. It may also mean MARV warheads."

The admiral looked up. "Independently manoeuvrable and targeted re-entry vehicles? They do think up the most awful names, don't they?"

He put his eyes once more to the stereoscope. "What else?" The commodore considered the question. "We've accepted that the Soviet Navy is moving ahead of the US Navy in ballistic missile range. If they take the lead in introducing MARV warheads into submarine missilry, well . . ."

"I know," the admiral waved a deprecatory hand. "I've

done the course, too. 'It will constitute a serious threat to the West.' Anything else in these?"

The commodore's pencil moved again. "Yes. The conning-tower or fin is further forward than in the Y class, and it has this semi-circular extension on its after side. Rather like half a pressure hull. Must be all of thirty feet—and about half the height of the fin. Too large for a radome."

"Any idea what it's for?"

"It's possible to hazard all sorts of guesses but we've no real idea. *Clematis* reported that the Delta Twos had this extension, but he hasn't been able to discover its purpose. The security rating is exceptionally high."

The admiral nodded. "I'm not surprised. Anything else?"

"Yes. Those semi-circular blisters right aft. They extend over the last fifteen metres of the submarine's length. Terminate either side of the tail stabilizer fin and rudder. Our boffins have worked at it but can't come up with anything helpful. It's not particularly good hydrodynamics, they say—so must have a pretty important function."

"The baffled boffins," said the admiral thoughtfully. "Good title for a book. And now, Mr. Commodore Intelligence ... what's your proposal?" The VCNS and the commodore were old shipmates.

The small man frowned, pulled at his chin and contemplated the Mall beyond the admiral's left shoulder.

"Point one, sir." He threw in the occasional "sir" for good measure. "Information about the new Delta Two is vital to the West if the balance of maritime nuclear capability is not to be upset."

The admiral looked at him with renewed interest. "Go on, Rathouse," he said. "This is splendid stuff. Worthy of the senior war course."

The commodore said, "Sorry. But it's important to see this thing in perspective."

"I'm sure it is," said the admiral. "*Whose* perspective often provides the problem."

"Point two." The commodore was unabashed. "I think

50

we should keep this off NATO's plate. At this stage at any rate."

"Why?" VCNS's voice, eyes and chin combined in a single challenge.

"NATO is in a state of disarray. For various reasons. The Middle East affair. Tricky Dick's alert to US armed forces round the world. His incredible failure to consult with NATO before embarking on that face-to-face with the USSR. Then there's trauma between the major NATO powers—and the US—about oil. You know. Chauvinistic pursuit of short-term aims vis-à-vis the Arab-Israeli war because of dependence on Arab oil." He paused to see what effect all this was having on the Vice Chief of the Naval Staff.

"Go on," said the VCNS. "You fascinate me."

"I feel—we feel," amended the commodore thinking of his staff, "that if we take this to NATO the US, as leading nuclear power in the West, is going to demand a major say in any intelligence operation."

"Leading is an understatement, Rathouse. Of course they will. So would we in their situation."

"I agree, but we're not happy about it. Washington may forgo exploitation of the opportunity rather than risk damaging the détente with Moscow. And, frankly, I don't think they're capable of the subtlety, the low profile, this demands."

"Come, come, Rathouse." The admiral made a clicking noise. "That's a chauvinistic statement if ever there was one. Anyway, what about the Norwegians? The submarine is aground on their territory. They're highly sensitive about territorial rights. For my money they've already decided they'll handle this themselves. They'll tell NATO to lay off."

The commodore said, "I agree they'll not want NATO to butt in. But in my view the Norwegians won't do any intelligence gathering. What they will do is give the Russians every assistance in getting the *Zhukov* off. Her presence is highly embarrassing. Norway is most anxious to preserve good relations with the USSR. Certainly they're in no mood to take risks."

51

The VCNS tried again to balance a paper knife on the paperweight. "I think I go along with that."

"We know Roald Lund, Norway's director of service intelligence," continued the commodore. "Freddie Lewis is a close friend. Both airmen. They've done staff courses and NATO war courses together. So we know him well. How he thinks. How he works. He regards NATO Northern Command as a leaky intelligence sieve. The US have a CIA unit there. Civilians. Ostensibly for security purposes only. But," the commodore spread his hands and shrugged his shoulders, "you know how these things work, particularly as the US have no service intelligence units in that set-up."

The admiral looked relieved. He'd succeeded in getting the paper knife to balance. "What is your proposal, Rathouse?"

The commodore looked the VCNS squarely in the face. This was the crunch. "I believe we must exploit the opportunity to the full. Do it on our own as a purely British venture."

"Have you thought of the implications?"

"Yes, sir. What I—we—have in mind won't put Norwegian interests at risk although her territory is involved."

"Our interests?"

"It won't be known at any stage that it is a British operation. If anything its stamp will be Chinese."

"China in Norway." The VCNS raised a critical eyebrow. "Little far fetched isn't it?"

"Not when you hear the details, sir." The commodore's smile was indulgent. "What we want is a private venture with service support in the background. Very much in the background. And it's no more than an intelligence gathering operation. We've done some rough outline planning. Not much." He looked at his watch. "Only two hours since we got *Daffodil*'s message. And we can't really get down to the nitty gritty until our people are on Vrakoy. It'll be a case of looking for leads and following them."

"Sounds rather cloak-and-dagger," said the VCNS doubtfully. "Tell me more."

The commodore did and, half an hour later when he

stood up to go, the VCNS said, "Well, Rathouse, I'll have to discuss this with the First Sea Lord once you've cleared it in principle with ICC and Maltby." ICC was the intelligence co-ordinating committee in Whitehall. Maltby of the Cabinet Office was its *éminence grise*. "But remember," the VCNS wagged an admonitory finger. "If I do put it to One-SL it will be on the strict understanding that it is no more than an intelligence gathering operation. To be carried out in such a way that neither the Norwegian nor British Governments can possibly be involved. In other words, if you get the go-ahead you're on your own. Your party will be without official support or recognition and if things go wrong we shall not hesitate to repudiate them, and—" his grey eyes narrowed into a cold stare, "we'll sack you."

"Thank you, sir." The commodore seemed happy. "You won't forget about HM ships in the area? And the bodies we'll need?"

"No. I'll have a word with C-in-C Fleet, Northwood, and the Naval Secretary. By the way have you thought up a code name for this?"

"We have. *Daisy Chain*."

"*Operation Daisy Chain*. I rather like that," said the VCNS. "Very Enid Blyton."

"Glad you like it, sir."

The admiral looked at the commodore speculatively. "I suppose I needn't tell you that this will have to be done at the double. The *Zhukov* news is out now. The Soviet Navy will be rushing to help their comrades on the rocks. I imagine high altitude air space over Vrakoy will soon look like Piccadilly Circus. You know—the Russians, US, French, British, NATO, the lot. All busy clicking their little shutters. Not to mention some shady characters on the ground—no offence to your lot, Rathouse—casting for a scent."

The commodore nodded. "Yes, sir. We do realize that speed is the essence of the operation."

# Eight

Hjalmar Nordsen, a saturnine man still in his dressing gown, removed the traces of an interrupted shave and gestured his visitors to sit down. It was a largish room with its books, files and typewriters—more like an office than a study.

"Good morning, gentlemen," he said. "Unfortunately I do not speak Russian. You speak Norwegian?"

"I do, *Ordforer*," said Krasnov introducing Milovych and the sub-lieutenant.

"Well, now. What can I do to help you?"

"Tell him," said Milovych, "that a technical problem and subsequent failure in communications systems obliged us to put our submarine aground off Knausnes. We tried to reach Uklarvik but this proved impossible. Explain to him that the submarine is a first generation nuclear boat, used now only for training purposes. Emphasize that we were on a training cruise, outside Norwegian territorial waters, when the trouble occurred."

Krasnov, speaking fluent Norwegian, reported this to the *Ordforer* who replied, "Please tell your captain I am extremely sorry to learn of this misfortune." He dabbed his face with a shaving towel. "What does he wish me to do?"

The lieutenant translated. Milovych said, "In the name of the Soviet Union we ask for every possible assistance from the Norwegian Government. First, we must request that this . . ." he took from his pocket the coded message he and Yenev had drafted, ". . . be dispatched at once to the Soviet Embassy in Oslo."

Krasnov translated and handed the message to the *Ordforer*, explaining what Milovych had said. Hjalmar Nordsen pointed to the clock on his desk. "It is now seven-twenty in the morning. Our postmistress comes on duty at eight-thirty. The message will be sent as soon as she arrives. She is the only person able to transmit."

Milovych spoke again to Krasnov. "Tell him that we wish the news of the stranding of our vessel to be kept confidential as long as possible. We must ask him to take immediate steps to keep sightseers away, both to landward and seaward."

When Krasnov repeated this in Norwegian, Nordsen's response was guarded. "Tell your captain that we will do what we can. There are already rumours in Kolhamn that a submarine has gone aground on the Dragetennene—the rocks off Knausnes. I heard them early this morning. There is no law in Norway which forbids citizens to look at ships which have stranded on our shores, nor any censorship of such matters. However, I will communicate with the authorities to whom I am responsible and act in accordance with their instructions. You must understand," he spoke with some asperity, "that this is a small island. We have only four hundred people here. Mostly fishermen and their families. We are a *herredskommuner*—a rural district—and I have very limited facilities. Only a bailiff, a policeman, a harbourmaster and a part-time postmistress."

Krasnov translated. Milovych said, "Ask him who is actually in charge of this island." Krasnov put the question, the *Ordforer* answered and the lieutenant explained. "He says there is a *herredstyre*—a council—over which he presides. They are the local authority. They in turn are responsible to the Nordland Fylker—the county council—in Bodo."

During the course of further conversation it was agreed that the Russians should accompany Hjalmar Nordsen to the council office, the *radhus*, when he had completed dressing.

While he was doing this Mrs. Nordsen, a large pink and white woman with a deep voice, gave the uninvited guests fillets of cod, mugs of coffee and buttered rolls. She wasn't very pleased about this because her hair was still in curlers and she didn't like Russians, particularly the plump man with the high pitched voice who seemed to have so much to say.

On arrival with Milovych and Krasnov at the *radhus* the *Ordforer* called in Odd Dahl, the bailiff, Olaf Petersen, the harbourmaster, and Dr. Gustav Kroll, his deputy, the *vice-Ordforer*. Bluff, genial, bearded and rotund, Kroll was a retired teacher of mathematics. He had lived on the island for many years.

Krasnov, an observant young man, soon gathered that Hjalmar Nordsen was not only Vrakoy's leading citizen but represented important fishing interests on the mainland. He was responsible for buying the catches and arranging their shipment. In an aside to Krasnov, Kroll had said, "We call Hjalmar Nordsen 'the little king'." He looked at the *Ordforer* with admiration. "He owns or has a say in just about everything in Vrakoy."

Before the discussions ended it was agreed that Krasnov and the sub-lieutenant would remain in Kolhamn at least until replies were received from the Soviet Embassy in Oslo and the Norwegian authorities on the mainland.

The *Ordforer* pointed out that the westerly end of the island where the *Zhukov* lay was too mountainous for human habitation. It was unlikely that many people, if any, would see the submarine there. They learnt from him, too, that the island enjoyed a daily air service from Harstad. This brought mails, passengers and urgent supplies. Other supplies were brought by the inter-island coaster service.

The Russians left the *radhus* early in the forenoon and returned to the harbour. There attempts were made to establish communication with the *Zhukov* by means of the walkie-talkie berthing sets but though the distance was under ten kilometres the high mountain between Kolhamn and the Knausnes rocks made this impossible.

Milovych and Krasnov discussed the communications problem. Eventually Milovych said, "I will go off to the *Zhukov* now and send the skimmer back to you. As soon as a reply is received, or you have other important information, send it out."

"Yes, commissar."

"In the meantime," Milovych dropped his voice and looked round the quay where fishermen were coming and going. "You and Gerasov must get to know the town. Find out where the locals gather. Particularly the fishermen. Listen to their conversation. Find out what they know about the *Zhukov* and her stranding. Take every opportunity to stress that she is an unimportant vessel. One of the first generation ballistic missile submarines, no longer operational. You know the story. Never mention her name. Be discreet in all things. Trust no one. Remember . . ." the commissar ran his tongue round thick lips, "you represent the Soviet Union."

Krasnov jerked his chin forward and upwards as if to escape from his collar. "We will carry out your instructions, commissar."

The lieutenant was delighted. He and Gerasov were good friends. A day ashore in Kolhamn would be far better than one in the stranded submarine where the normal discomforts of life on board had been aggravated by pounding seas, flooding, the failure of the air-conditioning plant, the smell of chlorine gas, burnt rubber and other remnants of the disaster.

Standing on the quay, he and Gerasov saluted smartly as the skimmer's engine came to life. The small craft sped out of the fishing harbour, down the fjord towards the sea. "I think the commissar is worried," said Gerasov.

"He has a great deal to worry about," replied Krasnov.

The two men gave each other questioning, uncommitted glances. Neither liked the commissar.

Krasnov said, "Well. Now let's take a look at Kolhamn."

"Wine, women and song," Gerasov laughed. "Pity I can't speak the language."

"None of that," said Krasnov. "We're here on duty." But he too laughed. "Who knows what the night may bring?"

"If we're still here," said the sub-lieutenant. "Not that Kolhamn looks very promising."

Hjalmar Nordsen's report to the county authorities at Bodo was passed with little delay to Northern Command Headquarters. The GOC at once discussed it by scrambler with Military Headquarters in Oslo. The Chief of the General Staff informed the Ministry of Defence. There was consultation at cabinet level, decisions were taken, instructions issued.

Hjalmar Nordsen was authorized to give the Soviet submarine's captain all possible assistance and to make such arrangements as he could to keep sightseers away until assistance arrived later in the day. A Norwegian minesweeper with military personnel on board would, he was told, arrive in Vrakoy from Harstad in the late afternoon. The soldiers were to establish a cordon on the landward side of the approaches to Knausnes, while the minesweeper protected the seaward approaches. The submarine was not, recorded the Oslo message, to be harried by sightseers, media representatives, photographers, or other unauthorized persons. The message to Vrakoy's *Ordforer* concluded with: "Major Lars Martinsen from Military HQ Oslo will fly in by helicopter in the afternoon to take general charge."

At eleven-thirty that morning the Norwegian Foreign Minister in Oslo received the Soviet Ambassador at the latter's urgent request. In a brief meeting, notable for its friendly tone, the Foreign Minister informed the Ambassador of the steps being taken by the Norwegian authorities. He assured him that all possible assistance would be given to the stranded submarine.

The Ambassador conveyed to the Minister the desire of the Soviet Government that their warships should, without delay, be permitted to enter Norwegian territorial waters to assist the submarine.

The Foreign Minister said that his Prime Minister, anticipating the request, had discussed it with the Cabinet. The Cabinet had decided that Soviet salvage vessels, naval or otherwise, would be so permitted but unfortunately Soviet warships could not. The Minister was apologetic but reminded the Ambassador of Norway's NATO commitments. The Norwegian Government would, however, be happy to make available its own salvage vessels and experts to assist. The Soviet Ambassador thanked the Minister for the offer, undertook to convey it to his Government but believed it would not be necessary to impose in this way upon Norwegian generosity. He did, however, express concern that Norwegian territorial waters and air space might be used by foreign powers anxious to obtain photographs of the stranded submarine. The Minister assured him that his government would do all it could to prevent incursions into Norwegian air space.

There was discussion about the dangers of radiation. The Soviet Ambassador gave his assurance that there was no present danger. It was fortunate, he said, that the vessel was used for training purposes only. Thus the missiles did not have nuclear warheads. The Ambassador's nose twitched involuntarily as he told this lie. As far as the nuclear power plant was concerned, he continued, Soviet salvage experts would give radiation control overriding priority.

The meeting concluded. The Minister rose from his desk to escort the Soviet Ambassador to the door.

"By the way, Ambassador," he said. "You haven't mentioned the name of your submarine. I wonder if I might have it for reference purposes?"

The Ambassador smiled affably. "I am afraid, Minister, that is not possible. You see the vessel has no name. Only a number."

"And that is?"

"Seven-three-one," said the Ambassador, acting on instructions from Moscow. "One of our first ballistic missile submarines. Not a very successful class, I fear. Obsolescence is so rapid in these ships. She's no longer suitable for operations. As I've explained, our navy use her for training purposes only." He paused, hand over mouth, his eyes on a picture on the wall—the "Trollfjord in Winter." "Prior to that she was used experimentally. For testing various designs. Matters of hydrodynamic efficiency, you know. For that reason a somewhat unusual hull configuration, they tell me."

"Yes, of course." The Minister opened the door for his guest. "In these days of advanced technology, design and capability change so swiftly."

"Indeed they do," said the Soviet Ambassador. "Goodbye and thank you, Minister."

"Not at all, Ambassador. Please assure your government that we are only too anxious to help."

At the headquarters of NATO's Northern Military Command in Kolsas, outside Oslo, the senior Norwegian representative told his NATO colleagues of the stranding of the submarine and the action being taken by his government. "I have been instructed to inform you that, should any assistance be required in any form, my government will not hesitate to ask for it."

To his listeners—the representatives of the United States, Britain, Germany and Denmark—it was evident that the Norwegian representative was in fact saying, "Norway will handle this. So lay off." Nor were they in any doubt as to the reasons for this stance.

Roald Lund, Director of Norway's service intelligence and former colonel in the Norwegian Air Force, went to the window and looked out over Oslofjord, the wide expanse of water dominating the city which takes its name. Its surface reflected the cold greyness of a wet and cheerless October day. "I think that's about all, Martinsen. Is there anything you're not certain about?"

The tall man with greying hair turned away from the wall map of Norway. "No. Your instructions are quite clear." He looked at his watch. "Twenty minutes to one. That leaves about three hours in which—," he breathed deeply. "To make contact, change into uniform, lunch and pack." He was about to go on when something occurred to him. "Just one point, sir. How d'you know it's the *Zhukov*?"

Roald Lund continued to look out over Oslofjord where wind gusting across it left swathes of shimmering water. In the foreground two sail-training ships lay alongside each other, dwarfed by an oil rig under construction on the other side of the basin. It was nearing completion, a strangely unnautical structure, vast steel tubes joined in geometrical patterns like a huge building toy. The bright glow of welding arcs flared and faded, ferries came and went, a streamer sounded its siren, and at the quay in front of the City Hall a big Soviet merchant ship warped alongside, red flag fluttering in the breeze, its reception committee a knot of stevedores.

"Sometimes, Martinsen, it is better if the right hand does not know what the left is doing."

"I'm sorry. It was idle curiosity."

"In our job curiosity is a virtue, Martinsen. Never apologize for it. But let me say this. If I didn't know it was the *Zhukov* I wouldn't ask you to let them know."

"It won't be any trouble," Martinsen smiled. "And I'm sure your reasons are sound."

"I'm sure it won't be—and they are." Lund rearranged things on his desk in an absent-minded way, then looked up. He was smiling. "Well, some people have all the luck. You may carry on, Lars." It was a good sign. He didn't often use Martinsen's first name.

The tall man drew his heels together, gave the suggestion of a bow and left the room. He wondered what the colonel would think if he knew just how lucky he was.

It was known only to Roald Lund and his close associates that Lars Martinsen, an air force officer seconded for staff duties to Military Headquarters, Oslo, was an important member of Norwegian Intelligence.

## Nine

Martinsen got back to his office, picked up a phone and dialled a number.

"Who is it?" asked a woman.

"Me. Lars."

"Oh, Lars. How super. Where've you been?"

He ignored the question. "Marvellous to hear your voice, Karen. Listen! Can I lunch with you?"

"When?"

"Now. Today."

"You mean here? Yes, of course. But there's nothing to eat."

"Want me to bring something?"

"No. Bring yourself. That'll do. I suppose you know the time?"

"Ten minutes to one. I'll be with you in fifteen minutes."

"Make it twenty. I've got to fix the lunch." She laughed. "And drag on some clothes."

"I shouldn't worry too much about that."

"What, the lunch or the clothes?"

"The clothes."

"You haven't improved, Lars."

"Want me to?"

"No. See you."

"See you, Karen."

It was over a month since he'd last visited the flat but she hadn't forgotten the things he liked: strips of raw sild,

Jarlsberg cheese, oatcakes and butter, akvavit and beer with which to chase it. He'd brought chocolates. Karen adored them.

As always she'd set out lunch on a coffee table in front of the studio couch. Its cottage weave stirred pleasantly erotic memories.

She was wearing blue slacks, a high-necked white jersey, and looked very desirable. She was, he decided, one of the nicest, most undemanding and unacquisitive women he'd ever known. And always incredibly pleased to see him, notwithstanding the long intervals between visits.

"Akvavit?" She raised an inquiring eyebrow.

"Please. You've not forgotten."

"No." She filled two spirit glasses, passed one to him.

"Skol," he said, raising and lowering the glass in mock ceremony.

"Skol," she inclined her head. "Lars, where have you been all this time?"

"Here and there."

"That's what you always say."

"It's true."

"I suppose you tell that to your other girl-friends?"

"That's not true."

"I won't cross-examine you. It's fabulous having you here." She held her head on one side, her eyes inquiring. "What time do you have to go?"

He looked at his watch. "In one hour and ten minutes exactly."

"Bloody hell," she said. "It's always the same. Why do I bother?"

"I wonder about that too. Know something, Karen?"

"What?" she challenged, still upset, unsure of him.

"Nothing really. Sounds silly put into words. Oh hell, I don't know. But when I'm with you I feel so relaxed. Out of the rat race. In a sort of dream world. You do something for me."

"Do I?" She touched his hand. "I like to hear you say that."

He put down his glass, then hers, pulled her across his knees, cradled her in his arms.

63

"Lars," she protested. "You'll upset . . ." He smothered the rest of the sentence with his mouth.

"Oh, God," she said. "I want you."

Later in the bedroom, after they'd made love, they lay in each other's arms talking in subdued tones. Half sentences about their relationship, their emotions, the lives they led, the things they did and hoped to do. Time caught up with them and he was late and worried as he stood in front of the mirror dressing, seeing her reflection as she lay naked on the bed, thinking how attractive she was, how lovely her body. And he thought how good it would be if things were different. If I didn't have to use her in the way I do.

She, watching him dress, thought what a lean strong body he had, what a resolute face, how marvellously he made love, what good company he was. But I hate using him like this, she decided. I wish it could be different.

When he'd gone she went to the window, watched him come out of the building, hurry up the street, flag down a taxi. After it had disappeared she stood there, naked, thinking. She put on a caftan, went to the telephone and dialled a number.

A man with a North American accent answered.

"Can I speak with Jo Carless?" she said.

"Sure," said the American. "Hold a minute."

While she waited she thought of Lars Martinsen. Why, she asked herself, do I have to get emotionally involved with the bloody man when it's the last thing I want? She didn't know that at the same moment Lars Martinsen, travelling down Drammensveien in the taxi, was thinking much the same thing.

Her thoughts were interrupted by a voice on the line.

"Joe Carless here. Who is this?"

"It's Karen, Joe."

"Hi, Karen."

"Joe, I've got that hi-fi catalogue at last. Would you like to collect it?"

"Why that's great, Karen. I'll come right up if that's convenient."

"It is, Joe."

"Okay. See you then."

"Bye, Joe. See you." Her voice trailed away.

"You all right, Karen?"

"I'm okay, Joe." She replaced the receiver, slumped on to the studio couch, buried her face in a cushion. "Oh, Christ!" she said. "Oh, bloody hell!"

## Ten

The clock on the wall showed two-twenty when the Commodore (Intelligence) got back to his office from lunch with the Vice-Chief of the Naval Staff.

He rang for Briggs. The lieutenant-commander appeared with customary alacrity, file in one hand, clipboard in the other, brisk, alert, nose well forward like a hound on the scent.

"Well, Briggs. What progress with *Daisy Chain*?"

"Everything more or less under control, sir. C-in-C Fleet has diverted *Aries*—returning to the Clyde from an Icelandic patrol—and *Bluewhale*, outward bound on an Arctic patrol. They were between fifty and seventy miles north of the Faeroes at noon. *Aries* has been ordered to a position in area GXF—approximately one hundred and twenty miles southwest of the Lofotens. *Bluewhale* to a position seventy miles north of the Shetlands. She will later receive instructions to rendezvous with *Aries* for an anti-submarine exercise. Purpose—to test new equipment. The equipment to be flown to them by helicopter from

*Belligerent* with ASW specialists from Portland." Briggs turned a sheet on the clipboard.

"*Belligerent*, at present off the Forth, is to proceed to a position sixty miles east of the Shetlands to embark the ASW equipment and the specialists. She will rendezvous with *Aries* and *Bluewhale* in area GXF and take charge of the exercise. All other details—the Liang Huis, Special Branch, the yacht, etcetera—in hand as planned."

"Good for C-in-C Fleet," said the commodore trying not to look delighted. Not only had the First Sea Lord approved *Daisy Chain*, but C-in-C Fleet was providing more background support than Naval Intelligence had requested. The importance of exploiting the *Zhukov* disaster had not been lost anywhere along the line—even Maltby and the ICC, suspicious of nonintegrated operations, had liked the idea. *Aries*, a Leander class frigate, *Bluewhale*, a Porpoise class submarine, and *Belligerent*, an assault ship, couldn't be a better trio for the job.

"And now," he said, using his low key voice. "What progress with the *Daisy Chain* party?"

Briggs put the clipboard on the desk and consulted the manilla file. "Rather good, sir. We've had a bit of luck. Liang Hui and his sister Tanya, Secret Intelligence Service agents based on Hong Kong, are here for debriefing. On leave in London at the moment. I think you know them, sir. They helped us close that massage parlour leak in Kowloon two years ago. Before my time here, but I've read it up."

"Yes, I know them, and I'm quite sure you've read it up, Briggs. The parlour where dishy Cantonese birds treated our sailors to hash and saki preparatory to swapping pelvic massage and other eroticisms for classified information." The commodore was thoughtful. "So the Liang Huis are here. Well, they couldn't have come at a better time."

Briggs nodded absent-mindedly. He was thinking about the massage parlour. The dossier on it—polaroid photos, tapes, the lot—had long been a popular and hilarious diversion for night duty staff when things were quiet.

Gems like that didn't often come the way of naval intelligence.

Briggs returned the notes to his file. "The Liang Huis' background seems tailor-made for this assignment, sir. Grandmother, a white Russian *émigrée* in Shanghai. Spin off from the Bolshevik revolution. She married a Cantonese, the Liang Huis' grandfather that was. The son married a Cantonese girl. They produced Li and Tanya Liang Hui. Their father insisted they spoke Russian as well as Chinese. They are equally fluent in either. The Liang Huis are in Linton's parish. He gives them a high rating."

The commodore's face gathered in seams which Briggs knew to be approval. "Who else have we got?"

"Collins and I checked through the Naval Secretary's list of interpreters. We looked for Norwegian, Russian and Chinese speakers. We also checked on RN personnel with one or more parents, of non-British origin. From that sifting we made up a list, checked it against service history sheets. We had to have at least one man with BMS service. We then made inquiries about sailing experience. Having sieved through that lot we made up this short list. You'll see I've made background notes about each name on it. Of course, it's subject to your approval, sir."

"Very considerate of you, Briggs." The commodore took the list, bunched bushy eyebrows and began to read:

*Lieutenant-Commander Stephen Nunn RN. 31. Married. No children. Weapons Electrical Officer. Four years' service in ballistic missile submarines of which eight months with USN. Father English, mother Cantonese. Qualified interpreter in Chinese, Japanese and Korean. In addition has sound knowledge of Russian and Scandinavian languages. Member of the RN Sailing Association. Has crewed and skippered for ten years.*

"Good God," said the commodore. "Wonder what he thinks in?"

"They come like that, sir. Quite a lot of bodies in NS's list are qualified in three or four languages."

The commodore read on:

67

*Chief Petty Officer Sven Sandstrom, 38. Married. Three children. Gunnery Instructor (gunnery and missiles). Ten months' service in ballistic missile submarines. Mother and father Norwegian. Latter served in Norwegian destroyer attached RN, WW II. Qualified interpreter in Russian and Norwegian. Good sailing experience.*

*John Boland, Leading Marine Engineering Mechanic, qualified diver, 28. Two children. Father Ulsterman, mother Chinese. Qualified interpreter in Chinese.*

"Extraordinary mixture," said the commodore. "Children must be Catholic Buddhists." He went back to the list. "Ah—the bait."

*Julie Saville, 24. Third Officer WRNS. Unmarried. Daughter of former Norwegian diplomat, now dead. Mother came from North Russia. Saville has taken stepfather's name. She speaks fluent Norwegian, fair Russian. Good sailing experience.*

"I expect that's not all she's good at," said the commodore. "What is her stepfather's background?"

"Oh. Sorry, sir. I forgot to record that. He's a captain RN retired. Three terms junior to you."

"Saville. Saville. Probably J. J. He was a submariner."

"Yes, sir. That's him."

"Good. Well, I can't fault your list, Briggs. They're just names to me. Other than the Liang Huis. But they sound a pretty useful lot. When do we get them together?"

"We're busy on that now, sir. The briefing is scheduled for ten o'clock tonight."

"Secure venue?"

"A farmhouse. It's near . . ."

The commodore's hand shot up like a pointsman's. "For heaven's sake don't tell me. I'm not supposed to know." His pucklike face became preoccupied, worried. "They won't know, I take it?"

"No, sir. They'll arrive in a closed van."

"General security?"

"Special Branch have it wrapped up."

"Good. I want *Daisy Chain* off the ground by noon tomorrow at the latest. Tonight there won't be a newspaper or TV station not carrying the *Zhukov* story. And don't

68

forget the Soviet salvage lot. They're not going to waste time."

"D'you really think the media will know it's the *Zhukov*, sir?"

"No. I hope not. But they'll report a bloody great Soviet nuke high and dry on Vrakoy. That'll stir the pot."

The commodore looked at his notes, then at Briggs. "You'd better get the charter message off. The yacht to be available by 1800 tomorrow."

"It's drafted, sir. Just waiting your go ahead."

"Right. Dispatch it."

Briggs went to the door, stood there undecided. "By the way, sir. You said you'd let me know who was to take operational command of *Daisy Chain*."

The commodore frowned. "I know you'd like to, Briggs. But you lack the essentials. Russian, Norwegian and an intimate knowledge of that part of the world. That rules you out, I'm afraid." He scribbled a name on a slip of paper and handed it to the lieutenant-commander. 'Planted in Norway twenty years ago. You won't find him on any retired list. But he's the man for the job. Afraid I can't tell you more just now."

Briggs looked at the name: *Lieutenant-Commander James Harold Craddock, RN (retd)*. He returned the slip of paper to the commodore who put it in an ashtray and burnt it.

"How do I contact him, sir?"

"You don't," said the commodore. "I do that."

In Bodo that afternoon Gunnar Olufsen's travel agency received a request by teleprinter from Thos. Cook and Sons's West End office requesting the charter of an ocean going yacht for a party of four arriving the next day. The teleprint message recorded that three of the tourists were experienced yachtsmen. The boat would be required for about two weeks, during which time the charterees planned a sailing holiday in and around the Lofoten and Vesteralen Islands. Since time was limited, an auxiliary engine capable of providing a speed of at least eight knots without sail was essential. Gunnar Olufsen attended to the request personally. Within a few hours he had selected the forty-foot ketch *Kestrel* from the list provided by Halvorsen Brothers, yacht brokers and hirers. Its 60 HP diesel gave it ten knots without sail. She was lying in Bodo.

That done he flew down to Oslo and transferred to the night flight to Heathrow.


The Rover slowed down for the hairpin bend, took the humpback bridge and turned left along a farm road, its lights sweeping fields and hedgerows before steadying on the iron gates ahead. It squealed to a stop. A dark shape appeared from nowhere. In the headlights it became a man, sheepskin coated and tweed hatted. He opened a door, searched inside the car with a torch, checked the registration plates and licence disc. At the driver's window he spoke to the sole occupant. "Let's see it, then."

Briggs produced an identity card. The torch focused on it then shifted to Briggs's face. The man passed back the card, spoke into a walkie-talkie. "Okay, sir," he said. "Mr. McGhee's waiting."

Briggs let in the clutch and the Rover bumped down the track towards the farmhouse. He parked it behind a cowshed.

At the back door another man checked Briggs's face against the identity card by torchlight. "Mr. McGhee's in the living-room, sir," he said. His breath smelt of a recently finished meal.

The superintendent was sitting on a stool in an inglenook where broken necklaces of plaster hung from the ceiling.

"Good organization, McGhee."

"Cold for the time of year," said McGhee warming his hands in front of a log fire. "Might as well be comfortable."

" 'Fraid we're going to be late," said Briggs. "One of our lot's been delayed."

"Not the first time," said the superintendent. "Nor the last I'll warrant."

"He's had to come rather a long way," said Briggs apologetically.

● ● ●

They were all there by midnight. Six rather ordinary looking civilians. Unnotable save, perhaps, for the Cantonese brother and sister and the faintly oriental flavour of two other members of the party. All were dressed in a casual nonconformist way. The usual run of denim jeans, jackets and woollen jerseys. But for the brother and sister, they were unknown to each other, as were their faces until they'd reached the living-room. The van's interior light hadn't worked.

The late arrival came in the van on its second journey. He was a lean man with greying hair and a lined weathered face. He sat alone at the far end of the table, silent and immobile except when turning an aquiline nose and large questioning eyes on those who spoke. Occasionally the eyes and lips combined in a smile and the face was transformed.

"I'm Martin," said Briggs. "Please introduce yourselves."

All but the late arrival did, and from somewhere a Special Branch man produced hot coffee. Not that they knew he was Special Branch. Lighters flared, cigarettes were lit, and they stood about chatting warily as strangers do, drinking hot coffee from earthenware mugs and feeling slightly self-conscious. Later Briggs gathered them round the solid farmhouse table. He took the chair at its head. "I want to kick off," he said, "by repeating what you've already been told by your commanding officers. This is a private venture. Get that clearly into your minds. A private venture. If you get into trouble you'll be repudiated by the British Government. There'll be no official support or recognition. The Ministry of Defence will deny any knowledge of you. There'll be no reward for success. No compensation for failure. And whichever way it goes you'll have to be forever silent." He stopped for a moment. "You know the penalties if you're not. You've all been accepted as volunteers—repeat volunteers—for what may be a dodgy operation. It's of the utmost importance to the West or we wouldn't be bothering with it. Then there's . . ."

71

Briggs stared at the girl. She was scrabbling in her shoulderbag like a terrier looking for a bone. "You listening?"

"Yes. I am actually." She saw his eyes on the bag. "Sorry. Looking for a file. Broke a nail." She held up a slender finger.

Briggs gave her one of his specially baleful looks. "As I was saying, it's vital to the West. It shouldn't take long. Five to six days we estimate. It'll be carried out in a foreign but friendly country." Feeling he'd been over formal he added, "Should be rather fun, I think."

He looked round the table. "If anyone wishes to pull out, now's the time. Before we get on to the detail. Pulling out won't affect your service career. And if you do, we won't ask any questions because we know you'll have good reasons. Anyone?"

There were no takers, just a murmur of noes.

"That's great," said Briggs. "Now for one or two preliminaries. First, the name of the operation is *Daisy Chain*. Remember that, will you? Next, you're all civilians with no RN or other service background or connections. Just a party of friends who've decided to charter a yacht for a week or so of sailing in and around the Lofoten and Vesteralen Islands." He grinned. "So you'd better get to know each other pretty quickly."

The girl said, "Are you coming with us?"

"No, I'm not," he said, wishing he were. She had friendly eyes, an inviting smile. "Passports are being prepared. The essential facts—names, dates and places of birth, etcetera—will be correct. Your occupations will be relevant but they won't suggest any tie up with the Royal Navy. For example, Lieutenant-Commander Stephen Nunn,"—Briggs looked at the man with the pallid high-cheekboned face and almond eyes—"is a weapons electrical officer. He'll travel as Mr. Stephen Nunn, electronics engineer. He, like all of you, will get his passport, tickets and travel cheques, a written summary of his background, firm which employs him, home address—we've fixed them in case of inquiries—and so on. That summary is to be committed to memory before you leave, then destroyed."

"If we're friends we ought to be on first names, oughtn't we, sir?" The man who'd spoken looked faintly oriental, notwithstanding the Irish accent.

"Yes, John Boland, we bloody well ought. And don't use *sir* again. Either to me or anybody else while on this *Daisy Chain* operation. Get me, John?"

"Yes." The leading seaman looked embarrassed.

"Yes, what?"

"Yes, Martin."

"Right. Now we'll have a look at some slides and you'll be given a general outline of things as we go along. There's no operational plan. Just an objective, a set of options, and the means available. Put quite simply the object is to learn certain things about *Zhukov*. I'll deal with them in a moment. But this thing will have to be played by ear. So much depends on what you find when you get there. On the opportunities that present themselves."

Briggs turned to the man on the projector. "Ready, Harry?"

"Okay. All set."

"Good. Lights out. Let's go."

The first picture on the screen was a map of the Lofoten and Vesteralen Islands, Vrakoy arrowed. Next a large scale map of the island itself, followed by numerous shots of the fishing village and harbour mostly taken from tourist postcards. Then a chart of Kolfjord and a plan of the small harbour town; photos of the cliffs and rocks at Knausnes were followed by enlargements from stereoscopic projections. These showed the long slim line of the grounded Soviet submarine. There were slides of missile submarines of various types, ending with an artist's impression of the new Delta Two class.

To most of the slides Briggs provided the running commentary. For those of Vrakoy, the late arrival was commentator. Stephen Nunn did the commentary on ballistic missile submarines and their technology.

The slides, the running commentaries, the questions and answers and Briggs's summaries provided the hard core of the *Zhukov* briefing.

The last slide had been shown, the penultimate question answered, when the inevitable came from Stephen Nunn. "Who'll lead *Daisy Chain* once we're on the ground?"

Briggs, nettled at the forestalling of his *pièce de résistance*, looked aggrieved. "I was about to deal with that," he said. "You'll be led by a man who has considerable knowledge of the terrain . . ." he paused. "And other things important to *Daisy Chain*." Briggs pointed to the late arrival. "His name is Gunnar Olufsen."

The beaky nose and questioning-eyes of the late arrival encompassed them all, the sensitive mouth and eyes crumpled into a smile. "Hullo," he said.

One way and another it was after four in the morning when members of the *Daisy Chain* party climbed back into the van. All except Gunnar Olufsen. He and Briggs stayed in the farmhouse with McGhee after the others had left. Later they said goodnight to the superintendent, climbed into the Rover and followed winding lanes down through West Clandon to the A3. Once on it, Briggs pointed the car's nose for London and hit the accelerator hard.

## Eleven

As the skimmer drew away from Kolhamn and headed for the open sea, Milovych was unusually thoughtful. He was not sure about Hjalmar Nordsen. The *Ordforer* had been studiously polite but at no point had the man dropped his guard. That he would not bend the rules for the *Zhukov* was evident. Everything would have to be referred to higher authority and that meant delay. Milovych, by nature and training suspicious, mistrusted Nordsen, sensed a lack of sympathy. It was calamitous indeed that all communications had to be passed through Vrakoy's post office. Nordsen would have access to them. So would Norwegian Intelligence. The code was no protection. Had *Zhukov*'s transmitters been working there'd have been no problem. Computer-scrambled high-speed transmissions couldn't be deciphered. For those reasons the message to the embassy in Oslo had not been anything like as explicit as Yenev and the commissar would have wished, but Leningrad would understand. The response would be immediate and effective. Of that Milovych had no doubt.

The skimmer cleared the headlands at the mouth of the fjord, bumping and spraying its way past the bay at Uklarvik and on towards Fyrbergnes. The sky was grey and oppressive, and the mountain which dominated the western end of the island loomed darkly under snow-capped peaks. Beneath them steep flanks led to cliffs rising vertically from the sea.

No wonder Nordsen had said the western end of the island was uninhabited, difficult of access. At least that was something in the submarine's favour, decided Milovych. The lighthouse at Fyrbergnes, its black and white ringed tower stark against the mountain, came up to starboard and passed astern as the skimmer rounded the point. It was only then that the submarine, a few kilometres away, came into view. The glistening black fin and hull were scarcely visible against the jagged rim of the Drageten-nene and the clouds of spray which leapt skywards as seas broke against them. A knot formed in Milovych's stomach. It was a mind-bending spectacle. This marvellous product of USSR technological genius stranded like some dying whale on a foreign shore. There would be a court martial of course. Would the court take the view that *Zhukov* should have been abandoned and destroyed? That he, Milovych, should never have agreed, however reluctantly, to Yenev's proposal?

As Milovych tussled with this problem the high whine

of the skimmer's engine dropped to a lower pitch. Soon afterwards it coughed and died as the little rubber craft entered sheltered water in the lee of the submarine and drifted alongside. Milovych climbed a rope ladder and went down to the control-room through the free-flooding door at the foot of the fin.

In the security of the captain's cabin the commissar reported on the morning's events. He finished by outlining the arrangements made with the *Ordforer* for Krasnov and Gerasov to remain ashore for the time being.

Yenev in turn told of the work done that morning, of progress made with emergency repairs, with containing flooding and controlling radiation and chloride contamination. "We've got some of the radar on stream again," he said. "And Uskhan has rigged an emergency radio receiver. It's a small set. Brought on board by a seaman and impounded. Otherwise there has been little change in the electronics situation."

"The forward torpedo-compartment?" Milovych ran his tongue round his lips.

"Completely flooded. We can't risk opening the W.T. doors and vents. Nor can we enter by the forward escape hatch. It's awash most of the time."

"The men there?"

"We can do nothing for them. All must have been dead for a long time. Outside assistance is essential to deal with that compartment."

"The salvage vessels?"

"Of course."

"By now Leningrad will have had our signal from Oslo. They in turn will have passed it to C-in-C Northern Fleet. How long have we to wait, comrade Yenev?"

"A *Nepa* class submarine rescue and salvage ship can make eighteen knots. The Fleet salvage tugs a little more. If they clear Polyarnyo by fourteen hundred today, and the weather holds, they should be here within thirty-six to forty hours."

Milovych looked at his watch. "That means some time tomorrow night."

Yenev nodded. "We should have a reply from Oslo shortly. I have given instructions for the skimmer to make the trip to and from Kolhamn at two-hourly intervals, at least until we receive it."

"How are the injured?" For reasons probably known to psychiatrists Milovych's inquiry was accompanied with a smile.

"There are seven receiving treatment. Three for burns, three for minor fractures—and Kossuth of course. He has been decontaminated but still suffers from shock." Kossuth had been on duty in the emergency communications room at the time of the explosion.

Yenev scratched his head. "The doctor says none are serious. We can treat them better on board than would be possible on the island. And it mustn't be known ashore that there's been a radiation leak."

Milovych crossed his legs and sat back in an easy chair. Yenev, at a small desk beside the bunk, sat facing him. "There is something I do not like, Commissar. Our radar and research receivers picked up several reconnaissance aircraft this morning. Uskhan identified four of them by their radar signatures."

"They were?"

"One was US. Probably a Lockheed SR-1A from the Keflavik Air Base. Operating at 22,000 metres. The first to arrive was British. Almost certainly a Nimrod. It did some low flying to the west. We couldn't see it for cloud. There was one of ours. A Tupolev TU-16. Operating at about 16,000 metres. Probably on surveillance patrol. There was also a Breguet-Dassault at about 15,000 metres."

"It may be chance," said Milovych. "The US, British and French may also have been on routine patrols."

Yenev shook his head. "Radar tracking shows they were concentrating on this area. Photographing, I expect. I've no doubt we'll be receiving more attention during the day. The Norwegians are not going to stop their own military flights. I'm only surprised we haven't seen more of them."

"How is it known so soon that *Zhukov* is here?"

"I'm sure they don't know it's the *Zhukov*. But the news that a big Soviet BMS is aground on Vrakoy is already being broadcast. Uskhan heard it on the emergency receiver."

"How did they get it?" Milovych, head cocked on one side, watched Yenev closely.

"Somebody in Kolhamn must have talked. Fishermen perhaps. Such news travels fast. It is something for which we cannot be responsible."

"It might be said, comrade Yenev," Milovych smiled amiably, "that your decision not to destroy *Zhukov*, to put the ship in a place where Western reconnaissance could observe her, *was* responsible."

Yenev's pale eyes held the commissar's. "Our decision, I thought."

"Made on your advice, comrade."

"Somehow," said Yenev, "I don't think that argument would carry much weight at a court martial."

Milovych winced. It seemed Yenev's unblinking eyes could peer into his brain, read his thoughts. The commissar changed the subject abruptly. "What do you think of the weather?"

"The glass is steady but broadcast weather reports from Oslo are not encouraging."

Milovych kneaded the flesh under his eyes with his knuckles. He felt tired, despondent. These matters were not susceptible to political treatment. If they were, how different everything would be.

Later that afternoon the Norwegian minesweeper from Harstad arrived. It landed two platoons of infantrymen and left immediately for Knausnes to patrol to seaward of the *Zhukov*.

One platoon of infantrymen was billeted in the town with a lieutenant in charge; the other, under the command of a young captain, embarked with their equipment in a fishing vessel commandeered by the *Ordforer*. Forty minutes later they were landed in a small cove in the deserted bay at Uklarvik, near the Fyrberg lighthouse. From there they set out to cover the three kilometres to

Knausnes, led by a guide provided by the *Ordforer*. The journey involved climbing the lower slopes of Fyrberg before making the descent to the cliffs above the Drägetennene. It took all of two hours.

It was raining and almost dark when they arrived at their destination. After posting sentries along the cliff, the captain returned to the site where patrol tents were being erected for what promised to be a miserable night. His orders were to keep sightseers, journalists, photographers and other unauthorized persons away from the submarine. He regarded the whole operation as a waste of time. Who on earth, he asked his second-in-command, a bespectacled young lieutenant with lanky hair which belied his toughness, would be crazy enough to make the journey across the mountain to see a submarine aground?

"That's right," said the lieutenant. "But what a size. Bloody fantastic, isn't it?"

At about the time the minesweeper disembarked its load of soldiers in Kolhamn a helicopter of the Norwegian Air Force flew in. From it stepped Lars Martinsen. He went immediately to the *radhus* where he had a brief discussion with Hjalmar Nordsen.

Soon afterwards, accompanied by the harbourmaster, Olaf Petersen, he climbed into a launch and they headed down the Kolfjord towards the open sea.

The helicopter had brought three other passengers. These men, civilians, didn't disembark. They sat in the helicopter behind drawn blinds talking in low voices. On the tarmac outside an armed military policeman stood on guard. He, too, had come in the helicopter.

Krasnov and Gerasov spent most of that day walking round Kolhamn, visiting the *radhus* at regular intervals to see if the reply from Oslo had come in. Their uniforms attracted attention but this was not serious. The news that a Russian submarine was aground had circulated quickly and they had no need to explain their presence.

By four o'clock that afternoon there was still no reply

from Oslo. The two Soviet officers now had a fairly good idea of the small harbour town and its activities. They had observed that it spread like the foot of a large sock round the head of the fjord and was dominated by the mountain which cradled it, its dark slopes leading to rocky summits mantled with early snow.

The wooden houses of the fishermen—for the most part perched on stilts—lined the fjord. They were fronted by quays of rough-hewn wood on which nets, dan buoys and other fishing gear were stowed. Above and beyond them small houses traced irregular patterns in the foothills. Toylike in the distance, they were painted in bright colours: terracottas, beiges, greens, blues and creams. All had white doors and window frames and were modest in size and appearance. A single dirt road threaded its way round the fjord between the houses. There were bicycles but no cars. Krasnov had learnt that it was the time of year when most of the fishermen were up in the Barents Sea cod fishing. Thus women and children predominated.

There were two general stores housed in old clapboard buildings. In strange contrast to its exterior, one was organized as a supermarket. Krasnov and Gerasov had made small purchases in both. By design the task had taken a long time for Krasnov did not then admit to speaking Norwegian and changing money had presented problems.

His instructions from Milovych had been clear—*listen to the gossip in the town. Find out what the locals know.* And so he and Gerasov set themselves the task of finding out where local gossip could best be overheard.

It was this they were now discussing. "The two stores, I reckon," said Krasnov, "and this place." He looked round the small *kafeteria* in which they were sitting. They had eaten there at midday. The only other occupants were two young men, fishermen it seemed, who were at a pin-table, two old men sitting in a corner smoking pipes and engaging in brief monosyllabic conversation, and three teenage girls whose whispered sentences, sudden giggles and sidelong glances were directed at the Russians.

Gerasov refilled his beer glass. "Yes. I agree." He belched quietly. "The stores and the *kafeteria*. Wish they sold spirits here. This beer would go well with vodka or akvavit."

"You're lucky to get beer," said Krasnov. "We're not here to sample the booze. Concentrate on the job, my lad."

They'd found in the course of what seemed a long thirsty day that the *kafeteria* was the only place in Kolhamn which served beer for drinking on the premises. Spirits could not be bought on the island, the population being too small for a state liquor shop. Many of the fishermen apparently made their own spirits—*hjemmebreut*—and drank them at home, but these could not be bought. Krasnov had made casual but calculated inquiries about local drinking habits in the belief that where locals congregated to drink gossip would be plentiful. But there was nowhere other than the *kafeteria* and that seemed poorly attended.

He looked at his watch, emptied the glass and reached for his cap. "Come on. Drink up. The skimmer's due at five. We've only ten minutes."

Gerasov swallowed the last of his beer, took a uniform cap from the table and looked at the teenagers. "Think they'd part with it?"

"Better ask them," said Krasnov. "But not now. We must get cracking."

"Sorry," said Gerasov. "Must have a pee first. This beer goes through a man like a knife."

"Well shake it up. There's little time." The lieutenant stood waiting while Gerasov went through the glass door at the back marked *Toileten*.

# Twelve

The harbourmaster's launch taking Martinsen out to the *Zhukov* emerged from Kolfjord as the submarine's skimmer making its 1700 trip entered. Leaping and spraying it passed within a hundred yards of the launch. Had the men known each other rain, spray and distance would have concealed their identity. Martinsen had no idea that one of the hunched figures in the skimmer was Milovych; and Milovych, unaware that the launch was bound for the *Zhukov*, didn't know it carried Martinsen with the reply from Oslo which the commissar was hoping to find in the *Ordforer's* office.

The apparent comedy of errors was not as uncontrived as it appeared. On arrival in Nordsen's office Martinsen had said, "My orders are to go at once to the submarine to discuss with Commander Yenev the steps we are taking to assist him. Can you arrange transport for me?"

"Most certainly," said the *Ordforer* who'd already been briefed by telephone from the county governor's office in Bodo. "The harbourmaster's launch is at your disposal." He took a sealed envelope from a desk drawer. "This coded message for Commander Yenev has just come in by teleprinter from the Soviet Embassy in Oslo. Please hand it to Yenev personally."

"Of course." Martinsen pocketed the envelope. "I shall go at once."

The *Ordforer* said, "Two officers from the submarine have been ashore all day waiting for this message. They call here regularly to see if it has arrived."

"Then they will no doubt be grateful to us for expediting its delivery."

Nordsen's serious face managed a smile. "No doubt."

Martinsen knew that transmission of the message had been delayed by Norwegian Intelligence, that the *Ordforer*'s briefing from Bodo had included an instruction to hand it to him for delivery immediately on arrival. For their part the Russians, having no illusions about the integrity of foreign intelligence services, had couched the message in guarded terms. It did no more than inform Yenev that Soviet salvage experts would fly in to Kolhamn that evening, and that salvage vessels and tugs from Polyarnyo would arrive off Knausnes about midnight on the following day. It recorded also that a Norwegian minesweeper and military personnel were being sent to Vrakoy by the Norwegian authorities to assist in security measures.

*These measures*, concluded the message, *have been agreed on a government-to-government basis and the authorities have been instructed to give you every assistance.*

As the harbourmaster's launch rounded Fyrbergnes it was intercepted by the Norwegian minesweeper on patrol and ordered alongside. "Who are you and what is your business?" shouted the captain by loud-hailer.

Olaf Petersen cupped his hands. "I am the harbourmaster of Kolhamn. My passenger is Major Lars Martinsen from Oslo. He has instructions to visit the submarine and discuss security arrangements with the captain."

"Very well. You may proceed."

The captain of the minesweeper had already been informed by radio that Major Martinsen would take general charge of security arrangements on Vrakoy. The minesweeper turned away and headed for Knausnes, informing the submarine by signal lamp of the launch's mission.

The launch approached Knausnes and the submarine showed up suddenly through the rain. "Christ," said Petersen. "She's as big as a cruiser. I never expected to see one of them on those rocks."

"Don't suppose they did either," said Martinsen.

83

It was low water and a good deal of the submarine's hull was visible. As the Norwegians drew closer they saw sailors on the casing hanging fenders over the side while armed sentries, automatic rifles slung over oilskins, stood at guardrails which had been rigged on either side of the fin and the long hump which extended aft from it. The launch went alongside and two officers emerged from the door at the foot of the fin. They turned out to be the captain and his interpreter ... Yenev and Gallinin. The latter spoke indifferent Norwegian but understood it well.

"What do you want?" he shouted to the Norwegians.

Martinsen said, "I wish to come on board. I am responsible for security arrangements to protect your ship and must discuss these with your captain. I have also to deliver a message to him from your embassy in Oslo." Martinsen held up the envelope. He was himself a fluent Russian speaker, but did not yet intend to let it be known.

Gallinin engaged in earnest conversation with Yenev. "My captain's regrets," he said. "It is not permitted for you to come aboard. This would be contrary to Soviet security regulations. We shall come down into your boat."

The Russians climbed down into the launch, Gallinin first, then Yenev. Martinsen handed over the sealed envelope. "I understand this message is from your embassy in Oslo," he said.

Yenev put it into his pocket unopened. No doubt he knew it was coded. Martinsen said, "My government has sent the minesweeper to patrol to seaward. It will keep away all unauthorized craft. In addition military personnel have been landed on Vrakoy. They will take up their stations above you," he pointed to the cliffs. "To keep unauthorized persons away from this area."

Gallinin translated this to Yenev. After a brief exchange with him Gallinin said, "My captain wishes to thank your government for this assistance. It is greatly appreciated."

"Is there anything else we can do for you?" asked Martinsen.

Yenev and Gallinin conferred again in low voices. "The captain thanks you but there is nothing more at the present time." The Russians shook hands with the Norwegians and climbed back on to the casing. The launch cast off, drew clear of the big submarine and set course for Fyrbergnes. Rain was falling more heavily now and the sky had darkened.

"Hospitable lot," said Martinsen, buttoning up the collar of his military raincoat.

"A vodka would have been welcome," said Olaf Petersen, wiping the rain from his face with the back of his hand. He looked back at the submarine. "Sorry for that captain. He'll finish up in the salt mines."

"D'you think they'll be able to get her off?"

Petersen said, "It's difficult to say. She's hard and fast but it depends on the underwater damage, and what salvage assistance they get. There's a spring tide in six days. That'll be their best chance."

Martinsen said, "I see." He couldn't yet tell Petersen that salvage experts, vessels and tugs were on the way.

"It's a big job," said Petersen. "And a lot depends on the weather. I wouldn't like to bet on their getting her off."

Martinsen was silent. He was thinking of what he had seen. Nothing more than a huge steel hull, that towering fin, the long extension behind it. Norwegian Intelligence's plan for getting him into the submarine had failed. The Russians weren't going to let foreigners on board. He thought of the men in the helicopter on the tarmac in Kolhamn. A motorboat from the minesweeper would go into the harbour after dark to embark them. They were nuclear scientists and had with them electronic and other equipment for measuring many things, including radiation. They had, too, cameras with high-powered telephoto lenses for obtaining close-ups of the submarine.

"By the way," said Olaf Petersen. "Did you notice the trail of bubbles astern of her as we left?"

"No. What of them?"

"Scuba divers," said Petersen. "They're operating an underwater patrol."

"You're very observant."

"Spent most of my life fishing. Makes a man notice what's going on in the water."

"What's the purpose of that long extension—sort of deckhouse—on the after side of the fin?"

"No idea," said Petersen. "Haven't seen anything like that before, even in pictures of nuclear submarines."

After the launch had left, Yenev sent for the executive officer. When he arrived the captain pointed to the empty chair. "Sit down, Lomov." He paused. "I didn't much like having that launch alongside. Most unfortunate."

Lomov nodded. "I agree, Captain. But we had no option. In any case they've only seen something of the hull and superstructure above water. No more than the men in the minesweeper have already seen, and the soldiers on the cliff will see when daylight comes."

"I suppose so," said Yenev. "But all the same I don't like it."

"Our divers are checking along the hull and over the sea bed beneath where the launch was," said Lomov. "They've found nothing so far."

Yenev scratched his head absent-mindedly. "Good. The anti-swimmer patrol is of exceptional importance, Lomov. Make sure it's maintained at a high level of efficiency."

"I will do that, Captain."

There was a knock on the door and Uskhan, the communications officer, came in. "I've deciphered the Oslo signal, Captain." He handed the message sheet to Yenev who read it. He passed it to Lomov. "Our people are not wasting time. They'll be here soon."

In the *Ordforer*'s office Milovych, through Krasnov, was expressing his displeasure that the Oslo reply had been taken out to the submarine by Martinsen instead of being handed to the Russian officers who had been left in Kolhamn expressly for that purpose.

"Major Martinsen had instructions from Oslo to visit the submarine to discuss security arrangements with your captain," said the *Ordforer*. "It seemed only sensible to hand him the reply for delivery. Your officers were not here at the time. It avoided delay."

"Tell him," Milovych said to Krasnov, "that in future all communications intended for our ship must be handed to you or Gerasov. We are not permitted to allow foreign vessels of any sort alongside the submarine."

Krasnov conveyed this to Nordsen. Milovych then said, "Tell him that we wish to protest most urgently at the action of US, British and French aircraft in carrying out reconnaissance flights over Vrakoy today. This is a flagrant disregard of Norwegian air space by the imperialist capitalist powers."

While Nordsen listened to Krasnov's translation his saturnine features betrayed no emotion. But he was not accustomed to being rebuked, least of all by a shipwrecked foreigner, Russian or any other nationality, and he disliked the man's squeaky plaintive voice.

"Tell your commissar," he spoke with asperity, "that the necessary protests have already been made by my government, including one in respect of violation of Norwegian air space today by a Soviet Tupolev reconnaissance plane. Inform him that Norwegian military aircraft will, as a result of these violations, be carrying out patrols over the area from daylight tomorrow."

On hearing this the commissar realized that the ball was in his court. The prospect of Norwegian military aircraft patrolling air space above Vrakoy—no doubt photographing the submarine for NATO at the same time—was an unwelcome one but there was nothing he could do about it. In an attempt to mollify Nordsen's evident displeasure he put on his most engaging smile. "Tell the *Ordforer*," he said, "that we will be grateful if he can arrange suitable accommodation ashore for you and Gerasov for the time being. Possibly for several days."

Krasnov, who had difficulty in concealing his pleasure, passed the news to Nordsen.

"Facilities here are very limited," said the *Ordforer*. "There is only the Kolhamn *hospits*—a boarding house with rooms for a few visitors. It is clean and reasonably comfortable. For meals you have to go to the *kafeteria*. I will see if there is a room available." He picked up the phone and asked for a number. They heard a woman's voice. After a brief conversation he replaced the receiver. "They can give you a double-room."

"We thank you," said Krasnov, who then explained the arrangements to Milovych.

"That is satisfactory," said the commissar. "Now make it unmistakably clear to him that you will call regularly at the *radhus* for messages. They must on no account be sent off to the ship."

Krasnov reported this to the *Ordforer* who reminded him that messages could only be transmitted and received during the hours the telephone operator was on duty—eight-thirty to noon and three-thirty to five. Which wasn't quite true.

Down on the quay, well away from strangers, Milovych and his young officers sheltered from the rain in the lee of a warehouse. "It is common knowledge," said Krasnov, "that our ship is aground off Knausnes. Nothing that we have heard suggests it is known that it is the *Zhukov*. We have spread it about that she is old and obsolete—now used for training only."

Milovych dried the wet pouches under his eyes with thumb and forefinger. "We shall have to leave you and Gerasov ashore for some days I'm afraid. We cannot take the risk of giving these people excuses to send boats off to the ship again."

"We can manage, commissar." Krasnov pulled up the collar of his oilskins. "And while here we can keep in touch with what is being said and done locally."

"That, too, was in my mind," said the commissar. "You have done well." He looked first at his watch then through the rain at the dark banks of cloud moving in from the west. "Our salvage experts will be arriving by Soviet helicopter late this evening. The *Ordforer* will give you their ETA as soon as he receives the signal from Narvik. You are to meet them at the landing strip. Immediately on arrival send them off in the skimmer."

Krasnov said, "I will see to that, commissar."

"They are to spend the night with us on board so that we lose no time in discussing the problem. On arrival of the salvage vessels tomorrow they will probably be accommodated there."

Once again the commissar looked at the threatening sky. The wind was freshening and the rain came in stinging sheets. He didn't relish the skimmer journey. The sooner it was over the better. "Well, I must be getting back. It is important that I see the Oslo reply without delay." He puffed his cheeks as if to emphasize the importance. "I'll send Leading-Seaman Lenkin back with your shaving gear and other needs for the night. Never discuss the ship in your room or in any place where you can be overheard. *Never*, you understand."

Salutes were exchanged and he climbed into the skimmer. The Soviet officers watched it until it was well down the fjord. Then Gerasov, bursting with laughter, clutched Krasnov's arm. "Needs for the night," he mimicked. "Oh, comrade. If only he knew what I needed."

Krasnov pushed him away. "Stop arsing about," he whispered hoarsely. "Those men over there are watching."

Gerasov said, "Sorry, comrade Lieutenant. In the excitement of thinking about their women I forgot their men."

"You're a lecherous bastard," Krasnov said. "If you feel that way why don't you get married?"

"I do feel that way and I intend to get married. That's why I'm keen on getting practice now." He looked up at the sky. "Let's get out of the rain."


From the windows of his office in the big complex which housed the CIA, Rod Stocken, assistant to the Director of External Operations (Western Hemisphere), looked out on what he could see of the Virginian landscape in the late twilight. "So Joe gets it from Karen and she gets it from Martinsen and we know he's Roald Lund's front runner."

The man opposite him nodded. "That's right."

"So why does Martinsen have to tell Karen that it's the

*Zhukov?*" Stocken looked at the men sitting round the large scale map of the Lofoten and Vesteralen Islands.

A dark young man with an Annapolis fraternity ring and film star looks said, "Maybe I'm naïve, Rod. But I see it this way. Here's this one-off, never-again opportunity of checking their latest nuke first hand. But it's too hot for Norway to handle. They daren't offend Moscow. As it is they're not happy about their NATO commitment. We know that Soviet naval units in the Northern Fleet alone outnumber their NATO counterparts by five to one. There's constant Soviet naval activity off the Norwegian coast. But the Norwegians don't want the West to miss out on this. Without the West they'd lose their independence overnight. So they tip us off. They can't take the risk of doing it officially. So Lund gets Martinsen to pass it to Karen. He knows she's a CIA feedback."

"I go along with Ben." The man with the sad face of a bloodhound closed his eyes while he paused to think. "There's a close relationship between Lars Martinsen and Karen. Usual bed-time story. He lets the name *Zhukov* slip. Forget it, he says. Shouldn't have said that. You know. Standard bull. Karen picks it up. Feeds it back to Joe. And Keflavik's confirmed it's a nuke with unfamiliar configuration."

"I guess Ben's right. You're both right. That way it makes sense." Stocken lit a cheroot, examined the tip, stuck it into the corner of his mouth. "Right now the Norwegian Government is negotiating with the USSR on maritime problems. This is a highly sensitive area. Norway's northern continental shelf pushes way out into the Barents Sea. That's where the oil is. They can't risk fouling up those negotiations."

"So what do we do?" asked Ben.

Stocken examined the tip of his cheroot again. "We get busy, Ben. Right now." He looked round the table indulging his sense of theatre. He knew they were all wondering how, when and who? Well, he'd take them up to it gently. "You fellows heard of Laillard's Tern?"

They hadn't. But they looked at the stack of reference books on his desk. That was Rod Stocken. Always did his homework. "It's a variant of the Arctic Tern," he said. "Very rare. Breeds in only two places in the world. One is the island of Rost, south of the Lofotens. The other," he paused, leant back in his chair and exhaled a cloud of smoke. "The other's Vrakoy."

"Great," said Ben. "Where do we go from there."

That pleased Stocken. He smiled, which was something he didn't do easily. "Ed Ferret and Jim Plotz are going to learn a lot about Laillard's Tern," he said. "And they're going to learn fast. For a start they can read it up on the night flight to Bergen." He leaned over the map, the cheroot jutting aggressively, his finger on Vrakoy. "Now," he said, "let's get busy with the *Gemini* plan."

"So why's it *Gemini*, Rod?" Ben smiled indulgently. He knew Stocken's weaknesses.

"I'll explain that when Vince gets here. Call him in will you, Ben."

# THE SECOND DAY

## *Thirteen*

Four of them arrived in Bodo that afternoon with light
hand luggage. They'd travelled in different aircraft from
Heathrow: Nunn and Sandstrom by way of Oslo, Boland
and Julie via Bergen. At no stage in the journey had they
recognized each other. From Bodo airport they'd made
their way separately to the rendezvous, a café round the
corner from Olufsen's offices. There they'd joined forces
before going into the travel agency. Nunn spoke to the
girl at the counter. "You speak English?"

She smiled. "In this job, yes, of course." Her manner
suggested it was a silly question.

Nunn realized it was. "We're from England," he said,
waving a hand in the direction of his companions. "I believe Mr. Olufsen is expecting us."

"Oh, yes. You've come for the yacht?"

"That's right."

"Wait, please." She went through a door to the back
office. A moment later she re-appeared with a man with a

weatherbeaten face and large questioning eyes. "This is Mr. Olufsen," she said.

Nunn introduced himself, then the others. It was a convincing performance.

Olufsen bowed in a stiff, rather old-fashioned way. "I am glad to meet you. Come please into my office." He held open the door, they went in, he closed it behind them. "There's not much room," he said. "This is only a small business."

Nunn and Julie took the visitors' chairs. Boland and Sandstrom sat on the edge of the desk.

Nunn winked. "Got a good boat for us?"

Olufsen showed no sign of having seen the wink. It annoyed him. His training didn't permit that sort of thing. "A forty-foot ketch, *Kestrel*. In excellent condition. Sixty h.p. diesel. She makes ten knots without sail." The English, the trace of Scandinavian accent, the sometimes unusual word order, was not the English they'd heard at the briefing in the Surrey farmhouse.

"Charts, fuel, food?" said Nunn, now slightly humbled. "You know our plans. We want to sail round and about the Lofoten and Vesteralen Islands, starting in the north and working south with the prevailing wind."

"Yes. The message from Cook's made that clear. You will find your needs in the boat." He looked out of the window towards the distant harbour. "Including food for three days. After that you have to visit shops."

The girl said, "Good. That's my department."

"If you will sign these documents, Mr. Nunn—charter and insurance contracts—we can go to the harbour. I know you do not wish to delay."

"Yes," said Nunn. "We mustn't waste precious time. It was difficult enough to find two weeks in which we could all get away together."

Down in the yacht basin they had a good look over *Kestrel*, checked her sailing gear, started and stopped the engine, tested the VHF radio, the radio direction finder, Seascan radar, and the echo sounder. When they'd asked the innumerable and inevitable questions involved in taking over a strange boat, they followed Olufsen down the companionway to the small saloon. "We can talk freely here," he said. "Any problems?"

"The inflatable skimmers and outboards?"

"In their packs in the stern cabin with the skin-diving equipment. There are also two inflatable life-rafts. In the orange packs with double white stripes." There was no foreign accent now and the word order was normal.

"Good," said Stephen Nunn. "The fuel for the outboards? In the engine-room? Red tank on the port side?"

Olufsen raised an eyebrow. "Yes. Where I showed you."

"The charts?" said Nunn.

"Under the table." Olufsen pointed to the drawers under the small table in the navigator's space at the after end of the saloon. "Depending on tides and currents you should make Kolhamn within fifteen to twenty hours. You'll find the courses laid off on chart 2312. That's for the passage after you reach the Lofoten Wall. From Lille Molla up through Raft Sund to Hadsel Fjord. Then through Sortland Sund and Gavl Fjord to a position off the Anda Light. From there it's only seventeen miles to Vrakoy."

"Pity so much of it's in the dark."

"Yes. The most interesting part. The scenery is superb. Particularly the passage through the Raft Sund."

Stephen Nunn found the chart. He laid it on the small table. "How's the navigation? Difficult?"

"You'll have to watch the currents. They can be fierce. Read up the sailing directions before you get there. They're in the rack above the chart-table. There are lighthouses and light beacons all the way. You can't go wrong really, especially with radar. That Seascan has a range of sixteen miles. What there is in the way of wind at the moment is north-west. You'll be using the engine most of the time."

"What's her endurance at ten knots?"

"About seventy-two hours. She has large fuel tanks. Chose her for that. Among other things." Olufsen looked at his watch. His large eyes searched the faces round the table. "Any more questions?"

There were none so they went up on deck. The sun had set, twilight was deepening.

Nunn said, "When do we see you next?"

"In Kolhamn tomorrow. I fly over in the morning. To get news for my papers, you know. I may be there a few days."

"I'm sure you will," said Nunn, and then wished he hadn't. He wasn't, he knew, behaving like a professional.

They shook hands with Olufsen before he went up the brow to the quay.

"Good luck," he said. "And good hunting."

Bill Boyd, the competent but irascible lieutenant-commander who presided over the destinies of *Bluewhale*, saw the radio supervisor making for him with a signal clipboard. "What's it now, Blades? More buggering about?"

Blades handed over the signal. "From C-in-C Fleet, sir," he said, and grinned. The captain, he knew, was feeling pretty brittle about signals from MOD. At 1400 the day before they'd received one diverting *Bluewhale*, outward bound on an Arctic surveillance patrol, to a position north of the Shetlands to rendezvous with the assault ship *Belligerent* for an ASW exercise. This hadn't pleased Bill Boyd in any way. The Arctic patrol meant *Bluewhale* would be on her own and he liked being on his own. What was more she'd been bound for the Barents Sea and waters off the Murman coast where units of the USSR's Northern Fleet would be carrying out late autumn exercises. *Bluewhale* had orders to monitor these, which was something Boyd enjoyed doing. The Russians didn't like NATO submarines monitoring them and had ways of making things difficult, which was a challenge and really rather fun. It was a more attractive proposition than stooging round the Shetlands to a ASW exercise under *Belligerent*'s signal.

Bill Boyd frowned as he read *Belligerent*'s signal. *My Whirlwind has picked up two survivors from yacht sunk approximately twenty miles north of you. Helicopter's fuel*

*remaining precludes making Lerwick or returning Bellig-*
*erent with additional load. Stop. Surface now repeat now*
*and standby to receive survivors from Whirlwind.*

He handed the clipboard back to the radio supervisor.
"Bloody hell," he said. "You'd think we're a flipping hospital ship." He took the broadcast mike from its rack and
pressed the speak-button: "This is the captain speaking.
We've just received a signal from *Belligerent* ordering us
to receive two yacht survivors from her Whirlwind. They,
he, she or it, will probably require medical attention." He
replaced the mike and turned to the officer-of-the-watch.
"Pipe hands to diving stations. I'm going to surface."

Soon after *Bluewhale* surfaced the Whirlwind was
sighted coming in on her port quarter. The sound of the
engine rose as the helicopter grew larger until, nose down,
it took station abreast of the casing abaft the fin. Three
seamen and a petty officer wearing lifejackets stood by to
receive the transferees. The noise of the engine was
deafening and beneath the helicopter the down draught
from its rotors created a circle of shimmering sea. The
petty officer signalled "come in", the Whirlwind crabbed
in sideways and hovered over the casing. A line was
dropped and a figure wearing an orange lifejacket was
winched down and grabbed by the men on the casing.
The procedure was repeated and another figure winched
down. The survivors were helped along the casing and in
through the door in the fin.

The helicopter swung away bound for *Belligerent* some
eighty miles to the east. A signal was made to the assault
ship reporting completion of the transfer, whereafter Boyd
gave the order to dive. Blades was busy again with an incoming signal from *Belligerent*: *Well done* Bluewhale.
*Proceed with dispatch to rendezvous with* Aries *in position Lat 67°30′N Long 8.30E. You will receive instructions for transfer of your survivors in due course.*

"That's bloody helpful, isn't it?" said Boyd to his first
lieutenant. "Who are these characters, Number One?"

"Frank Brough and George Hamsov, sir. Lecturers
from London University."

"What sort of shape are they in?"

"Wet and cold. Suffering a bit from shock. But the LMA says fit otherwise. We're fixing them up with dry clothing and a hot drink."

"Where are you putting them?"

"In the senior ratings' mess, sir."

"Good. What's their story?"

"There were three of them in the yacht. One chap was lost when she capsized in a squall. The Whirlwind picked up the inflatable dinghy on radar while exercising a square search. Sheer chance."

"Have you got details of this? Names, addresses, name of yacht, port of registration, etcetera. We'll have to let MOD know."

"Not yet, sir. I thought you'd like to see them first."

Nobody in *Bluewhale* knew—nor anyone in *Belligerent*, save her captain—that Brough and Hamsov had not met with a yachting accident. It was only when he interviewed the survivors in the privacy of his cabin that Bill Boyd learnt the truth: that Brough and his companion had been flown from Lerwick in the Shetlands by a Special Branch helicopter which had dropped a self-inflating life-raft into the sea before winching them down into it. There they had observed conscientiously the instructions to make themselves wet, tired and dishevelled in the half-hour of waiting for rescue by the Whirlwind. Sea seasickness had helped. It was the captain of *Belligerent* who'd ordered the square search "for exercise"—in the area where he knew the life-raft to be. He knew, too, that its occupants were members of the Special Branch.

At about the time the Whirlwind was lifting the two survivors from the North Sea another helicopter landed on *Belligerent*'s flight deck with three scientists and their equipment. These men, it was understood in *Belligerent*'s ward-room, had been flown to the Shetlands that morning from the undersea warfare research establishment in Portland. The buzz on the messdecks was that they were to test ASW equipment with *Bluewhale* and *Aries* in an ex-

98

ercise due to begin in a day or two. The equipment evidently had a high security classification for it was locked in a storeroom with an armed sentry outside. The scientists, three rather ordinary-looking men, took their meals in the captain's quarters and were incommunicado as far as the rest of the ship's company were concerned.

By late afternoon accommodation for visitors in Kolhamn had become something of a problem. The fishing village bustled with new arrivals: Press, TV reporters, and cameramen, a whole gaggle of media representatives jostling with each other for beds, meals and the hire of boats. The *hospits* could not help them with accommodation. It was full. Krasnov and Gerasov had moved into one of the double-rooms the night before. On the second day two United States ornithologists had flown in from Bodo in the Wideroes inter-island flight. They had taken the remaining double-room which had been booked for them by telephone by the Ornithological Society of America, New York. A press and tourist agent from Bodo, a man well known to the manageress of the *hospits*, had arrived in the same flight as the ornithologists. He had taken the remaining single-room. Inga Bodde, the telephone operator, had booked it for him the night before.

The media men had resolved their accommodation problems in various ways: some were making do with rented *rorbu*—fishermen's cabins not used at that time of year—others, more fortunate, had made arrangements for bed and breakfast with local householders.

They then joined in the frenetic hunt for information but soon found that to get anywhere near the stranded submarine was impossible. The Royal Norwegian Navy had reinforced its minesweeping patrol with a Storm class gunboat, and the cordon of soldiers precluded any approach to the cliffs above Knausnes—even for those not daunted by climbing the mountain in mist and rain. The Norwegian Air Force was operating fighter patrols over the island and its territorial waters, these having been declared prohibited air space. All aircraft wishing to land on Vrakoy had now to obtain preflight clearance from Royal

Norwegian Air Force H.Q. in Bodo. This in effect ruled out just about anything other than Norwegian military aircraft and normal commercial flights operated by Wideroe's.

The weather was deteriorating. The *Zhukov* shook and trembled as the seas struck her, notwithstanding the partial breakwater of the Dragetennene. So mentally did Milovych. "What's your opinion, comrade Feodor?" he asked. Dark bags had formed below the small eyes. Milovych was a tired man.

The salvage expert fingered the plans on the desk in Yenev's cabin. "I don't yet know enough about the damage to form one. But it's obviously serious. A difficult salvage task. Worse than your message suggested."

Milovych stared at Yenev. "It would have been better perhaps not to have stranded her."

Feodor regarded him thoughtfully. "I believe the decision had your approval, comrade Commissar." He turned to Yenev. "Your divers report a good deal of damage forward where the explosion occurred, but they don't find much evidence of other external damage. We know it's there of course. The flooding tells us. But we haven't the facilities for a thorough check."

"We need the salvage vessels for that," said Milovych.

"Of course." Feodor disliked the obvious. "They'll be here in the morning."

"I don't like the look of the weather. The glass is still falling." Yenev looked at him gloomily. "Wind and sea rising."

Feodor said, "These October gales usually blow themselves out in forty-eight hours."

"It's a long time," said Yenev.

"The weather's too much for the skimmer," said Milovych. "All right once round Fyrbergnes, in the lee of the island. But from the lighthouse to those rocks ... phew!" He shook his head. "We should hire a local fishing vessel."

"Yes," said Yenev, who'd proposed this the day before only to have Milovych turn it down. "And man it with our own sailors. I'm not having foreigners alongside again. No knowing who they are or what they're after."

Feodor said, "I agree. It won't be as fast as the skimmer, but it'll operate in all weathers. Commissar Milovych will no doubt make the necessary arrangements when he visits Kolhamn this afternoon. Once the *Nepas* arrive we can use one of their motorboats."

Milovych smiled uneasily. He didn't relish travelling in the skimmer in bad weather. "Wouldn't you like to go into Kolhamn this afternoon, comrade Feodor? See what salvage facilities they have."

"None that could help us. I checked that before I left. You know the *Ordforer*. I suggest you go."

"You'll be able to get Krasnov's latest report," suggested Yenev hopefully.

That gave Milovych an idea. "What about you, comrade Yenev?" His small eyes brightened. "Isn't it time you met the *Ordforer*?"

"Dealing with the authorities ashore is a political task," said Yenev. "I don't leave my ship while she is aground."

"I see." Milovych stood up. "Once again the task of extricating us from this . . ." He hesitated. ". . . this difficulty falls on me. I shall go now."

"Take enough men to man the fishing boat. Say three. One of them a diesel mechanic." Yenev yawned. He too was a tired man. "Leave the skimmer in Kolhamn until the weather improves."

Milovych didn't like the edge of authority in the captain's voice. He stared back to show his disapproval. When he'd gone Feodor looked at Yenev thoughtfully. "A difficult man?"

"Not one I like," said the captain.

The *Ordforer* was co-operative and after some minor delays Milovych got the fishing boat; a sturdy craft, flush decked, high bowed, a comfortable wheelhouse and sound diesel engine. The Russian crew took it over and the skimmer was secured alongside in Kolhamn. Having seen to this, Milovych went for a walk to the fish racks accompanied by Krasnov and Gerasov. It was cold and uncharitable, rising wind moaned through the saplings of the racks, rain fell steadily and the Russians' oilskins gleamed wetly.

"What news?" Milovych wiped the water from his face with the side of his hand.

"A number of Western media people have arrived. Press, TV, cameramen. But they're not getting results. They can't get near the *Zhukov*."

"Don't call her that," said the commissar testily. "You are never to refer to her by name."

Krasnov accepted the rebuke in silence, the forward and upward thrust of his chin the only sign of the irritation he felt.

"Have they spoken to you?" Milovych gave him a sharp look.

"They've tried. We say nothing."

"Good. Anything else?"

"A Norwegian press and tourist agent from Bodo—Olufsen by name—has taken a room in the *hospits*. He seems well-known in the village."

"Anyone else of interest there?"

"Two Americans. Ornithologists from New York. Booked in by their society. They have the room adjoining ours."

Milovych looked alarmed and the high pitch of his voice became almost a squeak. "Watch them. What do ornithologists come here for at this time? I'll send Uskhan in later today. He'll fix a surveillance mike in your room. Gerasov, you speak English, don't you?"

"Yes, Commissar. I took it at university. I'll listen of course, but I think they're genuine."

"You have no means of knowing," said Milovych. "Treat everyone as suspect. That way you avoid mistakes. And remember—never discuss the ship in your room or near other people. Never."

Krasnov nodded. "It has been on the Norwegian news broadcast that our tugs and salvage vessels are on the way from Polyarnyo. They call our ship 'the Soviet Navy's ballistic missile submarine 731. A first generation nuclear vessel, believed to be used now for training purposes'."

"I know," Milovych smiled smugly. "We heard it."

"Where are they now, Jim?" The speaker was lying full length on the floor beside the wall, almost under the bed he'd just pulled clear.

The man at the window said, "Walking along the quay by the fish sheds."

"All three?"

"Yeah. Milovych, Krasnov and the young guy. What's his name?"

"Gerasov."

"What are they doing?"

"Up-dating each other on news, I guess."

"They're welcome to it. It's heavy rain, Jim."

"We should have brought a directional mike."

"They're too far for that."

"Think so, Ed?"

"I know. I'll put the needle through at floor level."

"Got the thickness of the wall?"

"Sure. Turn up the volume on the radio."

The man at the window turned it up.

The man on the floor chose the spot, triggered the drill and the thin bit ate into the wood. When the bit-check reached the wall he stopped with the bit just short of breaking the wall on the far side. He withdrew the drill, inserted the needle aerial, pushed it home and fitted the wooden plug into the wainscoting. When he'd rubbed it over with shoe polish he cleaned up the wood dust and moved the bed back against the wall. "That'll do," he said. "We can take out the plug, clip on the leads anytime. Listen or tape."

The man at the window said, "A characteristic of Laillard's Tern is its disinclination to breed in any spring which precedes a severe winter. This has given rise to much speculation and the belief that . . ."

"For Christ's sake, Jim. Must we have that?"

The two *Nepa* class submarine rescue and salvage ships with two naval salvage tugs arrived off Knausnes at half-past ten that night. During an exchange of lamp signals with the *Zhukov* it was decided that, in view of the weather, they should round Fyrbergnes and anchor in Uklarvik Bay to await daylight.

This they did and were anchored in the lee of the mountain shortly after midnight.

An hour later a ketch rounded Kolnoy Beacon and with some difficulty made her way down the Kolfjord under sail. The north-westerly wind gusted and eddied unpredictably from the slopes of the mountain and sail had to be shortened. In the early hours of the morning the ketch anchored off Kolhamn to the east of the slipway where the water shoaled. The anchor light was hoisted and an attempt made to communicate with the harbour by voice-radio and lamp. There was no response. Kolhamn seemed asleep.

"They'll register our arrival in the morning," said Stephen Nunn. "Let's get our heads down while we can."

"Marvellous," said the girl. "I've had it."

"We'd better set anchor watch," said Nunn. "I'll take the first two hours."

"I'll relieve you after that," said Sandstrom.

Boland came up the companionway from the saloon. "Have to work on that injection unit at first light," he said.

"You have to mislay a component," said Nunn. "A critical one."

"No problem. Normal routine for me."

"Remember where you hide it, mate. We can't afford to break down for real."

"Trust me." Boland's normally dead-pan, slightly oriental face broke into a grease-streaked grin.

Nunn looked round at the rest of the crew. "Remember the breakdown story. The engine packed up a few miles north-west of the Anda Light. After that we made a long haul to the westward before running in for the Kolfjord. That's why we took such a long time."

# THE THIRD DAY

## *Fourteen*

"That then," said the Commodore (Intelligence), "is the situation?" The fingers of his left hand beat time to Ravel's *Dance Macabre* which sounded persistently in the outer reaches of his mind.

Briggs thought the tapping was a conditioned reflex, the commodore's response to a problem. In fact the music was the response, the tapping its by-product, so he was partially right.

"By and large, yes, sir."

"So it could be staged at any time. Tonight for example?"

"Possible but improbable, sir. They only arrived this morning."

The fingered staccato continued. "I think Freddie Lewis must go to Oslo this morning. Chat up Roald Lund."

"About what, sir?"

"About what Lund knows. What if anything his lot are up to ..." The commodore hesitated, the tapping stopped. We're coming to the nub of the matter, Briggs decided. Rathouse always stops like that when he's made up his mind.

"And—to tell him," continued the commodore, "about our tip-off."

"I'm not with you, sir," said Briggs. "What tip-off?"

"The one we've had from an *unusually reliable source*. That a great power is laying on something rather special by way of an intelligence gathering operation. Lund will want some detail, a clue perhaps. Freddie will say he has none. The tip-off in those terms is all he knows. Comes from high up the tree. Lund is sure to ask if the 'great power' is a NATO power. Freddie will say he doesn't know. That way China is not excluded."

"You're not proposing to let Lund in on *Daisy Chain* in some round-about way, are you, sir?" Briggs's voice was flat, leaden.

"I should bloody well hope not. But if Lund suspects we're up to something, now or later, this should convince him we're not. We'd hardly pass on a tip against ourselves. And it won't do any harm if his speculations range over Asia as well as Europe and America."

That lifted Briggs. He looked quite cheerful. "I get it, sir. Very bright idea."

"Many thanks. Now perhaps you'll get Freddie Lewis down here so that I can brief him. The sooner he goes the better."

"Aye, aye, sir."

Lund said, "You've been quick, Martinsen."

"Chopper lifted me out of Kolhamn at 1700. I flew a Phantom on from Bodo."

Lund looked at the younger man with interest. "Fly it yourself?"

"Yes, sir."

"Still like flying?"

"I've a love-hate relationship with Phantoms, sir. Like to keep my hand in."

"What's happening on Vrakoy, Martinsen, that I don't

106

already know?" Lund held out a packet of cheroots. "Care for one?"

"I don't, sir."

"Sorry, I forgot." Lund lit a cheroot, sat back in the chair and puffed at it contentedly.

Martinsen stood at the window enjoying the view. He said, "The two *Nepa* ships arrived during the night. Plus two salvage tugs. There was a conference on board *Zhukov* this morning. All the big salvage and nuclear brass was there. The chief salvage officer from Murmansk and his two assistants who'd arrived the day before, plus another seven or eight from the *Nepas*. There's no shortage of technical talent."

"Any idea what's been decided?"

"None, I'm afraid, sir. Their signals to and from Murmansk are being handled by the *Nepas*. High-speed transmissions computer-scrambled. They're not using our telegraphic services."

"Have they made a start doing anything—anything we can see?"

"Nothing yet. The weather's too bad at present for external diving on the rockshelf. I imagine they've had divers in the flooded compartments. There's a steady traffic of ships' motorboats between the *Nepas* and the submarine. Hansen—he's in charge of the platoon on the cliff—counted eight corpses being transferred from the submarine to a motorboat this afternoon. They were wrapped in blankets but he was using high magnification artillery glasses. Says there's no doubt they were dead bodies."

"Interesting." With a critical eye Lund examined the smoke ring he'd exhaled. "Has he been getting photos?"

"Yes. Through an observation slit in the tent. I brought back a lot of film from him and from the scientists in the minesweeper today. Keppel has it. Prints should be ready shortly. No chance of skin divers getting a look at the *Zhukov*'s hull. The Russians are operating underwater patrols."

"That was predictable. Anything else?"

"Our scientists in the 'sweeper have carried out various

laser, infra, geiger probes in the last twenty-four hours. They say there *is* a radiation leak. Probably from the reactor. And she *is* carrying missiles with nuclear warheads." He paused to let that sink in.

"So she's not the surveillance/ECM outfit our photo analysts thought?"

Martinsen shook his head. "They drew the wrong conclusions. Probably the unusual hull configuration. That extension to the fin, and the tail pods."

"Any idea about those?"

"No. Our scientists admit defeat."

"Anything unusual happening on the island?"

"A lot of odds and sods have drifted in."

Lund said, "Such as?"

"Mostly media people. We're managing to keep them away from the submarine. The *Ordforer*'s got word round that boats are not to be hired to them. So they can't get out to where our 'sweeper would stop them anyway."

"There's no law on that."

"He's his own law on Vrakoy, sir. A tough cookie. And the air is well under control. Nothing can get in close. There's still some high altitude stuff about. Difficult to control. Too high and too fast for fighter interception. But the weather's making life difficult for them. Our fighters are getting all the photos we need."

"Good," said Lund.

"Among recent arrivals—apart from the media—are two US types. Ornithologists. Came in yesterday. Sponsored by the Ornithological Society of America. Headquarters in New York. Come to investigate the nesting and breeding habits of Laillard's Tern."

"I should have thought spring was the time for that. At least the terns would be there then."

Martinsen nodded. "Their story is they're going to survey last season's nesting sites. Make plans for next season's count and ringing."

Lund puffed at the cheroot. "That takes them along the cliffs and down the beaches."

"And on to Hausen I expect. Ornithologists have an excuse for carrying powerful binoculars."

"Who else of interest?"

"Apart from the two Russian officers—Krasnov and Gerasov—you know about them—two Frenchmen arrived yesterday at the *hospits*. From Bordeaux. Cod buyers."

"Sounds reasonable. France buys a lot of cod from the islands."

"Their credentials are okay. But they're keen mountaineers. Seems a little odd. Got their equipment with them. Anxious to climb Bodrag. If it's a close-up of the *Zhukov* they want, they'll be disappointed. Our cordon will see to that."

Lund said, "A lot of people seem anxious to climb Bodrag just now. Is that all?"

"Not quite. A yacht came in early this morning with engine trouble. Three men and a girl. English. On a fortnight's yachting holiday. Doing the islands."

"Anything unusual about them?"

"Nothing that I know of. The *Ordforer*'s quite happy. Gunnar Olufsen from Bodo—you know of him—the press and tourist agent? He's among the media men on the island. He's well in with the *Ordforer*. Old friends. Olufsen told him the yacht party are okay. They hired it through his agency. They intend to move on as soon as they can fix the engine. Olufsen's sent for a spare part."

Lund shook his head. "Don't know how you get this stuff so quickly."

"A lot of it comes from the *Ordforer*. He knows just about everything that happens on Vrakoy. And he likes co-operating with us. Enhances his status."

"What's Kroll like? His deputy."

"Cheerful, good-natured old boy. Lazy I'd say."

Lund said, "So staying in the *Ordforer*'s house has worked out well?"

"Excellently. They've given me a comfortable room, she's a good cook and he feeds me information. Couldn't be better."

"Splendid." Lund left his desk and joined Martinsen at the window. "It's a great view, isn't it?"

"Marvellous. I don't see it often enough."

Lund changed the subject. "Freddie Lewis called on me earlier today."

"Lewis from Whitehead, RAF intelligence?"

"Yes. You've met him. We're old friends. We had a long chat. Whitehall wants to know what we're doing about the *Zhukov*. They're afraid we're going to miss a fabulous opportunity."

"What did you say?"

"Said I couldn't give him chapter and verse but we weren't standing by doing nothing. Towards the end he told me something interesting. Very interesting. Something you should know," Lund paused, turned away from the window and smiled at Martinsen, "and your contact." Unnecessary though it was Lund dropped his voice. "Lewis says they've had a tip-off from an *unusually reliable source* that a great power is laying on something special by way of intelligence gathering on Vrakoy."

"Which power and in what way special?"

Lund lit another cheroot. "I asked him that. I said was it a NATO power? He said, 'Look Roald. The words used were definitely *great power*. That puzzled us too. It's rather old-fashioned. But that's all I know. Absolutely all. Shouldn't really have mentioned it. Far too vague. Only worry you. It could be something. Could be nothing.' That's all Lewis said. I couldn't get anything more out of him."

Martinsen made church steeples with his fingers. "Not very helpful. I imagine it's the CIA. After all we've tipped them off in the hope that they'll do something."

Lund said, "I'm pretty sure it is the CIA. The ornithologists could well be their advance guard. Though how Whitehall gets into it that fast I can't imagine. But there's just the chance—a very remote one—that it's the French or British themselves. They're neither really great powers today, but I wouldn't put it past them. They'd love to steal a march on the States. You know the CIA's not exactly flattering about French and British intelligence. Particularly in its militant form."

Martinsen thought for a long time. "D'you trust Freddie Lewis, sir?"

"In this game one trusts no one, Martinsen. But he's a good friend. He tipped us off that it was the *Zhukov* within a few hours of her stranding. We know now that he was right."

"D'you think he knows we're doing a feedback to the CIA?"

"Good God! I hope not. How could he? We daren't have that known. Imagine if the USSR got wind of it."

Martinsen ran his hands through his tousled brown hair. "So I feed Freddie's tip back through Karen."

"Through your contact," corrected Lund.

"Sorry, sir. I meant contact." His grin made the strong white teeth in the sun-tanned face look like a TV ad for toothpaste.

"The CIA must know," said Lund. "Just in case it's not them."

The rain stopped in the late afternoon but the northwesterly wind persisted, and with it the rough sea and fast-moving clouds that darkened the sky.

Milovych came in late in a fast launch provided by one of the *Nepa* vessels, the fishing boat hired for the Russians having been returned to its Norwegian owners. The commissar called on the *Ordforer* to report formally the arrival of the salvage ships. Two-way voice radio, he said, had been established between the submarine and the *Nepas*. Messages could now be transmitted between Kolhamn and the submarine, using the salvage vessels as link.

"So you will no longer require your officers to remain ashore in Kolhamn?" the *Ordforer* inquired.

"We have considered that," said Milovych. "We feel they must remain ashore for the present. Both to represent us and to handle messages which may arrive through your postal and telegraphic services." Milovych had not added that their principal duty would continue to be one of surveillance. To keep him and Yenev informed of what was going on ashore and what the local people knew.

He said, "I have to request that your authorities intensify the seaward and landward patrols. You must know

111

that Vrakoy is now full of Press, television reporters, photographers and other busybodies. Our lookouts have on several occasions seen observers on the mountain watching the submarine through glasses."

The *Ordforer* stiffened involuntarily. "It is not possible to keep people off the mountains. This is a democratic country. We are already doing our best to help you. The military cordon at Knausnes and the seaward patrols make a close approach impossible. We cannot do more."

On leaving the *radhus*, Milovych walked down to the harbour accompanied by his two officers. Krasnov reported on recent developments in Kolhamn. That day the American ornithologists had climbed the long moundlike arm of rock to the south of the village known as the Spissberg. Using the wall mike given them by Uskhan, Krasnov and the sub-lieutenant had heard the Americans in their room at the *hospits* discussing the beaches on the far side of Spissberg. It was there, on the southern side of the island, explained Krasnov, that Laillard's Terns had their nesting sites and it was these the Americans had been examining. The *Zhukov*, he emphasized, was stranded on the western side of Vrakoy, ten kilometres from the beaches.

"What else did they talk about?" asked Milovych.

"Personal matters. Their wives and families. Current affairs. They have a radio. Listen to news from the United States. They were discussing the allegations against President Nixon."

"His accusers are traitors," said the commissar sharply. "I don't know why Nixon permits that sort of thing. We certainly wouldn't. The KGB would soon deal with it."

Krasnov thrust his chin forward in a nervous gesture. He had his own views on the Watergate affair but he wasn't going to make them known to the commissar. "One other thing," he said. "They talked about the United States Oceanographic Service unit operating from Bodo. One of the USOS scientists is a friend of the man Ferret. At no time did they discuss our ship or anything to do with it."

"Very good," said Milovych. "But watch them. If they're espionage agents they'll assume their room is bugged. You must trust no one." He changed the subject. "Are the media people still pestering you?"

"Not like yesterday. They realize it's hopeless. We won't speak. They've taken a few pictures of us. We can't stop that. But we refuse absolutely to talk with them."

Krasnov made other reports: the activities of the two Frenchmen, so far apparently harmless. The arrival of the *Kestrel*, a Bodo-registered yacht on hire to English tourists, one a young woman. The yacht's engine trouble. The Russians had seen two crew members working on it during the day.

Before leaving, Milovych told Krasnov of developments on board the submarine. Although the lieutenant had long assumed that Borchoi and his torpedomen were dead, the news of the removal of their bodies through the escape hatch—forced by the *Nepa*—deeply affected him. On the general question of salvaging the submarine, Milovych said little other than to remark that the weather was not helping matters. "For reasons of security," he said, "it has been decided that no shore leave will be given to the crews of the submarine and the salvage vessels."

In the last few days the *kafeteria* in Kolhamn, usually a quiet place in October when most of Vrakoy's men were away, had become crowded and noisy. Journalists, TV reporters, cameramen, soldiers from the platoon billeted in the village, the US ornithologists, the Frenchmen from Bordeaux, the two Russian officers, some of the English from the *Kestrel*, and the usual sprinkling of locals had now to jostle with each other for tables, food and drink. Haakon Jern, the proprietor, and his wife could no longer manage on their own so their daughter and Mrs. Jern's sister had been brought in to help.

Above the din of voices, the dissonances of different languages, the shouts of laughter and disagreement, the bells of the cash till rang merrily. The Jerns knew it wasn't going to last and were making the most of it.

Additional food and beer had been brought across from

113

Sortland on Langoya, the adjoining island, and, whereas the *kafeteria* used to close at ten-thirty in October, it now kept open until eleven-thirty.

Shortly before ten o'clock, having spent two fruitless hours in the *hospits* waiting for the Americans to return, Krasnov and Gerasov went across to the *kafeteria*. They'd had their evening meal there earlier but the place had filled steadily since. It was a good time for beer and listening to gossip.

As on previous occasions the arrival of the Soviet officers in uniform created a small stir, but the media men whose attempts to secure interviews had failed studiously ignored them. Kroll, the *Vise-Ordforer*, was sitting at a table with Odd Dahl, the *lensman*, and Olufsen, the press agent, drinking beer. Kroll was looking fat, cheerful and hot and his gusts of hoarse laughter were frequent. He evidently found Dahl and Olufsen amusing. The *lensman*—the island's bailiff—was, apart from its one policeman, the sole representative of civil law and order on Vrakoy. Two of the *Kestrel*'s crew, one of them the young woman, were at a table with Olaf Petersen, the harbourmaster. The Russians had seen these people from the *Kestrel* down in the harbour several times that day but had not spoken to them.

Krasnov said, "I want to get near those two Frenchmen. Listen to their chat."

"You do that," said Gerasov brightly. "While I close up on the yacht's crew. I can't speak French. English is my line."

"You come along with me," said Krasnov firmly. "Milovych has said we are to keep together always."

"I was only trying to be helpful, Ivan."

"Balls. It's the English girl. You can't keep your eyes off her."

Gerasov sighed. "She's a smasher. Look at those boobs."

"Forget them," said Krasnov. "We've a job to do."

# THE FOURTH DAY

## Fifteen

A new moon hung like a crescent on the skyline of the Virginian hills. There was a remote beauty about the distant sickle of light which stirred memories of another moon on another night in another place; a night of danger ... Rod Stocken tugged himself away from the memory, left the window and went back to the table. He pointed his cheroot at the dark man with sleek hair. "Let me get this straight, Ben. Joe's message repeats the phrase *a great power*. So I guess that emphasis is important. Okay? We don't know who gave the Brits the tip-off. We don't know which great power it is. What do we know? That this guy Freddie told Lund it came from *an unusually reliable source*. That could be bullshit. It could be not. Take your choice. And why does Lund want to feed the tip-off back to us? Because we may be pre-empted? What d'you say, Gary?"

The man with a face like a bloodhound said, "Yes. That could be the reason. We know we are," he looked down at the message sheet in front of him, "*laying on something special by way of intelligence gathering.*" He paused, turned to Stocken. "And I guess we're a great power. So maybe it's us."

Ben said, "We haven't tipped-off the Brits. And with our security I doubt anyone could. So maybe it's a kite they're flying. Why? To get a reaction from Lund's outfit or some place else?"

Stocken said, "From Ed's report it looks like a crowded scenario out there right now. Could be the French or the Brits themselves. They'd both like to give us a kick up the arse." Stocken bit on his cheroot. "So what can we do? Nothing, except get in first."

Gary said, "We've got the headstart. That's certain."

"Nothing's certain in this game, Gary. We've just got to pass the tip-off to Ed and Jim. Let them use their judgement. They're right there on the ground."

Ben said, "I'll do that."

Stocken picked up a set of photos and thumbed through them. When he'd put them down he trained the cheroot around in his mouth like a tank gun. "What's the latest from Keflavik?"

"They were over this afternoon at 60,000. Got fair pictures. The weather's moderated. The two *Nepas* and the tugs have moved in. They're anchored in the lee of the Dragetennene. Close to the *Zhukov*. Plenty of small boat activity between them and the submarine. There'll be diving going on, I guess."

"What's the ETA for the camels?" Stocken's finger gyrated in his ear like a drill.

"An SR7 from Keflavik picked them up off the North Cape at 1617. Being towed in tandem. Making twelve knots. They should be at Knausnes within twenty-four to thirty hours."

Stocken moved round the table, bent over the chart. "Say 1800-2200 tomorrow."

"That's right."

"Once those camels are alongside things are going to. move. There's only two days now to spring tide." Stocken went across to the window. The sickle of moon had set

116

and the night was dark. He watched it for a moment, seeing only the stabbing beams of auto lights. The time had come. There was nothing to be gained by delay. "Right," he aimed his cheroot at the table. "Let's get rolling. Instruct Keflavik, USN, USOS and the fieldmen to activate *Gemini*. Chopper to go in at 1800 tomorrow. I want this thing pulled quicker than shit. Okay?"

The Ivy League man who'd majored in philosophy and didn't care for four-letter words said, "I'll see to that immediately."

The Assistant to the Director of External Operations (Western Hemisphere) waved his cheroot at them. "Okay, boys. That's all for now."

"They've gone," said Ed Ferrett as he disconnected the leads to the needle aerial, looped the ear plug wire round his fingers and slipped it into a soft leather container. He put it into his hip pocket, fastened the flap button and put on his jacket. "Let's go, Jim."

"Sure." Plotz pulled on a jersey and they left the room, locking the door behind them. From the *hospits* they walked east down the street towards the harbour. It was dark and there were few people about. They didn't speak until they were among the sheds, then only in undertones.

"Waste of time," said Plotz. "Listening to those kids. All they do is philosophize. Consequences of power. Fallibility of man. Inevitability of corruption. Pseudo intellectuals. They haven't read much. I suppose they can't. Good thing their bosses can't hear. Subversive stuff I'd say."

"Tape it next time," said Ferret. "Blackmail material."

"Yeah. I'll do that. They seem to be sounding each other out. You know ... 'what's your view on Solzhenitsyn?' ... 'is there justification for Sakharov's criticism of the Party line on Jewish emigration?' ... that kind of thing. They never mention the nuke except to infer what a bastard M is."

"Who the hell's M?"

"Milovych, I guess."

Ferret said, "Well at least that's more interesting than

117

the stuff I got. When I listened you'd have thought they were from the Bronx. Football, fornication and food. What they'd have to eat for supper in the *kafeteria*. What they'd give for some plain home cooking."

"Like caviar Romanoff, borsch and vodka," suggested Plotz. "But I guess it's better for our Russian than refreshers in the lab in Camp Peary."

"Stuff the language," said Ferret. "I dream it. Seven years in Moscow. Jesus!"

"Spoke it before I knew English. When I was a kid," said Plotz.

"You know English? You could fool me."

Plotz pulled a crumpled packet of Chestertons from his coat pocket, fingered one into shape and lit it. They stopped under a warehouse lamp and he took the cable from his wallet and read it again: *Suggest you examine nesting sites on Rost before returning. Harrison,* 1800/2000. It had been dispatched from New York at 1:37 p.m. that day.

He passed it to Ed Ferret who was exploring his mouth with a toothpick. "So it's tomorrow," said Plotz with heavy finality.

Ferret read the cable they'd collected from Inga Bodde, the postmistress, late that afternoon. "Yeah. It's the activate signal for *Gemini*. Harrison is tomorrow. Chopper's ETA 1800. Vince'll look for the towel at 2000."

"Rod's in a hurry."

"He knows what's on the line."

"Yeah. Vince'll update us on that."

"I guess so."

"Let's give the *kafeteria* the once-over."

" 'Kay. Let's do that."

It was a small wooden building, squat and solid on stone foundations. Its roof of semi-circular tiles dated it late nineteenth century. Even without the "POST" signboard and posthorn emblem, its function would have been sufficiently advertised by the double letterbox, the telephone and teleprinter lines feeding in under the eaves, and the whip-like R/T aerial standing proud of the roof.

A man walked up the steps, opened the glass-panelled door and went in. The universal smell of post offices, a compound of postage glues, the mustiness of old stationery, and ink franking pads hung in the air. Behind the small counter a switchboard stood sideways on, so that the operator could see the counter while at the board. For the woman who was postmistress, switchboard operator and radio-minder rolled in one, this was just as well. With only four hundred inhabitants, less than sixty telephones—all wired for direct dialling of local calls—and recording devices for incoming telephone, teleprinter and radio messages during off-duty hours, Inga Bodde managed the postal affairs of Vrakoy remarkably well.

Still in her thirties she gave an impression of severity until she smiled and her face filled with warmth. As it did when she saw the man who'd just come in. "Hullo, Gunnar." She came to the counter, her eyes bright.

"Hullo, Inga." He leant over and kissed her.

"You can't do that," she said with mock disapproval. "I'm on duty."

"I'm a customer," he said. "We have our rights."

"For you." She produced a small parcel from under the counter.

He took it. "The spare part for the *Kestrel*'s engine. They'll be glad. They're tired of waiting."

"I know. The girl told me. She's nice, Gunnar."

"She said that about you. It surprised me."

"You're a horrible man."

He took a telegraphic form from his pocket. "For my office in Bodo," he said. "They'll forward it on to the papers. It's urgent, Inga."

"I know. I know," she protested. "All Mr. Olufsen's messages are urgent. Wait." She read it. *Soviet salvage vessels and divers are now working on USSR nuclear submarine stranded off Knausnes. Local opinion suggests flotation attempt will probably be made in next few days to coincide with spring tides. Norwegian naval, military and air units patrolling area where submarine is aground keeping shipping, small craft, aircraft, media representa-*

119

*tives and sightseers away. Message ends. Pass to local and foreign press. Daffodil Y 1627.*

"I've forgotten what *Daffodil* Y means, Gunnar."

"It's simply a code. We represent a number of newspapers. This tells my office which papers are to receive it and in what order. Sometimes I use X. Sometimes Z. Sometimes *Primrose*. Sometimes *Dahlia*. Sometimes nothing."

"Yes, I remember. You told me when you were here in the spring."

"Did I?" He took her hand and squeezed it. "Did I tell you anything else?"

"What else?"

"That I loved you."

"No. You never do. I have to guess it."

He dropped his voice. "Anything interesting, Inga?"

She looked through the window into the street. "Yes. I've made copies for you. You must destroy them afterwards."

"Of course. I always do."

She unlocked a drawer in the counter, took several message sheets from it and passed them to him. She sighed. "It's terrible that I do this. Wish I didn't love you."

He glanced briefly at the messages before thrusting them into his pocket. "I know. It's marvellous of you. But it does no harm and it helps me so much in my press work." He was preoccupied, thinking about something. "That telegram for my office, Inga. Can you let me see it again. I think I want to amend it."

She gave it to him. Before *Daffodil Y* and the time of dispatch he wrote, *Expect more positive news within twenty-four hours.* When he handed it back she read it, looked at him curiously. "Funny man," she said, shaking her head.

Over Olufsen's shoulder, she saw a face staring at them through the glass panel of the door. It was Gustav Kroll. He swung the door open and came into the office. "Good morning, Mr. Olufsen." His smile exuded warmth and geniality. "Hope I'm not intruding. I've come for some stamps." The relationship between Olufsen and Inga Bodde was no secret on the island.

In his room in the *hospits* Olufsen re-read the message sheets before burning them. One was the Ornithological Society's telegram to Plotz and Ferret about visiting Rost, another telegram from the *Ordforer* to the county governor in Bodo summarizing Milovych's non-committal salvage reports.

The *Ordforer*'s reports to the county governor were a formality. He knew that Martinsen's daily dispatch by sealed airbag to Military HQ in Bodo gave considerably more information, for the major received reports twice daily from the naval vessels on patrol and the soldiers on the cliffs.

A third message was from the US Consulate-General in Bodo informing the *Ordforer* that a helicopter of the United States Oceanographic Service would be landing in Kolhamn at 1800 that day. It was engaged on an oceanographic survey in conjunction with the Norwegian authorities.

The fourth and final message was from Military GHQ Oslo informing the *Ordforer* that a Soviet ocean-going salvage tug with two "camels" in tow would be arriving off Knausnes within forty-eight hours.

In the *kafeteria* that night Gunnar Olufsen stopped for a moment at the table where Nunn and Julie were sitting. "Hullo," he said. "How are things?"

"We're tired of waiting," said Nunn.

"All for a titchy spare part," said Julie. "Our holiday's coming apart at the seams. It's traumatic."

Olufsen's sympathetic eyes widened. "I know," he said. "I'm sorry. It's unusual for a boat hired from Halvorsen Brothers to give trouble. These things happen with the best of engines."

"I'm not blaming you," she said. "It's not your fault."

He smiled and she felt strangely drawn to him in spite of the gulf of years. In the short time she'd known this

121

man, his eyes, the warmth and kindness they conveyed, were like a caress.

Then, as if there'd never been a smile, the line of his mouth tightened. "Well. By tomorrow you'll know the land of the midnight sun." His eyes held theirs for a moment before he said, "Bye now."

When he'd gone Nunn said, "So it's tomorrow night."

Julie shivered. "Yes," she said. "I heard."

It was dark down in the harbour where the *Kestrel* lay. The single lamp on the warehouse shone dimly through the pall of rain, its light reaching the outer edge of the wooden quay. The night was quiet and still but for the lap of water against the ketch's hull and the chug-chug of a distant diesel as Gunnar Olufsen went down the ladder on to the ketch and made his way through the cockpit to the saloon.

"You're punctual," said Nunn looking at his watch.

Olufsen frowned. If he'd stayed in the Royal Navy he might well have reached flag-rank by now. Of course he was punctual. His training, his conditioning, his life were based upon punctuality. It could mean the difference between success and failure, sometimes between life and death. Was this young lieutenant-commander trying to patronize him? Olufsen ignored the remark. "Mind if I sit down?" He did so without waiting for Nunn's, "Sorry. Of course."

In a manner which was disconcerting to strangers but very much a part of the man, Olufsen looked in silence at the faces round the table. After a pause long enough to be embarrassing he said, "Hullo," and put on the table the parcel he'd collected from the post office that afternoon. "The spare part," he said.

Sandstrom took it. "Now we've got two."

Olufsen said, "How long to re-assemble that fuel injector?"

"An hour at most."

"Good. Work on it tomorrow." He looked at his watch. "I mean today. It's ten minutes past midnight. Make a start in the forenoon. Take your time. Encounter problems. Appear not to have completed the job when darkness falls. In fact, be sure you have finished. That engine must be a hundred per cent long before that."

"I will." Sandstrom was about to say "sir" but checked himself in time.

Olufsen looked at each of them in turn. "I know it's been boring ... and worrying ... for you. This waiting. It's nearly over." He smiled and once again Julie, feeling the magic of his eyes, wondered about him. How and why he'd come to be where he was.

His mood changed suddenly and it seemed to her as if a cloud had drifted across the sun. "We execute *Daisy Chain* in about twenty-four hours." He leant forward. "Now listen carefully. This is the final briefing. It outlines what each of you has to do. When I've finished I want your suggestions."

It was close to three in the morning when he left the *Kestrel* and climbed back on to the quay. He stood there for a moment, pulling up the collar of his raincoat before making his way between the sheds to the road which led to the village.

After he'd gone a dark shape emerged from the pile of fishing nets and buoys which lay against the warehouse. As the shape moved towards the light cast by the solitary lamp it resolved itself into a man in oilskins. He stopped, looked up and down the quay, listened intently, then disappeared round the corner of the shed.

When he was well down the road which led to the village he took off his tweed hat, produced a large handkerchief and mopped his forehead. It was sweat more than rain which worried Gustav Kroll for he perspired freely at the best of times and the oilskins had trapped the heat of his ample body.

# THE FIFTH DAY

## Sixteen

The divers from the *Nepa* salvage ships stopped external work on the *Zhukov*'s hull with the end of daylight, but inside the submarine patching and reinforcing of welding fractures continued throughout the night. The purpose of these was to reduce hull leaks to manageable proportions as quickly as possible. With the aid of the "camels," due the next day, it was hoped that flotation would be accomplished within the ensuing forty-eight hours when spring tides were at their zenith. Damage to the forward torpedo-compartment being too extensive to tackle in the time available, the salvage experts had planned other means of achieving positive buoyancy forward.

On arrival the "camels" were to be placed on either side of the submarine, abreast of the fin, and sunk by flooding. Chain cable bridles would be passed under the submarine's hull from one "camel" to another. This accomplished, compressed air would be forced into them, expelling the water ballast. At the same time *Zhukov* would blow all tanks and with the positive buoyancy provided by the "camels" she would lift clear of the bottom. The *Oktober* salvage tugs would then haul her clear of the cove and take her in tow for the 600-mile journey to Murmansk. The naval dockyard there could make good all damage, including building on a new bow section and undertaking such other reconstruction as might be necessary. These were long-term plans. The preoccupation of the salvage experts was to get the *Zhukov* afloat and haul her clear of NATO territory, so that she might with the aid of tugs and her main engines reach the safety of Murmansk, the nearest Soviet naval dockyard.

At thirteen minutes past two in the morning of *Zhukov's* fifth day aground, the sonar operators on watch reported the presence of unidentified underwater swimmers. They were approaching the submarine's port bow from the direction of the Dragetennene rocks.

The officer-of-the-watch sounded the alarm immediately, the captain was called and emergency state *Dobra*—repel enemy frogmen—was assumed. The two scuba divers already in the water on routine patrol were ordered to intercept the incoming swimmers. Two standby divers were in the water within less than a minute, and two more were made ready for instant action.

The sea around the submarine was illuminated by arc-lights and ratings with automatic rifles, explosive charges and underwater mortars manned the casing fore and aft. This was an emergency which had been expected.

As the arc-lights came on and night turned into day, leading diver Rostoff—one of the divers on patrol when the alarm sounded—sighted two dark shadows ahead of and beneath him. They were little more than fifteen metres away, swimming abreast close to the bottom of the sandy cove. It was the whiteness of the sand which had enabled him to pick them up so quickly. The incoming swimmers, blinded by the arc-lights ahead, had evidently not seen him. Soon after his sighting he saw them hesitate, then turn away. As they did so he fired an underwater mortar with a proximity fuse. It burst between the two swimmers, killing them instantly. He was joined soon afterwards by two more *Zhukov* divers and within minutes of the alarm having been given the bodies of the unidentified swimmers were in the control-room.

"Strip them," ordered Yenev grimly. "Examine each item of equipment for its place of origin."

While Yenev, Milovych and several other officers and men watched, the bodies were stripped. The wetsuits, the skull caps, the goggles, the back-packs, the compressed air cylinders, the breathing apparatus, the buoyancy compensators and air tank regulators, the weight-belts, the underwater cameras, the films in them, the powerful underwater lights, the stainless steel diving knives, the diving watches—every item of equipment was of United States manufacture.

The dead men had been killed by concussion—the hammer effect of the mortar explosion—and their bodies were unmarked. There were no tattoo marks, no artificial dentures . . . nothing by which they might be identified.

Milovych smiled. "Americans of course. They came to photograph the hull underwater. I expect the nose radome and the after blisters were the attractions. Hope they enjoyed their little adventure while it lasted."

Yenev addressed the executive officer. "Maintain state *Dobra* until further orders, Lomov. There may be other attempts before daylight." He turned to Rostoff. "You have done well, Rostoff."

"*Comrade* Rostoff," suggested Milovych.

Yenev's stare was too much for Milovych. He looked away. "You have done well, Rostoff," continued the captain. "You showed courage and initiative. You will be recommended for accelerated advancement."

Rostoff, wetsuit dripping, goggles pulled up over his forehead, looked with disbelief at the dead bodies, the staring sightless eyes, the half grins on the blue-white faces. He was trembling. It was the first time he'd killed a man. "Thank you, Captain," he said uncertainly. He was thinking, poor bastards—if they'd seen me first, it could have been me.

Yenev spoke to Lomov. "I want Krasnov and Gerasov brought off at first light. If these men came from the island they may be able to identify them. Furthermore, what has happened is to be treated as strictly secret. Those responsible for sending these swimmers must never know why they didn't return."

Milovych shook his head. "The U.S. wouldn't be so naïve as to send men from the island. These swimmers must have come from a submarine or helicopter."

Yenev said, "You may be right, Commissar. We shall see." He gave Milovych one of those looks which suggested to Lomov that his captain had detected a bad smell.

The Commodore (Intelligence) re-read the message clipped into the *Daisy Chain* file. Briggs, in his neat rather small writing, had endorsed it: "Most Urgent. From *Daffodil*, Bodo. 1627Y." The commodore read the words of the final sentence slowly, separating each with a deliberate pause. "*Expect more positive news within twenty-four hours.*" He looked up. "What exactly does all this mean, Briggs?"

Briggs was well aware that the commodore knew exactly what all that meant. It was the little man's custom to test him with such ingenuous questions. "The alert, sir. *Belligerent*, *Aries* and *Bluewhale* to proceed at once to their stations. *Bluewhale* to be twenty miles north-west of Vrakoy at 0200 tomorrow morning."

The commodore looked back through recent additions to the file. "*Belligerent* transferred the boffins to *Aries* last night, I see."

"Yes, sir. With their equipment."

"I trust so, Briggs." The commodore regarded him thoughtfully. "It would be rather sad if they'd left it behind."

Unabashed Briggs said, "The transfer went well, sir. *Aries* cleared upper deck for a nuclear fall-out exercise. The Wessex V winched down McGhee and his lot and they were taken via the mortar and one-nine-nine wells to the laundry."

"Which had been evacuated I trust. No Cantonese laundrymen left behind."

"Yes, sir."

"Yes, what? D'you mean they had been left behind?"

"No, sir. I mean the laundry had been evacuated. The laundrymen had not been left behind."

"Good," said the commodore. "I'm glad we understand each other."

"The quarterdeck aft of the hangar including the mortar and one-nine-nine wells have been put out of bounds to all hands except the flight crew when dispatching or recovering the helicopter. *Aries'* captain told the ship's company over the broadcast that it was for top security reasons. Highly sophisticated ASW weapons undergoing their first sea trials."

"Splendid. I always thought the *Daisy Chain* scenario was rather good. Hope it works as well as it reads."

"I'm sure it will, sir." Briggs looked rather pleased with himself.

The commodore's pucklike face gathered itself into a frown. "Nothing is sure in these rather dodgy operations, Briggs. Too many imponderables. If you'd been in a war you'd know that. I only hope our chaps have the luck they're going to need."

Briggs, who was an incurable optimist and felt the commodore fussed too much, smiled politely. "Yes, sir."

"Brough and Hamsov still in *Bluewhale*?"

"Yes, sir. They'll transfer to *Aries* with the ditched aircraft survivors in the morning. After the ditching has taken place."

"Quite," said the commodore. "It would be difficult to be a survivor before it had."

Briggs grinned. "Sorry, sir. My wife says I tend to emphasize the obvious."

The commodore handed the file back to him. "You do, Briggs. Not a bad fault. In planning repetition is an irritant, but omission is the kiss of death."

The *Nepa* launch delivered Krasnov and Gerasov on board *Zhukov* shortly after daylight. Both were unshaven.

The petty officer who called at the *hospits* to collect them had said his orders were to take them out to the submarine immediately.

Yenev and Milovych were in the control-room when they arrived.

"The bodies are in the sick-bay," said Yenev. "We'll come with you."

The sick-bay was a fair-sized compartment with four bunks in two double tiers. The centre compartment was dominated by an operating-table with surgical arc-lights above. Along two bulkheads stood stainless steel cabinets for medical supplies, in the corner a stainless steel washbasin and faucets; X-ray, shower and decontamination rooms led off the sick-bay. Five of the bunks were occupied by Russian crewmen who'd been injured in the explosion. One with radio-active burns moaned intermittently. The hiss of air-conditioning ducts was the dominant sound, iodoform the dominant smell.

*Zhukov*'s doctor and two medical attendants stood by the operating-table like officiates at a funeral. On the table alongside them lay two corpses, brightly illuminated by the arc-lights. Very close together because the table was intended for one person, very still because rigor mortis had set in. "Recognize them?" asked Yenev.

"Yes, Captain," said Krasnov. "They are the Frenchmen who were at the *hospits*."

Yenev's pale eyes switched to Gerasov. "And you?"

"Yes, Captain. The cod buyers from Bordeaux."

Krasnov said, "We saw them leave the *hospits* yesterday. With their climbing packs. They told the manageress they were going to climb Bodvag, the highest peak on the island."

The Wideroe's daily flight from Harstad brought in a mixed bag of passengers at midday. Three were Kolhamn residents returning, one a Norwegian fisheries man from Narvik, another the doctor from Harstad on his weekly rounds. The remaining two were tourists; a brother and sister visiting the Arctic islands of Vesteralen and Lofoten.

They went at once to the *hospits* where they were obliged to share a double-room owing to the shortage of accommodation. It had been booked for them some days earlier. After lunch in the *kafeteria*, followed by a brief rest, they explored the village. They were particularly interested in the harbour, the fishing vessels, the fish-drying racks and the *rorbu*—the house-cum-fishing sheds used by fishermen and largely deserted at this time of year.

They had signed the *hospits'* register as Li and Tanya Liang Hui from Hong Kong. Their passports showed their nationality to be Cantonese.

The light was failing as the big white Sikorsky came in low over the sea. The roar of its jets and the beat of its twin rotors were like the sound of an approaching storm. When it reached the shore it turned and swept down the beach below the Spissberg. At the end of the beach it climbed steeply, lifting over the rocky ledge which guarded the Kolfjord's southern flank like an outflung arm, and slowed its pace on the approach to the airstrip. On arrival there the Sikorsky turned into wind and hovered like a great white bird before lowering itself on to the tarmac where it sank on to its haunches as if to underscore its intention to fly no more.

For some time the rotors continued to turn, the navigation and dimension lights to blink. Then a door in the forward end of the podlike body opened and three men stepped out carrying hand luggage. In the gathering gloom it was just possible to discern the red-lettered inscription on the fuselage: UNITED STATES OCEANOGRAPHIC SERVICE.

Plotz took the red and yellow bathing towel from the cupboard and hung it out of the window facing the harbour. He closed the window, the sash jamming the towel in place.

Ferret looked at his watch. "Two minutes to eight," he said. "That's close enough to eight."

"I guess so." Plotz stood at the window looking down on to the dark street. The nearest light, dim in the gathering mist, was some distance away. "Could be fog tonight," he said.

"Yeah. It's looking that way."

"Better go down on the street. Check if he'll see it okay."

"I'll do that," said Ferret.

He came back in a few minutes. "It's fine. Light from the window's enough without the street light."

"Great."

They heard footsteps in the passage outside, voices, a door opening and closing.

"Jesus!" said Ferret. "They're back early. Pull in that towel, Jim."

Plotz turned off the light as Ferret finished the sentence. He opened the window and pulled in the towel. "Guess we better listen," he said, switching on the light again.

Ferret pulled the bed clear of the wall, removed the plug from the wainscoting and clipped the mike leads on to the needle aerial. He inserted the earpiece, cupping a hand over his vacant ear, pushed the bed against the wall and lay on it.

Plotz read a paperback and chain-smoked Chestertons. Later they swopped places. "Anything?" Plotz whispered as he took over. Ferret shook his head. "Usual bull."

It was not until close on ten o'clock that Ferret clicked his fingers and nodded to his companion. Some minutes later came the sounds of a door opening and shutting, of a key turning, of voices and footsteps receding down the passage. Ferret disconnected the mike, put the plug back in the wainscoting, the bed against the wall. "They're going to the *kafeteria*. Put the towel out, Jim. Vince'll be peeing himself."

The towel had been out for about ten minutes when there was a discreet knock on the door. Ferret opened it and a man came in. Ferret shut and locked the door. The newcomer wore a cloth cap and raincoat, and carried a canvas grip. He took off the cap and stood in the light. A tall, lean man with the brown skin of an American In-

132

dian. High cheekbones, dark intense eyes, black hair over an immobile face.

"Hi, Jim. Hi, Ed." He thrust out a hand, shook each of theirs in turn.

Plotz said, "Good to see you, Vince. Sorry for the balls-up. These guys would have to change their routine *this* night."

The newcomer smiled and the deadpan face came alive. "Guess it's kinda wet and cold our there, even for October. Maybe there's fog coming."

"Jesus," said Ferret. "We don't need that."

"I don't know. Could be useful. Depends."

"Where you been, Vince?" Plotz inclined his head towards the window.

"Holed up in the lane between the sheds. See your window from there without being seen."

Vincent Strutt put the grip on the floor, unbuttoned his raincoat and sat on the bed. He took a cigarette from the packet Plotz offered him, lit it and lay back, puffing whorls of smoke at the ceiling.

"Any troubles?" said Ferret.

Strutt shook his head. "No. Chopper landed on time. I came into the village with two of the crew. Later we separated. I've already covered the route from here to the main quay by the cold store. It's okay."

"And the rest?"

"All set." He looked at his watch. "*Rockfish* is surfacing about now. She'll dive immediately she's launched the skimmer. Then she'll head for the RV, twenty-five miles north of Nordnes—that's the most northerly point on Vrakoy. The skimmer will lay off the beach two miles east of the Ostnes Beacon from midnight waiting for our signal. We checked the layout coming in with the chopper."

"Fine. What's the back-up?"

"A *Charleston* support ship with three Belknap frigates one-fifty miles west of Vrakoy at midnight. *Rockfish* will RV with them round noon tomorrow. We'll make the transfer by chopper."

"Sounds okay."

Ferret turned to Plotz. "You better be getting along to the *kafeteria* in a few minutes, Jim. Be joining you soon." He looked at Strutt. "They usually stay on till the place closes at half eleven, then head back this way. Keep to themselves. They're there to listen."

"And drink beer and look at the birds," added Plotz.

"Talking of birds," said Strutt, "how's Laillard's Tern?"

"It should get stuffed," said Plotz, putting a lot of feeling into what he said.

"When these guys get up to leave I'll push out ahead of them." Ferret bit a thumbnail with fierce concentration. "We'll be sitting as close to the door as we can get. Jim'll come right along after them. Okay Vince?"

Strutt nodded. "When they've been back here for about ten minutes I'll knock on the door. Give Krasnov the message. He'll follow me down. Maybe the other guy too. We're organized to take care of both." He paused, examining the cigarette and his nicotine-stained fingers. "You boys'll be waiting down behind the cold store by the main quay. As we pass you come out. Okay?"

"Okay," said Ferret.

"You ask me the time in English. I tell you in Russian, *I don't speak English*. Right?"

"Right," said Ferret.

"Then we take him," said Strutt.

"Or them," said Plotz.

"Or them," repeated Strutt.

"One thing, Vince." Ferret eyed him curiously. "Why did Stocken call this the *Gemini Plan*?"

"*Gemini*—twins. Right?"

"I get it. Because there are two of them."

Strutt shook his head. "I guess not. If for any reason we don't get one or other of these guys—if that fails—Rod Stocken has given me an alternative objective."

Ferret said, "First I've heard of it."

"You and Jim are not involved, that's why. And that's the way it's got to stay."

"Okay. Okay." Ferret waved a deprecatory hand. "Suits me. We're not looking for hay."

"Anyway, that's why he called it *Gemini*," said Strutt flatly. "Twin objectives. See?"

Plotz yawned noisily. " 'Kay. Guess that's all. I'll get moving." He looked at the grip on the floor. "In there?"

Strutt nodded. "Yeah. But we don't want it rough. Unless it has to be."

Plotz opened the grip and took out three .38 calibre Colts in their shoulder-holsters. He took one, put the others on the bed. He strapped his on, slipped into his jacket, patted the gun where it snugged under his left armpit. He grinned. "Feel better dressed now." He put two spare clips of ammunition in a jacket pocket and went to the door. "Bye, fellas. See you."

When Plotz had gone Strutt took two miniaturized radio transmitters from the grip, and the uniform of a leading-seaman of the Soviet Navy. The ribbon on the cap was lettered VOLGA in gold. It was the name of one of the two *Nepa* salvage ships off Knausnes.

While he and Ferret talked he changed into the uniform. Before pulling the blue jumper over his head he strapped on a shoulder-holster. "It's difficult getting your hand to it in this rig," he explained. "They showed me how in Camp Peary. Look." He slipped his hand under the jumper and pulled out the Colt. "Jumper's not strictly according to Soviet naval regulations. Got a concealed elastic pleat."

They laughed. "You look great," said Ferret. "Kinda handsome in that rig."

"Get lost," said Vince. He was putting his own clothes back into the grip. "They've got your name on them, Ed."

Ferret said, "Kay. It's a verbal message, huh?"

"Yeah." Strutt broke into impeccable Russian. *"Lieutenant Krasnov? I am leading-seaman Pliyev, coxswain of the Volga's launch. I have been sent in to take you off to your ship. Captain Yenev's orders. You are urgently required on board."*

"That's quite something," said Ferret. "Your Russian's as good as mine."

"There's plenty more," said Strutt. "Like what I say if

135

he tries to check up, or if the other guy insists on coming along. I won't bother you. It's all taken care of."

Ferret lit a cigarette, took two photos from his pocket, passed one to Strutt. "That's Krasnov. This is Gerasov. Nice guys. Quite normal. Gerasov goes for the birds. Randy as hell right now. Just been telling Krasnov what he'd like to do to the Limey girl who crews for a yacht down in the harbour. She's around the *kafeteria* most nights."

Strutt studied the photos carefully. "Krasnov's not a bad-looking guy." He returned the photos to Ferret.

"He's a small-time intellectual. Doesn't like the navy." Ferret put them back into his wallet. "That makes two of us. It stank for me too."

"You're no intellectual, Ed."

"You could be right. How's Sara?"

"She's fine, Ed."

"And the kids?"

"Marvellous. Sammy's coming up six next week."

"You're kidding. Seems a few months ago he was that high." Ferret held his hand against his knee, palm down.

"Yeah. They certainly shoot up."

" 'Kay. I'll be getting along." Ferret stood up, strapped on ths shoulder-holster, got into his jacket and raincoat. He slipped one of the transmitters into an inner pocket of the raincoat and fastened the zip. "Bye now, Vince," he said as he opened the door.

"Bye, Ed. See you."

## Seventeen

More or less the usual crowd were in the *kafeteria* when Ferret got there. The media people, their numbers now down to six or seven, some Norwegian soldiers and sailors free from patrol duties for a few hours, with them a handful of local girls.

Petersen the harbourmaster was there with Dr. Kroll and Lars Martinsen. Three of the *Kestrel* crew had taken a table at the far end of the room, near the juke-box. Krasnov and Gerasov were as usual at a table on their own. Gunnar Olufsen, the press and tourist agent from Bodo, was at the counter talking to the proprietor. They seemed to know each other well.

It was a noisy, cheerful night. Behind the babble of voices, the laughter, the shouts of mirth and protest, the juke-box wailed and beat its sobbing message like a twentieth-century tribal drum.

As he threaded his way towards the counter Ferret greeted those with whom he had a nodding acquaintance. As always he responded to the English girl's cheerful smile. "Hi there, Julie. How's the *Kestrel*?"

"Fine," she said. "We've got the spare part at last."

"Leaving soon?"

"Tonight I hope. If we can get the engine going. How are the Arctic Terns?"

Ferret shook his head. "Guess they're way down south just now. In Africa mostly. We'll be ringing them next season. Tell you more then."

137

"Must be fabulously interesting. Knowing all about birds."

"It is," said Boland. "Ask any man."

Julie laughed through even white teeth. "Yes. I expect he knows a good deal about *them* too."

"Not me," said Ferret. "Married. Strictly lawn-mowing type."

"I wonder."

Ferret reached the counter; Haakon Jern apologized to Olufsen, turned to the American. The proprietor spoke little English, enough to serve customers and handle a modest chat. "Evening, Mr. Ferret."

"Evening, Mr. Jern. Two bottles of Mack lager and some Geitost cheese and biscuits. Those small square ones." Ferret pointed to the packets on the shelf.

Jern busied himself with the order. When he'd lined it up he said, "Your friend. He come tonight?"

"He'll be along soon, I guess."

"The work on the birds. Okay?"

"Yeah. Just about finished. We'll be moving on to Rost. Tomorrow maybe."

"Oh, Rost. Many birds there. A fine island. Beautiful, you know."

"So I hear. What's that I owe you?"

"Twenty-three kroner, please."

Ferret paid, put the beer, cheese and biscuits on a metal tray and made his way to the table by the door. It was an unpopular pitch, cold and draughty. Jim Plotz came in soon afterwards. He took a glass and poured a lager. "I need this. Long time no drink."

"Vince okay?"

"Yeah. He's on the bed reading."

Ferret looked at his watch. It was almost half past ten. Another hour to closing.

Plotz leant forward. "Seen them?"

"Yeah. Don't look now. Over in the corner. Opposite the *Kestrel* lot."

"What are they doing?"

"The usual. Drinking lager, talking a little, listening

mostly. Gerasov can't keep his eyes off the English bird."

"Don't blame him. The more I see her the dishier she gets."

"It's abstinence, Jim."

"You can say that again. Usual crowd here?"

"Just about. The French boys haven't shown up yet. They missed the evening meal too."

"That so? Maybe they're stuck on the mountain."

"Don't envy them. I reckon there's fog coming."

Just then Odd Dahl the *lensman* came in and joined Kroll and Lars Martinsen.

While he talked to Jern, Olufsen leaned against the counter, relaxed and casual, his wide eyes on the room, missing nothing. He'd seen the arrival of Ferret and Plotz, noted the absence of the Frenchmen and checked the position of the Russians' table relative to that occupied by the *Daisy Chain* party.

When the music stopped Boland slipped more coins into the juke-box and it started up again.

Nunn said, "Good. Keep the bloody thing going."

"Think there'll be fog?" Julie frowned.

Nunn shrugged his shoulders. "Looks like it."

"Could help," said Boland.

"Could be a flaming disaster." Nunn looked at Julie. She'd hung the sheepskin coat over the back of the chair. Her blue denim slacks were faded and patched and over the black sweater a medallion on a silver chain emphasized the curve of her breasts. "You're quite a dish, aren't you?" he said.

"You feeling well, Steve?" It was the first time he'd seemed to notice her. She'd long ago put him down as a misogynist.

"I've been watching Gerasov. Can't keep his eyes off you. I wondered why. So I checked. Simple as that."

"Bully for you. Such compliments."

"No. Don't get me wrong. He does, doesn't he?"

"Does what?"

"Looks at you as though . . ." he trailed off.

"He'd like to rape her," suggested Boland.

"For your information one of the reasons he looks at me as though he'd like to rape me," said Julie, "is that I've shown in a distant maidenly way that I'd like him to. Men always fall for that."

"How do you do this in a maidenly way?" asked Nunn.

Julie shook her head. "I give up. Hasn't anybody told you the facts of life?"

"Of course," said Boland. "But it was a long time ago. He's forgotten."

Julie looked at her watch. "Almost another hour," she said. "I feel all churned up."

"If you want to feel relaxed, watch Gunnar," said Nunn. "You wouldn't think he'd a care in the world." He looked across to where Olufsen was leaning on the counter talking to Haakon Jern.

"Or that he had a .38 Smith and Wesson stashed under that denim jacket."

"Mine feels like a socking great boil under my armpit," said Boland.

"I'm the fastest gun in the islands." Nunn did an imaginary draw. "Practised in the *radhus* loo this afternoon. Accidentally bashed the door three times. The attendant came and asked me if I was all right."

"Great," said Julie. "Gives a girl confidence."

Nunn looked at her. "To return to your charms, Julie." His eyes were on her medallion. "Don't forget when thanking our friends, you speak English to them—not Russian."

"For Pete's sake, Steve. That's the fourth time. I'm not a moron."

"No. But you got it wrong at rehearsal." He tweaked her nose gently. "Remember? You spoke Russian."

"A girl can make a mistake."

"They often do," said Nunn. "Sorry my twitch count's high tonight. Don't like waiting."

"Who does?" said Boland.

"The important thing," Nunn paused while the juke-box switched to *Raindrops Keep Falling on my Head*, "is that Julie gets out of here before K and G. The moment

140

we see them move she makes for the door. Gets well ahead."

"So kind of you," said Julie, "to remind me of my role. I hope you've not forgotten yours. Remember I haven't a gun."

"Just as well," said Nunn. "It's a dodgy do anyway."

"Get lost," said Julie. "And I don't approve of violence. I hope . . ."

"Look out!" Nunn did a stage hiss. "Don't look. K's on the move."

Julie reached for her shoulder-bag. Nunn put out a restraining hand. "Hold on. Gunnar's watching but he's not given the signal. K's going to the counter. No. No he's not. It's the loo. Christ! They're forgetting their drill. They usually go together. Old Russian custom."

"What'll I do?" whispered Julie urgently.

"You can't go with him," said Boland.

"Wait," said Nunn. "For chrissake, just wait."

Gunnar Olufsen was still leaning on the counter, one foot over the other, talking to Jern. For a split second his eyes held Nunn's. Then he turned back to the proprietor. As he did so his elbow caught the counter. The glass he was holding dropped from his hand, clattered to the floor. "The signal," whispered Nunn. "Stand by."

They saw Krasnov open the swing-door beyond the juke-box. It lead down the passage to the lavatories: men on the right, women on the left.

Gunnar Olufsen looked at his beer-stained trousers. "Excuse me, Haakon. I must fix these. I'm soaked." In a leisurely, unhurried way, he made for the swing-door. He passed the *Kestrel* table, winked at its occupants, went through the door. In a very quiet voice Nunn said, "Julie, give Gerasov the works." He turned to Boland. "Get moving, John."

Julie said, "I'm giving him all I've got. But he's fiddling with his wallet, blast him."

Boland emptied his glass, stretched, yawned, said a few words to his companions and walked slowly down the room between the tables and out of the front door.

Nunn said, "Okay, Julie. I'm off. Over to you." He stood up, went to the swing-door and passed through it.

Julie, left alone, busied herself with a mirror and lipstick. Looking up she caught Gerasov's stare and smiled. He smiled back. She got up, took her purse from the shoulder-bag, put the bag under her arm and made for the counter.

As she passed the Russian the shoulder-bag slipped and fell beside him. She stooped to pick it up, but he got there first, rose from the table, bowed awkwardly and gave it to her. Their hands touched.

"Thank you," she said. "So stupid of me."

"Not at all," he said. "It was my pleasure."

She looked surprised. "Your English is super. Where did you learn it?"

"It is not so good," he said. "In Leningrad University."

"I think it's fabulous. Wish I could speak Russian as well."

"You speak Russian?"

"Not a word, I'm afraid."

"Please." He indicated Krasnov's empty chair. "You sit down."

She looked uncertain, seemed hesitant, glanced back at the table she'd just left. "May I? Just for a minute. My friends will be back soon." Out of the corner of her eye she saw a Norwegian girl come out of the swing-door. God, she thought, she must have complicated things.

Gerasov said, "Some beer? Anything?"

She shook her head. "Nothing thank you. I've still got some over there."

"You are from the English yacht, yes?"

She nodded. "The *Kestrel*. You're from the submarine aren't you?"

"Yes. That is correct." He said it very formally and she sensed it was not something he wished to talk about, so she said, "Not a very exciting place Kolhamn, is it?"

"No." He smiled sympathetically. "Just this *kafeteria*. Otherwise nothing."

Two minutes have gone by, she thought. Please God, may all be going well in there. Things hadn't quite gone according to plan. They'd always assumed it would happen after closing, on the way down to the *hospits*. I must hold this chap's attention a little longer, she told herself. God, what if I can't? For a moment her head swam and she couldn't think what to do next. The Russian was saying something. What was it?

"Sorry," she said. "What did you say?"

"I asked what work you do in England. When you are not with your vacation."

"Oh," she said with relief. "I'm a secretary. I work in a shipping office in Southampton."

"Southampton," he said. "The seaport, yes?"

Above the blare of the juke-box and the din of conversation she thought she heard a muted cry from beyond the swing-door. She trembled. "Yes. It's a big port. Tell me," she leant towards him. "Do you often go to the ballet? You have marvellous ballet in Russia."

"Yes. I like ballet also. It is a strong part of our culture, you know. But I prefer to dance. Do you like dancing?"

"Yes, I love it."

"It brings a man and woman close together. Yes?" Gerasov looked into her eyes for confirmation, then at the medallion. She could feel his warm breath on her face and his eyes were bright. Thank God for my breasts, she thought. They're doing a great job.

The chat went on. After they'd exchanged first names Gerasov warmed to his task. He led the conversation firmly in one direction, she responded and the minutes ticked by, while under the table the pressure of his knee against hers became bolder. At last she saw the swing-door open. Through it came Olufsen and Nunn, calm and unruffled. Olufsen rejoined Haakon Jern at the counter and Nunn went back to their table. Perhaps nothing had happened. Her stomach churned.

It was only then that she noticed Steve Nunn's hair was disarranged. A few minutes later she excused herself. "It was fun talking to you, Mikhail. We must meet again."

"Of course," he said. "Goodnight, Julie."

143

Back at the table she whispered, "Your hair, Steve. Put it straight for God's sake. Was everything okay?"

"Yes," he said, brushing it casually with one hand.

She saw Gerasov look at his watch, frown, then leave the table and make for the swing-door.

"Now the balloon'll go up," said Nunn. "Hold on for a rough ride."

## Eighteen

Olufsen had moved swiftly down the passage to the men's lavatory. It was a small affair: an outer room leading to a washroom, off it a door to the WC.

He'd stood at the outer door waiting. Seconds later Nunn came in from the *kafeteria*. Olufsen nodded and they tip-toed into the washroom. It was empty.

Olufsen switched off the lights and they heard Krasnov's exclamation of annoyance. They stood, one on either side of the WC door, and waited. There came the rattle of the chain, the sound of water flushing, the door opened and a man came out. His features were undistinguishable but the light from the passage was reflected on the gilt of his uniform buttons and stripes.

The two men closed in from behind. Olufsen's gun pressed into the man's back, Nunn's into his neck. Krasnov let out a startled cry. With a large hand Nunn muffled it. "Keep quiet or we shoot," he commanded in Russian.

Krasnov attempted to turn his head to see his attackers. Nunn struck him on the temple with the butt of his gun. "Keep looking straight ahead," he hissed. The two men each seized an arm, pushed him into the passage. From the *kafeteria* came the throb of the juke-box, the buzz of many voices. They steered him round to the right, down the passage away from the swing-door. At its far end the passage turned and led to a fire exit. Olufsen slipped his hand over Krasnov's eyes as Nunn pulled the bolts and opened the door. Shutting it behind them, they pushed the Soviet lieutenant down the stone steps into the darkness of the street. Two men came from the shadows. In the faint reflection of light from a distant window their mandarin moustaches and peaked caps were the only discernible details. The caps were of the sort worn by Scandinavian seamen. With rehearsed precision they took over from Olufsen and Nunn, Boland poking the barrel of his gun into the Russian's back, Sandstrom pressing his into the man's neck. They each took one of the Russian's arms. In Russian, Sandstrom whispered, "Do what we tell you or you're a dead man. If we are questioned we are helping you back to your ship. The coaster which came in yesterday. You've had too much to drink. Now come on. Move." The rough brutality in Sandstrom's voice was as untypical of the man as the moustache he'd gummed on to his upper lip with theatrical glue.

Olufsen and Nunn returned their revolvers to their shoulder-holsters as they ran back up the steps into the passage. They bolted the fire-door on the inside, went into the lavatory, switched on the lights and washed their hands. The whole incident had occupied less than a minute.

Olufsen's wide grey eyes fixed Nunn's in an enigmatic stare. It was impossible to tell what the man was thinking. "Not bad so far," he said. "Let's get back to the *kafeteria*."

Boland and Sandstrom pushed their prisoner up a dark lane between the *kafeteria* and a warehouse. There they took off his uniform coat and put it into the shopping bag from which they produced a raincoat. Sandstrom said, "Keep your back to us and put this on." Krasnov did as he was told. Boland said something in Chinese.

The only street in Kolhamn, a dirt road, led past the front of the *kafeteria*. At the back, unlighted lanes threaded their way past warehouses, sheds, cold stores, and fishing racks. It was dark and the chances of meeting anyone coming up from the harbour at that time were remote, particularly as they were making for the eastern end of the fjord, away from the houses. They had gone several hundred yards when they heard voices. A man and a woman were coming up the lane towards them, talking quietly and laughing. The Englishmen ducked behind a pile of wooden fish-boxes, pulling Krasnov with them. For emphasis they pressed the barrels of their guns more firmly into him. They could feel his response, the trembling of his body, the laboured breathing.

The couple came abreast of the fish-boxes and stopped. They were Norwegians, much interested in each other and, unaware of the unseen audience, quite uninhibited.

For God's sake, thought Sandstrom, don't start anything like that against the fish-boxes. They'll never take your weight. There must be better places. Moments later the young couple must have come to the same conclusion for the girl said, "Of course I want to but not here. It's too uncomfortable, Nils. Let's go."

They went, and, when the sound of their footsteps had died away, Krasnov and his captors emerged from their hiding place and pressed on towards the end of the fjord well away from where the *Kestrel* lay. They came at last to a jetty in front of an old disused shed. A dark and deserted place without lights. The water lapped against wooden piles and the ancient structure squeaked and groaned as they moved across it. At the jetty's edge they stopped and before Krasnov realized what had happened, a chloroformed pad was pressed over his mouth, his nostrils were pinched and he lost consciousness.

Kolfjord was shaped like a sock, the long channel which led in from the sea being the leg, and the elongated basin which formed the harbour the foot. The fishermen's houses—the *rorbu*, a combination of dwelling house and store for fishing nets, buoys and other equipment—had their stone foundations on the shore, but the jetties which stood like verandahs in front were on stilts to take care of the rise and fall of the tide and to provide a safe mooring for the owners' fishing boats.

The foot of the fjord ran east and west for close on two miles. At its widest it was half a mile, narrowing to nothing at either end. The village, and almost all the *rorbu*, were strung along the northern side of the fjord in the lee of the mountain. On the southern side the shore line was almost deserted but for three *rorbu* set well apart. Two of these were derelict and crumbling, though their stone foundations were still sound. The third, that nearest to the village, was occupied by a fisherman's widow.

Sandstrom sat in the fibre-glass dinghy while Boland lowered the bound, still-unconscious body of Krasnov with a rope turned round a bollard, easing it away gently until Sandstrom had the Russian in his arms and laid him on the bottom boards. Boland came down the ladder to the boat and took the tiller, while Sandstrom rowed into the dark night with muffled oars. There was no wind, the surface of the water was glass smooth, and the mist had thickened so that the lights of Kolhamn flickered dimly for a while then disappeared. From the fish racks on the eastern shore came the odours of drying fish and Stockholm tar.

But for an occasional whispered exchange the men were silent. Sound travelled easily over water, especially in mist. After rowing for some time they saw dimly the flashing red beacon which marked the turn into the channel which led to the sea. "Not far now," whispered Boland. "We're closing the beacon. Can't be more than a couple of hundred yards."

Krasnov, disturbed by the voice, muttered and groaned, struggled feebly against the rope lashing which bound him, and vomited.

"Coming round," said Sandstrom.

"Listen!" There was alarm in Boland's voice. "What's that?"

From somewhere ahead came the drumming of a

147

diesel. He stopped rowing and the dinghy drifted. The sound of the diesel grew stronger and presently a green navigation light showed up to starboard, no more than fifty yards away. Seconds dragged by before it was swallowed up again in the mist and the noise of the engine receded.

Sandstrom said, "Phew. That was close." He began rowing once more.

The only sounds now were the slap of water against the dinghy's hull and the faint splash of oars. Soon Boland saw a flicker of white light ahead, tenuous and uncertain like a fluttering candle. He steered towards it and before long the rocky sides of Spissberg loomed up out of the night. The dinghy grounded and two dark shapes came from the shore. A man's voice enquired anxiously, "Everything all right?"

"Yes, Li. He's coming round now. There'll be no trouble. He's firmly bound. Suffering from nausea. Make sure he doesn't choke."

"When will Gunnar Olufsen come?" It was a woman's voice, soft and concerned.

"Within the next two or three hours. Long before daylight."

"You have the skimmer and the life-raft?" said the man in his high pitched reedy voice.

"Yes. In the dinghy. Also the outboard."

With the aid of the man and woman, the dinghy was hauled up into the shallows. Boland and Sandstrom lifted Krasnov and carried him along the beach to the *rorbu* which lay to their right, towards the flashing red beacon. Inside the derelict house they lifted floor boards and by the shaded light of a torch took Krasnov down a ladder into the basement. It was a dark, evil-smelling place, wet and inhospitable, the stone walls of the foundations moss-encrusted and dripping. They propped the Russian in a corner, checked his lashings, lifted his eyelids and examined his eyes by torchlight while he mumbled unintelligibly. The woman cradled his head in her arms and gave him water from a beaker, speaking to him gently in Russian as if he were a child. But he was still dazed, barely conscious, and the water dribbled from his mouth.

The men brought the inflatable skimmer, the inflatable orange life-raft, the outboard engine and the shopping bag from the dinghy, and put them in the basement. After a hurried consultation with the Liang Huis, Sandstrom and Boland pushed the dinghy clear of the shallows and climbed back into it.

There were softly-spoken "goodbyes" and the dinghy melted into the darkness. The man and woman went back along the beach towards the *rorbu*. When they got there Liang Hui went down to the basement, switched on a camp torch and sat on a plank near the prisoner. For reassurance he felt the bulge under his left armpit where a .32 Browning snugged in its shoulder-holster.

His sister, Tanya, sat on the floor of the deserted house watching through a broken front window as the gathering mist swirled through old and rotting timbers to add to the cold and damp of a cheerless night.


After his unsuccessful search in the lavatory, Gerasov hurried back to the table where Kroll, Martinsen, Odd Dahl and the harbourmaster were drinking beer and swapping stories. The sub-lieutenant's eyes were wild and his speech confused. Since he had no Norwegian he tried English. "He's gone. Disappeared," he said desperately, looking from one to the other to see if he were understood.

Martinsen said, "Gone? Who?"

"Lieutenant Krasnov. He was with me over there a few minutes ago." He pointed to the empty table. "He left me to go to the lavatory. When he'd been away for about five minutes I went to find him. But he's gone."

"He probably came back and you missed him," suggested Martinsen. "Maybe he's back at the *hospits*."

Gerasov shook his head. "He wouldn't go without me. Besides, he left his uniform cap on the table." But then he remembered that he'd been talking to the English girl at the time. Perhaps Krasnov had come back, seen him talking to the girl and—and what?

Kroll said, "I saw Olufsen and the Englishman Nunn come out of there. Perhaps they saw him?"

Pale, hesitant, filled with doubts and fears, Gerasov considered this. He looked from one face to the other as if trying to read their thoughts then crossed to the bar counter.

No. Olufsen had not seen him. There had been no one in the lavatory while he was there except Nunn. Nunn told the same story. Sorry. No one there except Olufsen.

Gerasov looked round the room again. But the *kafeteria* was a comparatively small place, there were not many tables and Krasnov was nowhere to be seen.

The sub-lieutenant went back to Martinsen's table. "Mr. Olufsen and Mr. Nunn say he wasn't in the lavatory." His voice was tremulous. He looked utterly defeated.

Odd Dahl, the *lensman*, said, "There's a fire-door at the back. Maybe he went out that way."

"No," said Gerasov. "It's bolted on the inside. I checked." He turned to Martinsen. "What should I do, sir?" It was a *cri de coeur*. Martinsen was thinking of Freddie Lewis's ... *a great power ... something special by way of intelligence gathering* ... Was this it? He kept his thoughts to himself. "I suggest you run across to the *hospits*," he said. "He may be there. If not come back to us. It'll only take you a few minutes."

Gerasov said, "I can't go alone, sir. My orders are never to be alone." He paused, his face drawn. "That's my problem. I should never have let Krasnov go to the lavatory alone."

Martinsen wanted to laugh at that but he controlled himself. "I see your point, Sub-Lieutenant. Very well. We'll accompany you." He looked at Odd Dahl. "You come along, too, Bailiff. After all, it's your problem."

"Of course, Major."

The three men left the *kafeteria* together.

When they'd gone Kroll said, "If Krasnov has disappeared we must report at once to the *Ordforer*. The consequences could be serious."

"He's probably with a girl," said the harbourmaster.

150

"Doesn't want the sub-lieutenant to know. Let's have some more beer."

Kroll's plump face, bright with perspiration, gathered itself into a smile. "Why? Maybe you are right."

Ferret and Plotz hadn't missed much. They'd seen Krasnov leave the table and go through the swing-door, followed by Olufsen and Nunn who'd returned later. They'd seen, too, how Gerasov had gone off in search of his companion, his agitation when he came back. It was then that Ferret had bought two more bottles of lager and gone back to the table by the door. "Jesus!" he said, his voice hoarse with emotion. "I think Krasnov's beat it."

Plotz said, "He's not come back through that door. Never had my eyes off it. But his uniform cap is still on the table over there."

"I'm going to check the lavatory, Jim. Watch things while I'm away."

Ferret was soon back. "He's not there. That's for sure. There's a fire-door at the back. It's bolted on the inside. It's the only way he could have gone."

"How come if it's bolted on the inside, Ed?"

"Because Krasnov wasn't there alone. Somebody let him out and bolted the door after he'd gone."

"Or pushed him out," suggested Plotz.

"Yeah. Could be. And that might mean Olufsen and Nunn. They went in after him."

"There's another possibility." Plotz leant over the table, lowered his voice. "Krasnov could have defected. Maybe he planned this thing. Norwegian accomplice. Right? Remember the girl. She came out soon after Olufsen and Nunn went in. Maybe she was around by the fire-door. She lets Krasnov out, bolts it and comes back in."

Ferret picked at a broken finger nail, then tried biting it. He was deep in thought. "Wouldn't Olufsen and Nunn have seen her?"

"Unlikely, Ed. If you check the time intervals. I guess they must have been in the men's for at least a minute when she came out that door."

Plotz laughed, a sudden explosive laugh, a combination

151

of nerves and discovery. "We're hypersensitive, Ed. It's an occupational hazard. Know what I think?"

"What's that?"

It *was* that girl we saw come out the loo. I guess Krasnov's laying her right now. Maybe over at the *hospits*. Maybe some place else."

"You could be right." Ferret abandoned the broken nail. "But it could also be he's defected. You know the way he talks with Gerasov. He doesn't dig the navy or the Party."

"And so," said Plotz. "What do we do now?"

Ferret's frown seemed to draw his small eyes closer together and the line of his mouth hardened. "If we can't take K, we take G. That's what *Gemini* says. So now we keep right on G's tail. Okay?"

At that moment Gerasov, Martinsen and Odd Dahl got up, walked their way through the tables and out of the *kafeteria*'s front door.

"Jesus!" Plotz's face froze. "What d'you know?"

"For Chrissake," said Ferret. "Why do they have to lay on a king's escort for that little bastard?" He stood up. "Tail them, Jim. I must see Vince. We're short on time."


By midnight the hue and cry, if it could be called that, had been raised, but in a minor key. It wasn't Kroll's fault. If he'd had his way it would have been very different. But the *Ordforer*—who'd made no attempt to conceal his displeasure at being called by his deputy from deep sleep—had other ideas. It was absurd, he said, to assume as Kroll had done, that Krasnov had been abducted. There were other, more likely possibilities. A woman probably. Or Krasnov had defected and was hiding somewhere in Kolhamn. If so, political asylum was involved and that was a matter for Oslo. Martinsen supported the *Ordforer*.

Kroll made the point that Oslo had instructed that the Russians be given every assistance. The disappearance of one of their officers was surely an emergency justifying special steps.

"That," said the *Ordforer* in a manner which brooked

152

no opposition, "is a matter for Major Martinsen. He's responsible for security while the submarine's aground on Vrakoy."

Martinsen agreed. He would, he said, do certain things at once. The few soldiers and sailors presently in Kolhamn on leave from patrol duties—mostly billeted with local families—would be mustered as soon as possible. They would conduct a house-to-house inquiry in the village, and search its environs. He would also alert the minesweeper off Knausnes and order the fast gunboat to carry out a sweep round the island—to challenge, and if necessary search, any strange craft encountered. Finally, he would arrange for a radio message to be sent to the *Zhukov*, informing its commander that Lieutenant Krasnov had disappeared and that a search for him was in progress.

Kroll then blurted out his suspicions: Olufsen had arranged the charter of the *Kestrel* for the English *tourists*, he emphasized the word. A day or so ago he had seen Olufsen go on board the yacht in the early hours of the morning.

What had Kroll been doing down there at that hour? challenged the *Ordforer*.

"I couldn't sleep," said the doctor. "So I took a walk. Sometimes I do this."

He explained how in the *kafeteria* that evening Olufsen and Nunn had gone through the swing-door to the lavatory soon after Krasnov. They'd returned a few minutes later. Krasnov had not. Indeed, since that moment he'd not been seen again. With a touch of dramatic emphasis Kroll pointed a podgy finger in the direction of the harbour. "I am certain Krasnov is a prisoner in the *Kestrel*."

The *Ordforer* was not impressed. He was a strong, stolid man, not one to jump to conclusions and he didn't like his deputy overmuch. In his opinion the doctor's air of geniality and goodwill masked a lazy, inquisitive character. But Kroll was popular locally and the *herredstyre* had elected him *Vise-Ordforer*. Nordsen had accepted the decision with misgiving.

Before the meeting broke up he made one concession

153

to Kroll—yes, the *Kestrel* could be searched. It must be done officially by Odd Dahl, the *lensman*, and Olaf Petersen, the harbourmaster. Kroll could accompany them in his capacity as *Vise-Ordforer*. The reason for the search was to be given as action following a drug tip-off. There was to be no reference to the missing Russian naval officer.

With a smile of satisfaction Kroll said, "Thank you, Nordsen. I'm sure that is a wise decision." Which wasn't the most tactful thing to say to Vrakoy's "Little King." Nordsen said, "You needn't thank me, Kroll. I think you'll be wasting your time. I'm more concerned with the disappearance of the two Frenchmen."

Martinsen said, "What's the latest news about them, *Ordforer*?"

"As you know, the search party found nothing on the eastern slopes. Low cloud and mist are making things difficult. There is no way of scanning the rock faces. We have notified the company in Bordeaux."

"I expect they'll turn up," said Martinsen. "They're probably shut in by the weather."

## Nineteen

Some time after midnight, the mist thickening and swirling wetly across the fjord, Kroll, Dahl and Petersen arrived at the jetty where *Kestrel* lay. They stood for some time looking down on her, wondering quite how to go about their business.

The ketch's cockpit lay between the double cabin aft and the companionway to the saloon forward. It was brightly lit. The hatches to the engine-space were off and two men, evidently unaware of the observers above, were working on the engine.

"Hullo, there," called Petersen. "Can we come aboard?"

Nunn's grease-streaked face looked up from the engine. "Who's that?" he asked.

"Petersen the harbourmaster, Odd Dahl the bailiff, and Doctor Kroll."

Nunn, who'd been expecting the visit, looked pointedly at his watch, then at the men on the quay. "Certainly. Come aboard if you wish."

Petersen and his companions came down into the cockpit, Kroll breathing heavily from his exertions. Nunn wiped his hands on a lump of cotton waste. "What's the trouble?" he said. "Our sailing clearance not in order?" Sandstrom left the engine where he'd been working, straightened his back and ranged himself along Nunn. He gave the visitors a long hard look. A big man with dark shaggy hair and rough-hewn features, he could look intimidating when he wanted to; this was such an occasion.

Petersen looked embarrassed. "We're sorry to trouble you at such a time, Mr. Nunn. But—well—we know you intend to sail tonight so we . . ."

"This morning," corrected Nunn tapping his watch. "Yes, we hope to sail soon. That was why I got clearance from you yesterday. As soon as we get this fuel injector properly adjusted we're off." He looked towards Sandstrom. "It's almost right, isn't it?"

"Won't take long now. Just some bolts to tighten."

"I'm sorry, Mr. Nunn." Petersen struggled with his problem. "But we received information . . . that is to say we had a tip-off."

"Bully for you," said Nunn.

Petersen didn't understand the idiom. "You say?"

"Nothing," said Nunn. "Carry on."

"Yes . . . we had a tip-off. About drugs on board your ship."

Nunn hesitated, allowing what he hoped would pass for a stunned silence. Eventually he said, "Drugs in *Kestrel*?

155

Good God! We've morphine—a syringe—and some Disprins in the medicine chest. Is that what you're after?"

"These tip-offs are often inaccurate," apologized Petersen. "Sometimes a hoax. Someone with a grudge. But we have to act on them. Just in case, you know."

Kroll evidently felt it was time to assert himself. He took a deep breath, puffed out his cheeks, then let it go with a wheeze. "I come in my capacity as *Vise-Ordforer*, Mr. Nunn. Odd Dahl is our bailiff. Now please. If you do not mind we must discharge the unpleasant duty of searching your ship."

Nunn affected surprise. "Search the *Kestrel*? At this hour?"

"I regret," said Kroll, arranging his fleshy chin into what he imagined was a pretty firm affair, "it must be done."

Nunn's sigh was a mixture of irritation and annoyance. "Very well. I'll get one of my crew to show you round. I'm too busy, I'm afraid. We must get this blasted engine fixed. We've already wasted three days of our holidays. Excuse me for a moment."

He went down to the saloon where Boland was lying on a settee reading. Julie had gone to her cabin.

Nunn explained the situation quickly—it was one for which the crew had been briefed—took the keys from the keyboard and handed them to Boland. "Show them everything. There's nothing to hide. Make it snappy. Sooner we get rid of them the better."

Boland followed him back into the cockpit. Nunn did the introductions, then rejoined Sandstrom on the engine.

Boland stared at the Norwegians with chilly unfriendly eyes. "Where d'you want to start? Aft?"

"Forward," said Petersen with the instincts of a sailor.

The search party moved off, Boland leading. He opened every hatch, every door, every cupboard and locker they requested. It was soon evident it was not drugs they were after. Little attention was paid to the contents of lockers where tinned food and ship's stores were stowed, or to bilges and other spaces too small for a man. For these reasons the search was soon over. It ended with a check along the upper deck where torch beams were directed into every nook and cranny. Kroll, at times on all fours, insisted on checking along the outside of the hull. Finally he directed the beam of his torch into the rigging.

"Bad place for drugs," suggested Boland. "Too much wind." Kroll glared at him. "You understand we have to be thorough."

"Quite." Nunn's face, high cheekboned and almond-eyed, betrayed no emotion. "Hope you're now satisfied. There is of course the hull underwater. You might care to look at that."

Kroll ignored the jibe. He turned to Petersen and Dahl. "Are you both satisfied?"

They'd not shared Kroll's obsession and were only too ready to abandon a search they'd considered unnecessary.

Kroll bowed stiffly to Nunn. "Goodnight, Mr. Nunn. I am sorry we had to disturb you. We were doing our duty."

"I am sure you were, Doctor Kroll." Nunn smiled at Petersen. He'd always liked the harbourmaster who was a bluff honest-to-God seaman. "We want to leave as soon as we get this injector working, Mr. Petersen. We'd like to get to Andenes at first light if possible."

"Of course," said the harbourmaster. "You've settled your harbour dues, completed the clearance papers. You are free to leave when you like."

"Thank you, Mr. Petersen."

There was an exchange of goodbyes and the Norwegians climbed up the ladder to the jetty and disappeared into the darkness.

Nunn watched while Sandstrom replaced the bolts in the fuel injector which he'd removed soon after dark. When he'd finished they went down to the saloon.

Julie—disturbed from sleep by the search party—and Boland were already there. Nunn drew a hand across his forehead and yawned. "So that little comedy is over. Christ, what a day."

Sandstrom said, "That was a bit dodgy. We got back less than ten minutes before they arrived."

"Don't tell me," said Boland. "I was sweating blood. The dinghy's only about thirty yards astern."

"Makes no odds. It's a local one. We left nothing in it. Tell you what. I'm going to have a beer. I'm bloody whacked." Sandstrom took a can from the locker beneath the settee.

"Yuk. That fat doctor." Julie shivered. "I wouldn't have him examine me. Those podgy fingers. Like a string of sausages."

Nunn looked at Julie curiously. The towelling wrap she was wearing was doing a poor job of concealment. She was getting into his hair and it disturbed him. His marriage was just recovering from a trauma for which he'd been responsible. It had been nearly wrecked by one Wren, he didn't want to repeat the experience with another. He wasn't looking for more trouble. His manner became brusque. "Okay, Julie. We read you. Now let's get down to business." He looked at the saloon clock. It showed one seventeen. "We sail at 0200. Olufsen and Co. move fifteen minutes later. See any snags?"

Sandstrom said, "Only the weather. The mist has thickened. Fog can complicate things."

"There are always complications," said Nunn. "Makes life more interesting."

Julie yawned. "I'm off to bed while the going's good."

It occurred to Nunn that it would be pleasant to join her there but he said, "In the Service we call it 'turning in'. I'll give you a shake five minutes before we sail."

"I call it bed," she said. "Sounds more exciting."

Her smile was a queer mixture of affection and mischief.


Dr. Gustav Kroll left the *Kestrel* a puzzled man. He was convinced that Krasnov had been abducted by the British. It was the sort of thing they'd do. Like the raid on the Norsk Hydro heavy water plant near Venmork. They were amateurish, their planning was half-baked, much left to chance, but their operations were always conducted with great determination. Kroll hated the British. He had suffered much because of that raid. What did they know

158

of the pressures to which a man had to submit in an enemy-occupied country? Britain hadn't been occupied for a thousand years.

Krasnov was not in the *Kestrel*. Where had they taken him? And where was Olufsen? Kroll's mind was at full stretch. Olufsen—Inga Bodde. Ah, that was it. He remembered seeing them together in the post office, their whispered conversation, the message sheets she'd taken from a drawer under the counter. Messages Olufsen had put into his pocket without reading. Kroll had had his suspicions then. The whole island knew of Olufsen's relationship with Inga Bodde.

What could be more simple? Having abducted Krasnov, where—if you were Olufsen—would you hide him? In Inga Bodde's house of course. And then, when the hue and cry had died down, you'd take him off the island under cover of darkness.

Because Inga Bodde was a much-respected woman on Vrakoy, Kroll was not prepared to share his suspicions with Dahl and Petersen. She lived with an invalid father. There was no one else in the house. It was a situation he could handle alone.

Back at the *radhus* they reported failure to the *Ordforer* and bade him goodnight. Kroll thanked Dahl and Petersen for their services and they parted.

When he had gone a short distance in the direction of his own house, Kroll turned away and set off up the hill, his mind full of resolve. It was dark and the mist had reduced visibility, but he knew Kolhamn like a book and he walked unhesitatingly along the path which led to the Boddes' house. It was steep going because the house was well up the slope. Land was cheaper there and the Boddes had little money.

Kroll was a heavy man, unused to exertion, and the climb made him breathless. Several times he rested. Once he thought he heard footsteps behind him and stopped to listen. But all was quiet except for the distant barking of a dog, the thump of the town's generator, and the sound of a fishing boat's diesel somewhere in the fjord. As he drew close to the house a new sound intruded ... the long drawn blare of the foghorn at the mouth of Kolfjord. A few minutes later the house loomed out of the mist. He stopped. It was then that he heard again something behind him. This time it was no illusion, for a man's voice called from the darkness. "Doctor Kroll. Doctor Kroll. Excuse me. I have a message for you."

When Ferret reached the *hospits* and reported events in the *kafeteria*, Strutt told him to join up with Plotz as soon as possible. "Krasnov has disappeared. Okay? So your objective now"—Strutt's dark eyes fixed Ferret's in compelling concentration—"is to get Gerasov. The prospects don't look too good, Ed, but keep right on that boy's tail. Maybe something'll come up for us."

Ferret sat on the bed, scratched his head and sighed. "What are you going to do, Vince?"

Strutt got up from the bed where he'd been reading, stubbed out a cigarette, put on a raincoat, and pulled a cloth cap low on his head. "I guess I've a job to do, Ed."

Ferret's expression showed only too clearly how much he'd like to have known what it was. Presumably the other leg of *Gemini*. He'd already been told it was none of his business. He sighed again. "Be seeing you some place, Vince?"

"Maybe. Maybe not." Strutt shrugged his shoulders.

Ferret looked at him glumly. "Things haven't been going for us, Vince. I wonder who the bastards are that snatched Krasnov."

Strutt shook his head. "Maybe the French boys. They've not shown up. Whoever it is, they've sure screwed things up for us." He went towards the door, put his hand on the latch. "Bye now. Look after yourself."

"Bye Vince. See you."

For Jim Plotz it was a night of endless frustration. After Martinsen, Dahl and Gerasov had left the *kafeteria* he'd followed them down to the *hospits*, kept watch while they went inside, latched on to them again when they came out, kept discreetly behind them all the way to the *radhus*.

There he'd waited outside in the cold misty night, miserable, bored and alone, until he was joined by Ferret. In brief staccato sentences they exchanged news before settling down to watch the *radhus*, Plotz in front, Ferret at the back. Some time later three men came out of the front door. Gerasov was not with them. Plotz recognized Kroll, Dahl and Petersen. They disappeared in the direction of the harbour. The American's assignment was to tail Gerasov. The sub-lieutenant had not left the *radhus*. For Plotz there was no alternative but to continue his miserable vigil.

From the *hospits* Strutt made for the *radhus*. He knew that sooner or later the principal characters in the hunt for Krasnov would collect there.

He hadn't long to wait, and he wasn't disappointed. From where he hid in the shadows he saw three men go in. He didn't know or recognize Martinsen and Dahl, but he'd seen recent photographs of Kroll at the CIA briefing. He'd have picked out the fat, bearded doctor anywhere. Later another man went in. Strutt didn't know that he was Hjalmar Nordsen, the *Ordforer*. In due course Kroll emerged with the two men he'd gone in with originally. Strutt tailed them down to the harbour, saw them go aboard the *Kestrel*. He waited patiently in a dark alleyway between fishing sheds until they'd climbed back on to the jetty. They set off and he followed them back to the *radhus*. For a man with Strutt's training and experience, shadowing in a fishing village with virtually no street lighting, on a dark misty night with most inhabitants in bed, was not difficult. But he took no chances and even Plotz and Ferret failed to see him when he moved into a doorway diagonally opposite the *radhus*.

Time went by. Three men came out. Kroll was one of them. They split, two going towards the western side of the village, Kroll to the eastern. Strutt followed Kroll, saw him backtrack, then turn up the hill. He lost sight of him in the mist, but the Norwegian walked heavily, breathed noisily, and the American was in no danger of losing him. At times Kroll would stop. Instantly, Strutt would do the same. The American, younger and fitter, moving silently in rubber-soled shoes, soon reduced the distance between them.

When Strutt was no more than twenty feet from the man ahead he heard him stop. As Kroll moved forward again the American slid a hand into a raincoat pocket and quickened his pace. In his haste he stumbled over a heap of loose gravel. The noise must have alarmed Kroll. He stopped and turned, facing the pathway. Strutt called out in Norwegian. "Doctor Kroll. Doctor Kroll. Excuse me. I have a message for you."

"Who are you?" It was a laboured, breathless voice.

Strutt moved forward in the darkness until he was a few feet from the doctor. "Major Martinsen asked me to give you this, sir. It's urgent." He held out the envelope. As Kroll took it, Strutt slipped an arm round the fat man's neck in a half-Nelson. The Norwegian's muffled cry changed to muted gurgling as Strutt plunged the knife deep into his throat, jerking it to and fro with sharp tugs. Kroll sagged, Strutt let him fall, watched the dark twitching shape for a few moments before taking it by the ankles and dragging it behind some rocks clear of the pathway. Strutt placed the envelope addressed to the *Ordforer* in the doctor's pocket, removed the surgical gloves, stuffed them into his raincoat, and disappeared into the mist.

As the American made his way east across the upper limits of Kolhamn towards Spissberg he did some mental arithmetic: time to make the five hundred foot ascent and descent to the beach on the far side; time to get along the beach to the RV one mile southwest of the Ostnes Beacon. Certain things were fixed in his mind: the blown-up aerial photo provided by the US Air Force Base at Keflavik which showed the ridge he had to cross and the section of beach on the far side; the diagram drawn by Plotz and Ferret who'd reconnoitred the route; the mental picture of what he'd seen from the USOS helicopter the day before when it had run down the beach and lifted over the Spissberg on the approach to the air-strip.

He recalled that the north-eastern end of the beach

ended in the rocky promontory of Ostnes. He planned to come down from the Spissberg just south of that. If he couldn't see the beacon for mist he'd back-track to the rock face, then turn about and travel the mile south-west to the RV. His watch showed one-forty-three. He reckoned he'd make the RV within the hour if all went well. Not that it mattered. The skimmer would wait if necessary until an hour before first light. That gave him to close on five o'clock.

He reached the slope and began the ascent. The going was wet, slippery, mostly rock with occasional patches of tundra. His rubber shoes though deep-treaded were not what he'd have chosen for that part of the journey. But he was strong and lithe. He'd walked, climbed and run in the Appalachians day and night in worse weather and over tougher terrain. That had been a year back, a routine part of the course at the "Farm" in Virginia.

Several times he stopped, set up the pocket compass and checked his bearings on its luminous dial. His task was simplified by the knowledge that he must keep his face to the upward slope. He reached the top and began the descent. The mist from the sea thickened and he checked his pace, coming down in long oblique contours, losing height slowly, slipping and slithering at times. Twice he fell. Each time he covered the metal-cased transmitter with both hands. His body could take the tumbles but the transmitter might not. It was vital to his mission.

Working his way down the slope, Strutt's thoughts turned back to the man he'd just killed. Kroll alias Charlsen, alias Rodsand, alias Sorensen, alias Lillevik . . . "Alias Christ knows who else," Rod Stocken had said after reeling them off at the briefing. It had long seemed that Kroll's past was buried in those aliases as securely as if he'd been buried beneath the earth, which was where a number of people would like to have seen him.

Strutt recalled Rod Stocken's run-down on Kroll: Born in Sweden in 1916 of Norwegian parents. Graduated from Malmo University in 1938 with a physics degree. Began teaching in a state secondary school in Oslo in October

163

that year. Collaborated with the Nazis after the occupation of Norway. Secured employment with the German scientific team working on the A-bomb project at Norsk Hydro plant in the mountains near Venmork. Stayed with them until late 1943 when Allied bombers destroyed the power station. When the Germans moved the project to a site in the Reich, Kroll opted out.

After the Russians had cleared the Germans from Norway, Kroll re-appeared in December 1945 in the Bergen district. Name then was Rodsand. KGB agents—tipped off by Norwegian wartime underground—picked him up, threatened to expose him as a Nazi collaborator unless he came clean on the Norsk Hydro project. Kroll told all he knew. Then, under pressure of blackmail, he was taken on as a KGB agent. After a long apprenticeship he became a useful low-key unit in the KGB *apparat* in Norway.

In 1963 Kroll, always a conceited man, decided the KGB had burned him out, weren't using him enough, weren't paying him enough. He contacted the CIA. Fed them sample information on the KGB network in Norway. CIA checked, found it reliable, classified him *potentially useful—unsafe—minimum access—possible double agent.* Over the next few years he was used to feed mixinfo to the KGB. CIA's confidence in him grew, he was re-classified *useful—probably unsafe—limited access—double agent.*

During this time he gained, of necessity, certain knowledge of the CIA Norwegian network: communications system, couriers, cipher-crypts, letter-drops, safe houses, escape hatches, channels for the procuration of false documents. For some time he continued to work for the KGB and CIA. He was proving useful to both sides, received reasonable rewards for information, and profited from dual expense accounts. He saved money and invested shrewdly.

In 1961, due to an administrative and security failure, Kroll gained access to a highly-classified CIA dossier. On learning this the Directorate instructed a deep-cover agent in Moscow to plant evidence that Kroll was feeding KGB systems material to the CIA. It was confidently anticipated that the KGB would liquidate Kroll. In the event, a senior KGB agent in Oslo confronted him with the evidence and the choice of liquidation or revelation. Kroll, anxious to live, told it all. As a result the cover of two contact men, long-established CIA agents in Norway, was blown; so was much else—including the communications system, the cipher-crypts, letter-drops, safe houses and escape hatches—before the CIA realized what had happened.

Kroll, now fearing both the CIA and KGB, did an overnight skip to Sweden, underwent cosmetic surgery, fattened on hormones and grew the beard which masked his face. He obtained employment in a Swedish secondary school teaching physics. For this purpose he used faked cover documents which he'd long before procured for just such a purpose.

Several years later he turned up on Vrakoy as Dr. Gustav Kroll, a Norwegian of private means, long retired from school teaching in Sweden. He chose Vrakoy because of its extreme remoteness from the main stream of people and events.

A few weeks before the stranding of the *Zhukov* the CIA had—by a strange chance arising directly from Kroll's vanity—discovered that he was on Vrakoy. If he were still active he was a potential threat. For that reason, and because of the damage he'd done to the CIA, it was decided to recommend his liquidation. It would serve, too, as a salutary warning to the KGB and their Norwegian agents.

"He's no great catch." Stocken had mouthed his cheroot aggressively. "Just a one-time Nazi collaborator and two-bit double agent. But he's a mean bastard and dangerous. He sold the CIA down the river and he's got to pay for it."

Thus, in somewhat unjuridical terms, was sentence of death pronounced upon Gustav Kroll.

Before there was time for the recommendation to be approved by the Directorate, the need to plan *Gemini* had arisen. It was then decided that if the main leg of the plan

165

failed—the abduction of one or more officers from the Soviet submarine—Strutt should liquidate Kroll before leaving Vrakoy, thus making unnecessary the dispatch of a hatchet man.

The envelope which Strutt had placed in the dead man's pocket contained a précis of all the CIA knew about Kroll. There was no indication of its origin or authorship.

By the time Strutt reached the beach mist had become fog. Visibility was down to fifty or sixty feet. There was no sign of the light at the Ostnes Beacon so he walked north until he reached the rockface. Then he reversed direction and set off towards the RV, a mile distant.

The tide was falling and with fog swirling wetly in his face, the sea at times lapping his feet, he made his way down the beach. Every thirty seconds he would hear the deep blare of the foghorn at the mouth of the fjord; but for that, the only sounds were those made by small waves breaking on the lee shore, the crunch of pebbles underfoot and the noise of his own breathing.

He was wondering whether he'd overshot when he stumbled over the line of stones Plotz and Ferret had laid across the beach to serve as a marker.

Strutt took the VHF transmitter from his pocket, extended the aerial and pressed the transmit button. He began to count in Norwegian, *en . . . to . . . fre . . . fire . . . fem . . .* , at ten he stopped, released the button, held the receiver to his ear. He heard a deep voice counting down in Norwegian, *ti . . . ni . . . olle . . . ayv . . .* , at five it stopped.

Strutt waited. Before long he heard the high note of outboard engines as a skimmer homed in on the bearing of his VHF transmission. He took the pencil torch from his pocket, switched it on and aimed it seawards.

# Twenty

The dinghy grounded. Olufsen stepped out, hauled it into the shallows. He walked along the beach in the darkness until he reached the stilts supporting the rough wooden jetty. He climbed the ladder and from its top flashed his torch three times at the dilapidated house. Answering flashes came from a front window.

He went through the empty door frame, his hand over the lens of the torch so that its light showed only a few feet ahead. The floor-boards creaked and groaned as he walked. From somewhere close came the anxious tones of a woman. "Is everything all right?"

"Yes. But they're looking for him. They searched the *Kestrel*. There was no trouble."

"Good." She sighed with relief.

"How is he?"

"Conscious now, but muzzy. He tries to keep awake."

"We leave in another fifteen minutes, Tanya. Has he changed clothes?"

"Yes. He refused to at first but Li persuaded him. It was not difficult. He's so weak and confused."

"I'll keep watch. Go down and give him the tablets."

Liang Hui shone the torch into the far corner of the basement. The beam revealed a man sitting on the earthen floor, his back to the wall. The combination of light and shadow emphasized the haggard features, high cheek bones and sunken eyes. He was wearing denim slacks, blue roll-neck jersey and canvas shoes. His wrists and ankles were tied with rope. Liang Hui got up from the wooden box and aimed the torch at the stone steps. Somebody was coming down them.

"It's me, Tanya." She spoke in Chinese. "Gunnar has come. He says we leave in fifteen minutes."

Liang Hui switched the torch beam back to the man in the corner, put the automatic pistol on the box.

"We must give him these now." Tanya unscrewed the metal cap of the Thermos flask, filled it with water and handed it to Liang Hui with the Sodium Pentothal tablets.

He went over to the corner. "You must take these," he said in Russian. "To offset the chloroform."

Krasnov looked at the Chinaman and the tablets with suspicion. "No." He shook his head. "I will not."

"Then we must inject." Liang Hui called to his sister. "The hypodermic."

The Russian's eyes lit up with sudden fear. "No," he said. "Please not."

"Good. Take these tablets. They will help you."

With a sigh of resignation Krasnov submitted. Liang Hui put the tablets in the lieutenant's mouth, held the metal cup to his lips. Within a few minutes he had slumped into unconsciousness.

They called Olufsen. With his help they took the skimmer pack to the water's edge, unrolled and inflated it and fitted the outboard. That done, they carried Krasnov up from the basement and put him in the skimmer. They loaded the orange life-raft pack, the VHF transmitter, the compass and the shopping bag. In it were Krasnov's uniform coat and trousers, the false moustaches and seaman's caps worn by Boland and Sandstrom.

Tanya got into the skimmer. Olufsen and Liang Hui pushed it clear of the beach and jumped in.

The mist lay thick over the fjord and they kept close inshore, the men using paddles while Tanya steered. The sound of the foghorn grew stronger and before long the flashing light of the beacon showed through the mist and they turned ninety degrees round it into the channel leading to the sea.

They stopped paddling and waited. Minutes passed before the noise of a diesel came from the lower end of the fjord. The sound grew stronger, came closer. Olufsen whispered, "There. Almost dead astern. They'll have picked us up on radar."

As they watched, the uncertain flickers of light resolved into a misty red and green, grew stronger, came closer, then faded and disappeared as the sound of the diesel engine passed up the skimmer's starboard side. A beam of light exposed for a few seconds by someone on board illuminated the name on the stern transom. It was *Kestrel*.

"Thank God for that." Olufsen breathed a sigh of relief. "Let's get cracking."

He started the outboard, barely opening the throttle. The skimmer moved ahead keeping the stern light of the *Kestrel* just visible in the darkness. Ten minutes later, still following the ketch, they rounded Kolnoy, the foghorn booming, the beacon flashing mistily. They remained close inshore until they reached the end of the channel. Once clear of the fjord, Olufsen steered north-east to pass along the southern coast of the island. The long rocky arm of Spissberg was close to port.

He said, "We couldn't have coped with this fog without *Kestrel*'s radar."

"They'd have had a hell of a job finding us," agreed Liang Hui.

"Take the tiller, Li." Olufsen moved aside in the darkness. "Keep her heading as she is. I must look at the chart."

Liang Hui took the tiller. Olufsen spread the chart on his knees, looked at it with the shaded torchlight. He'd already marked the courses to steer to the rendezvous, twenty miles to the north-east. He put away the chart, took over the tiller. "Right," he said. "We'll go ahead now." He opened the throttle, the note of the engine rose and the skimmer's bows lifted as it gathered speed. Above the noise he shouted, "We're steering north-east. Doing about thirty knots."

"Feels like it," said Liang Hui as the skimmer bounced, bumped and sprayed through the mist-laden night.

169

Before long they overhauled the *Kestrel*, passed up her starboard side, drew swiftly ahead.

Olufsen said, "As soon as we're past the Ostnes Beacon, we'll alter course to the north-west."

In the darkness Tanya leant over the body at her feet. She put her ear to Krasnov's mouth. He was breathing steadily. She felt his heartbeat and pulse. They were regular. The tablets would keep him heavily sedated for several hours. Long before that, she hoped, he would have been delivered to his destination. She felt a strange sympathy, a real sorrow for the Soviet lieutenant; and with it a sense of guilt that she'd been a party to it all. It was sad, she thought, that the world was like that. He was the son of some Russian mother, the husband or boy-friend of some Russian girl. What would they feel and think if they could see him now?

Olufsen's voice broke into her thoughts. "Drop that bag over the side, Li."

She heard the splash of the weighted shopping bag as it hit the water astern and sank.

*Bluewhale* arrived at the rendezvous twenty miles north of the Ostnes Beacon at 2200. Then began what was to prove a long wait for the signal from *Kestrel*. At first Bill Boyd occupied the time doing a square search round the RV. Submerged at "snort" depth, doing no more than five knots, the submarine ran on main diesels. That made possible full use of both radar and communications systems. Later he moved on to more interesting things, strange unpredictable manoeuvres to fox what he called "that nosey sod." The three-dimensional display on the sonar screen in the control-room showed everything in or on the water within forty miles capable of producing an echo, its range, bearing and depth and—if a moving object—its course and speed. The hydrophones and their amplifiers relayed all underwater sounds including propeller noises and sonar transmissions of other warships. The picture on the screen was dominated in the south by the coastlines of Vrakoy and the other islands of the Vesteralen group. Around the central spot of light—*Bluewhale* herself—

other specks, dots and smudges of neon showed up on various bearings and ranges. These were the ships, coasters and fishing boats in the area. The sonar operators on watch had reported and classified each as they appeared on the screen.

Soon after *Bluewhale* arrived at the RV the sonar operator had made a report which enlivened the otherwise rather dull proceedings. "New contact, sub-surface, bearing three-five-zero, range thirty-eight miles, classified submarine, depth two hundred feet . . ."

A ripple of excitement ran through the control-room as Bill Boyd acknowledged the report, altered course to the reciprocal of the bearing given, and ordered revolutions for three knots. "Until we know who he is, I don't propose to hand him our signature on a plate," he said, knowing that vital data had still to come.

Kingswell, the sonar officer, had joined the watch operator on hearing the report. He'd been hard at work since. His first report, "Contact's sonar transmissions are USN type, sir," pleased Bill Boyd. At least it wasn't Russian. A few minutes later Kingswell had more information. "Contact's course one-eight-zero, speed fifteen knots. We should get a sound signature soon," he added.

The first lieutenant checked through the NATO signal log. "NATO disposition signal for USN units in the Norwegian Sea at twenty hundred doesn't give a submarine anywhere near here, sir."

"Doesn't record us either," said Bill Boyd laconically. "At least it better bloody not."

Another seven minutes passed. The unidentified submarine came steadily closer. Kingswell reported, "Computer comparison with NATO sound signatures suggests *Finjack* hunter-killer class, sir. Appears to be heading for us."

"Appears be damned. The nosey sod *is* heading for us. Give him the NATO—IFF challenge, Kingswell."

"Will do, sir."

Kingswell switched the sonar transmissions to the IFF (identification friend or foe) pulsing challenge for the

day. Immediately the correct reply came from the unknown submarine, now twenty miles away.

"Well that's something," said Bill Boyd. "At least he's
an Atlantic cousin. All the same I wish he'd push off. We
don't want him sniffing round our arse for the next few
hours."

Around midnight *Bluewhale*'s sonar operator reported
that the US submarine had come up from two hundred
feet and was running on diesels at "snort" depth. In accordance with NATO radio identification procedures the
two submarines challenged, replied, and exchanged names
by means of coded high-speed radio transmissions. The
US submarine turned out to be the *Rockfish*. Carrying out
radar exercises, she said. *Bluewhale*, having revealed her
identity, reported that she was carrying out ASW exercises. Neither captain was tactless enough to refer to the
NATO disposition signal.

Thereafter the two submarines didn't communicate
with each other again, though they were never more than
seven miles apart. "Wonder what that nosey sod's up to?
Playing ducks and drakes with us," complained Bill Boyd
to his first-lieutenant.


The skimmer overhauled the *Kestrel,* passed noisily up
her port side and disappeared into the shroud of fog and
darkness, the sound of its engine fading rapidly.

Nunn took his eyes from the radar viewer. "The best of
British luck to them," he said.

"They're going to need it," said Boland. "Crazy without radar."

Sandstrom turned the wheel a few spokes. "Olufsen
knows the island well. That helps."

"What? At thirty knots, close inshore in this lot?
You're joking."

The three men could see nothing but the muted light of
instrument dials in the cockpit, fading and glowing as the
fog wrapped itself about them. The deep rumble of the
diesel, the creak and groan of the rigging, the slap and
splash of the bow wave and the periodic boom of the

Kolnoy foghorn wove an intricate and now familiar pattern of sound.

From where he watched the dials of the echo-sounder and the speed and distance log, Boland called, "Thirty-eight fathoms, Steve."

Nunn repeated the depth, read off the radar bearing and distance of the Ostnes Beacon, switched on the light under the hooded chart-table and plotted the position. He marked it with a neat pencilled circle and wrote the time against it.

"Ostnes Beacon bears zero-six-four, three point three miles," he said. "Allowing for the current against us it should be abeam in about twenty minutes. Not that we'll see it in this."

Boland said, "When do we make the stand-by signal?"

"Soon as we're past Ostnes and clear of the mountains. They mask these VHF transmissions."

"What time will that be?" Boland knew the answer but he was twitchy and chatting helped steady his nerves.

"Say three o'clock. First light's about six. Sunrise a few minutes before seven. There's plenty of time." He hesitated. "If all goes well."

In the silence which followed Nunn wondered if all would go well. There were Soviet naval units in the waters off Vrakoy, just outside Norwegian territorial limits, and there were the Norwegians: the minesweeper and the fast gunboat. Their beat was on the other side of the island, off Knausnes. But news of Krasnov's disappearance would long-since have been broadcast and a search at sea might already be on. His thoughts were interrupted by Boland's, "Forty-three fathoms, Steve."

Nunn acknowledged the report, went back to the radar viewer. "Let's see how Gunnar and Co. are getting on," he said. On the screen, luminous masses and contours marked the coastline to port. He looked along it until he found a tiny speck of light, glowing and fading like a fire-fly, moving towards the Ostnes Beacon. He turned to "large scale" and checked the speck's distance from the beacon. It was just over a mile. "Great," he muttered. "They're going fine."

173

Seconds later he let out a startled, "Christ!"

Another fast-moving speck of light had caught his eye. It was coming in from the north-east on what looked very much like a collision course with Olufsen's skimmer.

"What's the trouble?" asked Sandstrom.

"Just a moment." Nunn saw the two specks merge into one, then draw rapidly apart. "Christ!" he repeated. "That was a near thing. Must have been another skimmer. Going at a hell of a bat. Nearly collided with Olufsen's. It's heading for the beach now."

"Holy Mother o' Mary," said Boland. "What's going on?"

"Somebody's in a flipping hurry," said Sandstrom.

The *Kestrel* was almost abeam of the Ostnes Beacon when Julie's voice came from the companion hatch. "Coffee's ready. Any offers?"

"Plenty," said Nunn. "Bring it along." He kept his eyes pressed into the viewer. "Hullo. There's a new contact astern. Just come clear of Kolnoy."

There was tense silence in the cockpit as they waited, looking astern into the darkness wondering what was there, knowing it couldn't be seen. After what seemed a long time Nunn said, "May be following us. Doing about thirty knots. Overhaul us in fifteen minutes if it is."

Sandstrom said, "What d'you make of it?"

"Haven't a clue, Sven. It's small and fast. Same sort of blip on the screen as a *Gay Cavalier*."

"The Norwegian gunboat?"

"Probably," said Nunn. "Unlikely to be a Russian. We're well inside territorial waters."

A dark shape moved into the cockpit. "Come on," said Julie. "This coffee won't keep hot for ever. Take a mug and I'll pour."

Nunn took one and used the opportunity to squeeze her hand. She filled the mug and he went back to the viewer. The blob of light on the screen was growing steadily larger. "Expect it's coming to check up on us," he said. "Let's look suspicious."

"Not difficult for you," said Julie.

They laughed though they were worried. They knew their principal role in *Daisy Chain* was over. Krasnov had been taken and was on his way. Now they were involved in the secondary role. "Make the stand-by signal," Olufsen had said at the final briefing in Kolhamn. "If the skimmer calls for help go to its assistance. If at any time the need arises, create a diversion."

Once stopped for a search, the longer it took the better. At thirty knots the skimmer would soon be outside territorial waters and at the rendezvous with the submarine.

Nunn said, "Alter course thirty degrees to starboard, Sven."

"Thirty degrees to starboard." Sandstrom put the wheel over and the ketch's bows swung right.

"That ought to fetch them," said Nunn.

"Like a bird in a mini showing her . . ." Boland cut off short. "Sorry."

"I should think so," said Julie. "Really, what has the Navy come to?"

"It's always been like that," said Nunn. "Didn't you know? Now let's transmit the stand-by signal." He went below, switched on the VHF transmitter, took a cassette-player from the shelf, switched it on and turned up the volume. It was the Carpenters singing *Close to You*. He held the mike against the player, pressed the "speak" button and gave the transmission thirty seconds before switching off.

Almost immediately three sharp blasts on a referee's whistle sounded on *Kestrel*'s VHF speaker.

Julie came in from the cockpit. "That was great, Steve. We heard it on the cockpit speaker."

"Good," he said. "Come and be close to me."

"May I remind you, Lieutenant-Commander Nunn, sir, that we are being followed."

"Bloody hell," he said. "We're never left alone."

Olufsen shouted, "We must be less than a mile from the Ostnes Beacon." The wind made by their own speed carried the words away as the skimmer pounded and leapt through the night. Above the high-pitched scream of the

175

outboard they heard something approaching on the starboard bow. It came with frightening suddenness: first a sound like tearing linen monstrously amplified, then a dark shape shooting across their bows, twin wakes of tumbling foam marking its passage.

"Christ!" shouted Olufsen. "That was a near thing. No more than twenty feet ahead of us." The skimmer shook and bumped in the troubled water left by the intruder.

"What on earth was it, Gunnar?" Tanya's voice was timid, tremulous.

"A skimmer with twin outboards. Big ones. Must have been doing all of forty knots."

Liang Hui said, "D'you think they saw us?"

"I'm sure they did. Didn't you see the swerve to starboard? But for that we'd have collided."

"What d'you make of it?"

"Don't know, Li. One thing's certain. They're heading straight for the beach. Hope they know when they get there."

"Very strange," Liang Hui said it solemnly, as if pronouncing on some natural phenomenon. "At this time and place."

"A lot of strange things are happening at this time and place just now," echoed Olufsen.


When he estimated by dead reckoning that they had passed Ostnes, Olufsen altered course to the north-west. Clear now of the shelter of the land, the skimmer felt the swell and its motion at thirty knots had all the violence of a roller-coaster at a seaside fair.

In the next six minutes they covered three miles and he put their position as one mile off Randnes. Round that point the shore-line turned south and west to form the eastern side of Nordvag Bay. Still in thick fog, unable to see anything of the land, Olufsen piloted the skimmer into what he hoped was the centre of the bay. When he estimated they were half a mile offshore he closed the throttle. The bows of the skimmer dropped, it quickly lost way and he coaxed it inshore with short bursts of engine. They were still feeling the north-westerly swell and from

176

ahead came the sound of breakers. Olufsen realized then that they were too far to the east, heading for the exposed side of the bay. He altered course to starboard, seeking the lee of the long slope leading down from Bodvag to Nordnes.

The skimmer edged forward, the swell diminished, they entered calm water and he knew that the western side of the bay lay close ahead. Slowing the skimmer down to bare steerage way he ran in for a few minutes before switching off the engine.

"You've got the chart, the compass and VHF radio?" he said to Liang Hui. "Run out of here at full throttle and steer north-east. In five minutes you'll have done two-and-a-half miles. Alter then to north. Run on that course for twenty-five minutes. Allowing for the current, that'll bring you near enough to the RV. You know what to do when you get there? Quite happy?"

"Of course," said Liang Hui, putting a brave face on things.

"If for any reason you can't make it—engine trouble, some failure at the RV, whatever—call *Kestrel* on VHF and she'll come to your assistance. You've got the code words for that and she's got RDF. But remember it's a last resort and risky. Okay?"

"Yes, I don't expect to have any trouble."

Olufsen said, "Goodbye and good luck," and shook hands with both of them in the darkness before climbing out and wading ashore, a bundle of clothing under his arm. When he called out that he'd reached the beach Liang Hui started the outboard, opened the throttle and the skimmer moved out to sea.

Liang Hui was a man whose courage and determination had survived many tests but he was anything but happy. He had messed about in small boats in Hong Kong, crewed occasionally for yachting friends, but he profoundly mistrusted high speed in fog. It was one thing if you could see where you were going, but quite another to dash through the night at thirty knots with visibility down to fifty feet. He wondered if the *Daisy Chain* plan for the RV would work as well in practice as on paper.

*Bluewhale*, with radar, sonar, SINS and highly sophisticated communications systems had a lot of technology going for it. Briggs had stressed that at the briefing. The submarine, he said, would have no difficulty in finding the skimmer unless there were heavy wind and seas in which case that sort of operation would be impracticable anyway. But there was no wind, just a long swell under a mantle of fog.

Nevertheless, for Tanya who was very frightened and for his own peace of mind, he eased the throttle until the skimmer was doing twenty knots.

That would, perhaps, make them ten minutes late at the RV but the submarine would wait until shortly before daylight. There was plenty of time.

## Twenty-One

Olufsen waded ashore, stood waiting while the sound of the skimmer's engine faded. When fog and distance had swallowed the last faint note he moved on. Using the torch sparingly he climbed clear of the high-water mark, stopped and unfolded the bundle of clothing: the faded denim jacket and trousers, the worn plimsolls and Krasnov's uniform jacket. He arranged them among the rocks as if they'd been dropped, then kicked scuff marks in the sand-filled crevices. The makers' tags revealed that the shoes and denims had come from China. The wallet in the jacket had in it the papers of a Chinese seaman.

He moved along the beach until he came to the stream which flowed down the valley into the bay. Beyond it lay a rough footpath which wound up between Bodvag and

Landberg, dropping down into Kolhamn on the southern side. It was a journey of no more than two miles. He'd done it several times in the past with Inga Bodde but never at night or in fog. Even so he expected to reach her house by four. He would stay there until daylight, then after breakfast go down to the village.

Inga knew he was coming. She would if necessary testify that he had spent the night in her house after leaving the *kafeteria*. The alibi might be useful and would cause no surprise for he had on other occasions stayed overnight in the Boddes' house.

At three o'clock in the morning *Bluewhale* was still running submerged at "snort" depth when radar and sonar picked up a small fast-moving contact coming clear of the land echoes of Vrakoy. It was approaching at speed.

Boyd gave the order to surface. When the first-lieutenant reported "bridge clear," the captain opened the hatches and climbed the steel ladders through the fin to the bridge. *Bluewhale* rolled lazily as she moved through the water, beam on to the swell. The fog writhed and curled about the navigation lights like smoke from an invisible fire, the deep-throated rumble of the diesels at slow speed drowning the sounds of the night but for the distant blare of foghorns.

Reports of the fast-moving contact continued to reach the bridge from the control-room. Before long Boyd heard the waspish buzz of outboard engines approaching. He ordered the signalman to train an Aldis lamp in the direction from which the sound came. The lamp was switched on, but a curtain of fog hid the skimmer until it stopped, held in the beam of light close to the submarine. There were three men in it.

A man in the sternsheets shouted through a hailer, "Strutt here. We're coming alongside, Captain. Okay?" The accent was North American. The skimmer moved forward until it was a few yards clear of the submarine and heading in the same direction.

Boyd picked up the loud-hailer. "Sorry, mate. I think you're knocking at the wrong door."

179

"What's that?" came the puzzled reply.

"You're looking for *Rockfish*, aren't you?"

"Jesus! Isn't that her?" The shock in Strutt's voice was like that of a man who'd entered the "ladies" by mistake.

"I'm afraid not. Your parent has been hanging around like a bad smell for the last few hours. She's five miles to the north just now."

A whistle of surprise came from the skimmer. "Guess there's some confusion."

"Not up here, *mon vieux*. Would you like Father's bearing? Or shall I tell him you're with us? I've no doubt he's got you on radar, sonar, whatever, in that old tech tank."

"Thank you, sir," Strutt waved a hand. "That won't be necessary. We'll find our way back. Sorry to have troubled you."

"Don't mention it," said Boyd. "We like it." He paused. "You boys are out late aren't you? Been on the thrash?"

There was a pause before the man in the skimmer said, "Say again. I guess we don't follow."

"Not to worry. Just wondered if you'd been on a run ashore. You know. Booze and boobs."

"No, sir. Wish it had been that way. We're executing a radar exercise with *Rockfish*."

"Interesting. We're doing an ASW exercise."

"That so? Well—we must get busy."

"Yes. Hurry along. Father's sure to be watching. There's no percentage in stopping here."

"You can say that again. Bye now." Strutt pushed the tiller over, opened the throttles and the skimmer high-whined into the night.

"Just heard the Carpenters singing *Close to You*, sir," C.P.O. Blades, *Bluewhale*'s radio supervisor, grinned confidentially as he reported to the captain.

"Lucky you," said Bill Boyd. "Done your Match of the Day stuff?"

"Yes, sir. Three blasts on the ref's whistle."

"Well done." Boyd looked at the first-lieutenant. "Some

180

child at Northwood inventing new war games." It was said to satisfy the curiosity of the ship's company. He thought it would. He turned back to the radio supervisor. "Right Blades, make a signal: Immediate to *Belligerent* repeated *Aries* and C-in-C Fleet: Bluewhale *in all respects ready to execute exercise Kilo Zulu . . . time of origin 0315.*"

Before leaving the control-room he said, "Keep the hands at watch diving stations, Number One. We'll be surfacing within the next half-hour."

The Commodore (Intelligence) heard the discreet rat-tat-tat on the door. "Come in," he said, laying a mental 1,000 to 1 that it was Briggs. It was.

"*Bluewhale*'s signal to *Belligerent*, sir." The lieutenant-commander handed him the signal clipboard and top secret file marked *Daisy Chain*. "Interesting," said the commodore. "What does it mean?"

At his old game, thought Briggs, he knows perfectly well what it means. "That *Kestrel* was clear of the island at about a quarter past three this morning," he said, "by which time the skimmer should have been well on its way to the RV with *Bluewhale*."

"Splendid. What a memory for detail you have, Briggs. What do we do now?"

"C-in-C Fleet will instruct *Belligerent*, *Aries* and *Bluewhale* to search for survivors from a light aircraft reported down in the Norwegian Sea in area GVX."

The commodore thumbed through the pages of the *Daisy Chain* file. "Priority and security classification for that signal?"

"Immediate, sir. Squirt transmission, monitor proof, but plain language to HM ships reading. It'll be a below decks buzz right away in all three ships. Which is what it's intended to be."

"Thank you, Briggs. I recall suggesting that in the planning stage."

Briggs's left eyebrow rose perceptibly and he drew himself up to his full six feet four which always irritated the commodore who barely made five foot six. Briggs was pretty sure it had been his idea but he said, "So you did, sir." He was a man of considerable tact. It had been predicted that he would go far in the Service.

The sound of the gunboat's engines could be heard in *Kestrel* some time before its navigation lights showed up to port. Steering a converging course, she soon closed the distance. A searchlight beam leapt from the darkness and a voice amplified by loud-hailer shouted, "What ship? Where from?"

Nunn picked up the hand megaphone. "Yacht *Kestrel* from Vrakoy. Bound Andenes."

"Stop engines. We are coming alongside."

Nunn called down to Boland. "Stop engines, John."

The gunboat edged closer, sailors hanging fenders over the side. When she was almost alongside an officer and two ratings leapt across. The naval vessel drew clear, the searchlight beam still trained on the ketch.

The officer climbed down into the cockpit. One seaman went forward, the other aft. The Norwegian sub-lieutenant spoke good English. "This is a formality. We have authority to search vessels in our territorial waters."

"For what?" said Nunn.

The sub-lieutenant shone a torch in his face. "Are you the owner, sir?"

"No. The yacht is on charter from Halvorsen Brothers, Bodo. We are four British yachtsmen—in fact one is a woman—" he corrected himself. "We're on holiday. Sailing through the islands. We put into Vrakoy for engine repairs. Stuck there for three days. Left soon after two this morning. We hope to make Andenes by sunrise."

"May I see your charter papers—and sailing clearance from Vrakoy?"

"Certainly. What are you searching for?"

"The usual. Drugs. Illicit liquor."

You're lying, young man, thought Nunn, but you're doing it well. He shrugged his shoulders. "You won't find anything here but you're welcome to look. Come down to the saloon and I'll show you the papers."

The papers were in order and the search took place. A really thorough one, from stem to stern. Every cabin, locker and other stowage space was examined methodically.

The sub-lieutenant apologized for the inconvenience, thanked Nunn and his crew for their co-operation and signalled his ship alongside. The three Norwegians clambered aboard and the gunboat disappeared into the night.

"Holy Saint Patrick," said Boland. "They were indeed thorough."

"Suits us." Nunn looked at his watch. "That fun and games occupied thirty-three minutes."

Liang Hui shut the throttle, the skimmer lost way and came to a stop. There was nothing to be seen. Isolated and alone it climbed the long hills of the swells and slid into their valleys, lost in a limbo of fog and darkness.

A few minutes later they heard for the second time that night a threatening sound. It came swiftly towards them, the note subdued at first but rising, the compression of the sound waves transforming the distant rumble into a high-pitched screech, shattering the silence as it passed, the intensity diminishing as it drew away.

They had seen nothing. "Must be the same skimmer," said Liang Hui. "The one that nearly collided with us near the Ostnes Beacon."

"Again in a mad hurry," said Tanya. "Wonder what it's up to."

"They're probably asking the same about us."

When the last note of the outboard had faded all was silent but for the suck and splash of the sea against the rubber hull, the *tic-tic* of dripping water as fog condensed on thwarts and clothing, and the distant growl of foghorns.

"Those foghorns," said Tanya nervously. "Horrible sinister sound."

"Coasters and fishing vessels, I suppose."

"Will they worry us?"

"Not unless they see us. Shouldn't think it's likely."

"I'm frightened," she said. "This is the worst part of all."

"Don't worry. We've made the rendezvous without having to call for help. That would have complicated things."

"I suppose so." She crossed her arms over her breasts and shivered. "It's cold and spooky, Li. D'you think it's really worth it? All this?"

"Of course it is. Think of the stakes."

"At the end of the day they may get nothing from him."

"They'll get something. You know what interrogation's like nowadays. Not the old 'tell us the truth or else'. Much more subtle."

"It's cruel. The resistance course taught me that."

"Depends what you mean by cruel. It's not a physical thing is it? An assault on the mind, yes. It can be terrifying and humiliating. It's a risk we always run."

"Poor boy," she sighed. "Why should he suffer?"

"To keep the world safe. Sounds like a cliché but it's true." After a pause he said, "I don't know why you took it on if you feel like that."

"Oh, yes, you do. You talked me into it. And I've a grudge to settle. This is one way of doing it. And—let's be honest—I go for kicks and danger's the greatest kick of all. Even if I am frightened." She laughed in a timid uncertain way.

"I haven't time for philosophy. Must get on with the job." Using a shaded torch he un-zipped the cover of the orange life-raft, held the inflating lanyard in one hand and with the other threw the pack over the side. There was a steady hiss as the raft inflated and spread, growing larger by the second like the covered plant of a Bombay conjurer. The tubular walls filled and took shape and the canopy rose and became rigid. Eventually the raft loomed larger than the skimmer alongside it.

Liang Hui climbed in and turned it so that the canopy opening was opposite the stern of the skimmer, in which position he secured it. Krasnov was slightly built but it required all their strength to push, pull and claw him into the raft. Tanya got in next, while Liang Hui set about deflating the skimmer. Its buoyancy gone it sank, carried down by the weight of the outboard engine.

Apart from the life-raft's emergency equipment—flares,

a first-aid box, packs of iron rations, a torch and desalination kits—the Liang Huis had a passenger's flight bag inscribed ICELANDIC AIR LINES. In it were toilet and shaving gear, a flask of whisky, paperbacks, slippers and the other small impedimenta of air travellers.

They spent the next few minutes scooping water from the sea with a bailer, pouring it over themselves and Krasnov, throwing away their shoes, tearing their clothing and generally making themselves look as if they'd recently escaped from a ditched aircraft. Tanya took a large bandage from the first-aid box and wound it round Krasnov's head, covering his eyes. With Oriental solemnity Liang Hui gashed his own left forearm, rinsing the knife he'd used in sea water. The forearm bled copiously. With cotton wool from the first-aid box Tanya transferred her brother's blood on to Krasnov's bandage. By the time she'd finished the results were as convincing as Liang Hui's arm was painful.

They'd been in the raft for some time when they heard the deep throb of diesels. Liang Hui, fearing that it might be a merchant ship, checked that the red light on the canopy was blinking. After that he kept watch at the opening. A few minutes later the long finger of a searchlight poked the sea tentatively before settling on the life-raft. As suddenly as it had appeared it was switched off. The small light which took its place flashed a series of five longs followed by five shorts.

"It's *Bluewhale*," he called to his sister. The excitement in his voice reminded her of the games of discovery they'd played in their childhood.

"How marvellous," she said, and all her anxiety fell away.

With his torch Liang Hui flashed the agreed acknowledgement: a series of three shorts and three longs. They sat waiting, listening to the changing rhythm of engine movements, the sound of men's voices until, closer and higher than they'd expected, the submarine's navigation lights showed through the fog. A voice hailed them. "Stand by. We'll throw you a line."

185

It was close now, towering above the life-raft. In the reflected green of the starboard light they could see the shadowy outline of men on the casing. First attempts to pass the line failed. Eventually Liang Hui caught it and the raft was hauled alongside. Two seamen slithered down and with their aid and helping hands from above, Krasnov and the Liang Huis were transferred to the casing. They were taken along it, Krasnov on a stretcher, to the free-flooding door at the foot of the fin, then through it and down the hatches into the control-room.

Bill Boyd, well briefed by Brough and Hamsov, interviewed the drenched survivors and heard their story: how the light aircraft in which they'd been flying from Reykjavik to Narvik had developed engine trouble and come down in the sea. There had just been time to get off a MAYDAY but insufficient to give a position. Their friend who was both pilot and owner, Lars Rikdal, had failed to get clear. It had happened very quickly and in the darkness. The young man with them, Bjorg Edde, had suffered head injuries and some damage to his eyes. Fortunately, they explained, Tanya was a trained nurse and using the first-aid box in the life-raft she'd been able to bandage the injuries and sedate Edde. She was insistent that the bandages should not be disturbed and that he should be kept sedated until he could be transferred to a hospital.

Bill Boyd, understanding, puzzled and sympathetic at the same time, said, "Bit of a problem, but we'll sort it out. Great thing is we've found you. That's a slice of luck, anyway. We heard there was a light aircraft down but we hadn't a clue where you were. Sheer luck," he repeated, thinking that he was a pretty-accomplished liar. "I'll signal the senior officer of HM ships in company and ask for instructions. It'll probably be decided that you must be transferred to the nearest HM ship with adequate medical facilities."

Tanya said, "Bjorg Edde badly needs hospital assistance. Can't he be transferred to a Norwegian hospital?"

Bill Boyd pointed to the clock over the chart-table.

"It's ten to four in the morning and there's fog. The operation on which our ships are presently engaged is taking us away from Norway. By daylight we should be clear of the fog. We can then transfer you to *Belligerent*. She has surgeons and full hospital facilities."

"When will we be able to get to Norway, sir?" Liang Hui, wet and dejected, his forearm bandaged, was deferential but not to be ignored.

"That is for the Ministry of Defence to decide. No doubt proper arrangements will be made as soon as possible."

"Thank you," said Liang Hui. "Please don't think we're not grateful. It's just that we're worried."

Whatever you are, thought Bill Boyd, you and your sister are putting on a great act, bless you.

The little drama having been played out for the benefit of members of the crew in the control-room Krasnov was put in the captain's minute cabin with Tanya to look after him. Liang Hui was sent off to the small wardroom. It was already overburdened with Brough and Hamsov who were sleeping on settees.

"We've only got these people for a few hours," Bill Boyd explained to the first-lieutenant. "They'll have to make the best of it."

He sent for CPO Blades and gave him an "immediate" message for *Belligerent*, repeated *Aries* and C-in-C Fleet, reporting the recovery of three survivors from a ditched aircraft, one with head injuries. He requested instructions for their disposal. The reply came within a few minutes:

*Immediate to* Bluewhale. *Proceed with* Belligerent *and* Aries *to area GVF for Phase Two of exercise Kilo Zulu and for transfer of all repeat all survivors to* Belligerent *by helicopter as soon as possible.*

*Bluewhale* dived and made off to the north-west at seventeen knots. Soon afterwards Bill Boyd went to the sonar room, a screened compartment in the control-room. Petty Officer Stephens who'd been on watch while they looked for the *Daisy Chain* skimmer was still there.

"How's *Rockfish* getting on, Stephens?"

The petty officer looked at the sonar screen. "Bearing

187

two-seven-zero, twenty-one miles, sir. She's been heading to the westward since she picked up that skimmer."

"Bully for *Rockfish*," said Bill Boyd. "I was beginning to think we had her for keeps."

When things had settled down Boyd sent for the first-lieutenant. "Well, Number One, how are the lame ducks?"

"The Cantonese girl is looking after Bjorg Edde. Won't leave him. Doesn't want any help."

"Lucky Bjorg," said Boyd speculatively. "Nice-looking girl."

"Quite a dish, sir," agreed the first-lieutenant.

"Her brother?"

"Having coffee and nosh in the wardroom."

"Has he met Brough and Hamsov?"

"He's seen them. They're bedded down but they haven't lifted an eyelid for him."

"Sensible characters. Nothing like a good kip. Shan't be sorry to see all these bodies go. We aren't really cut out for this rescue-hospital ship scene."

"No, sir. We're definitely not."

## Twenty-Two

News of the disappearance of Krasnov reached the *Zhukov* in the early hours of morning. It came in the shape of a radio message from Major Martinsen using a *Nepa* salvage vessel as communications link.

Yenev, worrying about the progress of salvage operations, was lying on his bunk awake when Uskhan brought the signal: *Regret to inform you that Lieutenant*

*Ivan Krasnov cannot be found. He was last seen by Sub-Lieutenant Gerasov in the* kafeteria *at approximately 1100 last night stop Norwegian vessels on patrol off Vrakoy have been alerted and a search in and around Kolhamn is proceeding.*

Yenev instructed Uskhan to request the salvage vessel *Volga* to inform all Soviet naval units in the vicinity that Krasnov might have been abducted or be making an escape by sea. That done he sent for Milovych. The commissar, awakened from solid sleep, arrived in the captain's cabin wearing a towelling wrap. It concealed most of his plump body but when Milovych sat down Yenev could not, serious though the situation was, help observing how the commissar's belly settled round his middle in ample folds. The commissar, aware of the direction of the captain's gaze, drew the wrap more tightly about himself. He was still in a state of somnolent irritation. Among other things he was annoyed that he'd forgotten to put in his dentures. This introduced an unusual sibilance, a minuscule but embarrassing whistle when he spoke. Looking at his watch, he said, "I presume you have good reasons for sending for me at this hour?"

Yenev passed him the signal. "Judge for yourself."

As he read, Milovych's face paled visibly and seemed about to collapse. Recovering his poise, he stood up, pulled the wrap more tightly round his body and re-tied the girdle. "This is extremely serious, comrade." He waved the signal with one hand, gestured with the other.

Each man knew what the other was thinking. Defection.

The commissar's small eyes bored into Yenev's. "Have you had—ever had—any cause to doubt Krasnov?"

"Never," said the captain. "Knowing how thoroughly your department investigates the background, record and political behaviour of officers—especially those dealing with classified technology—I have never doubted him. Of course, as a seaman, I'm not enthusiastic about graduate entrants. You know that. I have, as you also know, been critical of Krasnov at times because he tends to be cocksure, too patronizing. But he's been a good officer and

189

that he should be insecure, politically unstable—well that I certainly have never thought."

Milovych pulled at the flesh beneath his eyes as if the gesture in some way improved matters. "I must say I never had any doubts about him. His political soundness. His loyalty to the Party."

You wouldn't have, you podgy dolt, thought Yenev. Officers who disliked the Party and its methods went to considerable lengths to conceal their feelings. Only occasionally were they identified and then almost always through informers—and no naval, army or air force unit lacked them. If anyone knew that the commissar should.

"And now," said Milovych. "What do you propose to do?"

"I've already asked the *Volga* to inform all Soviet naval units in the vicinity."

"Nothing else?"

"It is a political matter, comrade commissar. Abduction or defection on foreign soil. That is why I at once sent for you."

Milovych smiled. His thoughts were racing ahead. This was his scene and he was going to make the most of it. It was he who had urged that Krasnov and Gerasov should be armed when it was decided they should be left ashore. It was Yenev who had opposed the idea—on the grounds that it was a breach of protocol. Yenev's view had prevailed. That was something which Milovych would recall at the appropriate time and place.

"Please ask the *Volga* to send a boat across for me!" He said it with an air of bustling importance. "I must go into Kolhamn at once to see Major Martinsen and the *Ordforer*. I shall have to take charge of matters ashore. Ensure that everything possible is being done."

"Good," said Yenev rising from his desk. "But remember it is Norway, not Soviet Russia. What you can do is limited."

"I am well aware of that, comrade Yenev." Milovych eyed the captain sternly as if he had taken some unwarranted liberty.

"What are you going to do about an interpreter?"

asked Yenev, adding somewhat unkindly, "You've no longer got Krasnov."

"I will take Gallinin. He speaks Norwegian."

"I take it, then, that you will accept responsibility for radiation control failures," said Yenev.

"There are several experts in that field in the salvage vessels, comrade Yenev. I imagine they can do without Gallinin."

"Very well," said Yenev. "I accept your decision. But it must be logged as yours."

Milovych's small eyes glinted with animosity, and he made a mental note of Yenev's challenge before changing the subject. "When I am in possession of the facts I shall send a signal to the Vice-Admiral in command of the Political Department in Leningrad informing him of the occurrence."

"Yes. That would be advisable. He won't be pleased, of course." Yenev said this rather pointedly and with some relish. For a time it silenced the commissar, who had become thoughtful. No doubt Leningrad would not be pleased. They would want a sacrificial lamb. He would try to make it Yenev. But that might not be easy. He looked up, began a smile but cut it off when he remembered the missing dentures. "I must get into uniform," he said with sudden resolve. "Excuse me."

"Of course." Yenev was aware for the first time of feeling genuinely sorry for the commissar, who now had a heavy load of hay on his fork. "It is an extremely serious matter," said the captain. "I shall not rest until I hear your news."

This was something of an overstatement for within ten minutes of the commissar's departure Yenev was asleep.

When he reached the *radhus* during the early hours of morning the commissar found Major Martinsen with the *Ordforer* and Odd Dahl the bailiff. When Milovych explained that Gallinin would act as interpreter Martinsen said, "That will not be necessary."

Milovych found difficulty in concealing his surprise. Martinsen had spoken Russian. Initially, when he'd come off to the *Zhukov* with the message from the embassy in Oslo, and on subsequent occasions, he'd given no indication that he knew the language. Norwegian had always been used, Gallinin or Krasnov interpreting. Milovych was about to point this out, then thought better of it. Martinsen had been deceitful but that was a minor offence in the commissar's book. He would certainly have done the same thing if he could have turned it to advantage. No doubt Martinsen had hoped to overhear something of value. That he should now speak Russian suggested he hadn't.

"Nevertheless," said Milovych, returning to the point, "I would like Gallinin to be present during our talks."

"We have no objection," said Martinsen.

They seated themselves round the table in the *Ordforer*'s office and Milovych opened the proceedings. "I've had your disturbing message about Lieutenant Krasnov," he said, pinching the folds of his double chin. "What is the latest news?"

"We are still conducting a house-to-house inquiry," said Martinsen. "We've already searched the harbour area including a vessel about which Dr. Kroll had suspicions."

"Which vessel?"

"The yacht *Kestrel*. Crewed by British tourists. But there was nobody on board except the four crew members. The yacht sailed early this morning."

Milovych bristled. "That should not have been permitted."

Martinsen said, "It was a matter for us to decide, Commissar. This is a Norwegian port." He yawned, he'd been up a long time. "In any event, later she was stopped and searched at sea by our fast gunboat. It was a thorough search. The officer responsible says he would have found a hidden rabbit, let alone a Soviet naval officer."

Milovych was silent, weighing what had been said, wondering if the reference to the rabbit concealed something uncomplimentary. "Who is conducting the house-to-house search?" he challenged.

"It's not a search." Martinsen spoke wearily. "It's an inquiry. Our soldiers and sailors are conducting it."

"An inquiry is not enough," said Milovych. "Every house in Kolhamn should be searched from basement to attic."

Martinsen repeated this to the *Ordforer* in Norwegian.

Hjalmar Nordsen frowned, his mouth set firmly. "Tell the commissar this is Norway, not, with respect, Soviet Russia. We do not institute house-to-house searches to find men from foreign ships who go missing. We have already in my opinion over-reacted in our efforts to be helpful to his government. Krasnov may be in bed with a local girl at this moment while we are involved in all this fuss and bother."

Gallinin translated.

"No," said Milovych emphatically. "Our officers are too well disciplined. I believe he has been abducted."

Martinsen raised his eyebrows. "Abducted? Whatever for? Who would want to do that?" He watched the commissar's face with studied care before explaining to the *Ordforer* what had been said.

The commissar, aware that his reactions were under observation, attempted to control them by clenching his podgy fists until the knuckles showed white on the table. This was a question he should not have invited. Why indeed if the *Zhukov* was obsolete and used only for training would anyone want to abduct one of her officers?

"Well," he countered, "he may have been murdered." It was weak and everyone in the room including Gallinin knew it was.

"In which case a body will presumably be found and the matter becomes one for the police," said Martinsen.

Milovych's small eyes narrowed. I must, he thought, take a grip on myself. These Norwegians are being difficult. "The whole affair suggests that Lieutenant Krasnov has been the victim of violence," he said. "Gerasov tells me that when the lieutenant went to the lavatory he left his uniform cap on the table. So he intended to return." There was a glint of triumph in the commissar's eyes as he looked round the table. He'd made a good point and knew it. "Krasnov went through the swing-door to the passage leading to the lavatory and has not been seen since. The fire exit at the back was found bolted on the inside. If he went out of that door—which he must have done—someone bolted it behind him."

"I am not a detective, Commissar," said Martinsen, "but we cannot exclude the possibility that he has defected."

"Defected?" Milovych's attempt at incredulity was belied by the sudden fear in his eyes. Defection was the permanent nightmare of political commissars in the Soviet armed forces, more especially if the defector had access to highly classified information. And Krasnov had certainly had that. Of course the commissar had thought of defection. It had been his first reaction when he'd seen the signal in Yenev's cabin. But if Krasnov had defected where was he? Almost certainly somewhere on Vrakoy, most probably still in Kolhamn. Yet these wretched Norwegians were not prepared to take the elementary precaution of a house search. The situation was impossible.

"Yes. Defected," Martinsen was saying. "It may have been pre-arranged. Some girl perhaps. He leaves his cap on the table so that Gerasov's suspicions are not aroused. He goes out by the fire exit door and his accomplice—man or woman—bolts it on the inside."

Gerasov will have to account for this, the commissar was thinking. My instructions were unequivocal. They were never to leave each other. Always to remain together. Even on a visit to the lavatory. He turned to Martinsen. "At daylight we will land a party of naval ratings under officers to conduct a thorough search of the island. In the meantime I must take Sub-Lieutenant Gerasov back to the ship." The commissar smiled. "There will have to be an official inquiry on board and we shall need his evidence."

Poor little bastard, thought Martinsen.

Milovych got up to go.

Martinsen raised a restraining hand. "Before you go, Commissar, I must draw your attention to certain matters of protocol. In the first place please understand that Vrakoy, however small, is a part of Norway. We do not permit searches on Norwegian soil by the armed forces of foreign countries. If you wish to land a few naval ratings under an officer to carry out the normal duties of a naval patrol—that is to supervise and control the behaviour of your libertymen ashore, if any—" He stared at Milovych. Both men knew there weren't any—"you may do so provided the *Ordforer* has no objection. But your men will have no right of search. Neither of houses nor anything else on Vrakoy. I trust you understand?"

Milovych smiled. He knew when to give in. His bluff had been called. He was not so much a devotee of the Party as of Boris Milovych. He knew a good thing when he saw it, and when he did devoted his devious but capable mind to its pursuit. He was a successful member of the Party, but he could have been equally successful as a Wall Street broker or a brothel keeper in the Reeperbahn.

"You may rest assured, gentlemen, that we will do nothing improper. Perhaps I should have put it this way: if you would like the assistance of our men in the search for Lieutenant Krasnov, we shall be only too happy to co-operate."

"Your offer will be borne in mind, Commissar," said Martinsen gravely. "But I think we are capable of handling the situation. Of course, we will keep you informed."

Milovych rose, beckoned to Gallinin. "Well, goodnight gentlemen. We must be going."

Martinsen and the *Ordforer* stood up. "Goodnight, Commissar," said Martinsen.

Milovych's instinct told him they weren't sorry to see him go.


With the improvement in the weather salvage work on the *Zhukov* proceeded apace. The "camels" had arrived, been placed alongside to port and starboard and flooded. Divers passed lifting cables under the stern which was clear of the bottom for some twenty metres of its length, whereafter they were hauled forward as far as possible by wires taken through lead-blocks to the submarine's fin and winched in by the tugs.

At high tide the ballast in the "camels" was blown and with the aid of the submarine's own buoyancy they lifted two-thirds of her length clear of the bottom. Divers then passed another set of lifting cables under her hull, this time further forward. At low water the "camels", free of their load, were manoeuvred towards the bow, flooded and secured to the new set. Blowing of the "camels'" ballast tanks and lifting took place again at the next high tide. This operation was repeated on five successive tides until the "camels" and cables had arrived in the desired position to port and starboard of the fin. They were then flooded and the final set of lifting cables placed in position.

Towing wires were rigged between the submarine and the *Oktober* tugs—three of them now, an additional tug having towed the "camels" from Polyarnyo—and Feodor, the salvage expert, announced that all was ready for the final operation. On the following day at high tide the flooded bow would be lifted, full flotation achieved and the *Zhukov* would be towed stern first out of the cove.

The tow line would then be re-rigged so that the submarine could be towed bows first, the "camels" providing buoyancy forward. That done, the six-hundred mile journey to Murmansk would begin, *Zhukov* using her main engines at slow speed to supplement the towing power of the *Oktober* tugs and to assist steering.

During the operation she would be escorted by the *Nepa* salvage vessels, two *Kashin* and two *Kanin* class destroyers, and three patrol submarines.

The Soviet Navy's High Command was taking no chances with their crippled giant. Every effort would be made to ensure that she and her secrets were returned safely to the Soviet Union.


Gerasov was brought before Yenev and Milovych early in the forenoon. The sub-lieutenant had arrived back on board with the commissar and Gallinin at five o'clock that morning. Haggard, pale and red of eye, he'd not slept for some twenty-four hours and was close to breaking point.

Milovych questioned, cajoled, grilled, pleaded, threatened and bullied, but Gerasov stuck to his story: Krasnov had, notwithstanding Gerasov's protests, told him to remain at the table when he went to the lavatory.

"Why should he do such a thing?" prodded Milovych.

"I don't know, Commissar."

"Did this not arouse your suspicions? Why did you not insist on accompanying him? You knew he could not countermand my orders."

Gerasov had no satisfactory answer. He could not tell the truth: that the point hadn't arisen, that Krasnov had simply got up and gone while Gerasov had remained at the table. Why? To exchange glances with the English girl, hopefully to speak to her because he'd sensed she was interested. How could he tell these things to Milovych and Yenev?

Milovych pressed on relentlessly. In the few days they'd been together in the *hospits* had Krasnov given any indication of an intention to defect? Had he expressed views critical of the Navy or the Party? Had he said or done anything which raised the slightest doubt in Gerasov's mind?

No, lied the tired and frightened Gerasov, he had not. How could he tell them that Krasnov disliked the Navy, regarded many aspects of naval discipline and procedure as asinine, longed to get out of it into the academic world, into an environment where his doubts about the Party and its policies might not seem so out of place? Gerasov knew only too well that if he'd heard such things he should at once have informed Milovych. Nor had he remained neutral. Instead, in a mild indecisive way, he'd sympathized, shown some understanding of Krasnov's feelings.

Since he could not tell them these things he persisted with the denials. No, Krasnov had never done or said anything which could possibly have suggested defection. At least, reflected Gerasov, that was true. Krasnov had at no time hinted at defection.

Within an hour the inquiry had been completed. Gerasov was placed under close arrest and informed that he would be sent for court martial on *Zhukov*'s arrival in Murmansk. Milovych was leaving no stone unturned in his search for a scapegoat. If he couldn't implicate the captain, at least he could Gerasov.

During the afternoon Gerasov told the seaman on armed guard outside his cabin that he wished to visit the lavatory. When after some time he had not returned, the seaman gave the alarm and the door was forced. The sub-lieutenant was found hanging from a lamp bracket in the deckhead, his braces round his neck.

While Milovych was relieved to learn of this development, which he took to be an admission of guilt, he was disappointed that the sub-lieutenant had evaded a court martial. Before a naval court, in those circumstances, Milovych felt he could have done much to protect his own position.

In the early hours of morning there was considerable activity by Soviet naval units north-west of Vrakoy. It was through these waters that *Bluewhale* and *Rockfish* were travelling, now some twenty miles apart.

Both submarines had gone deep and had picked up at long range two fast-moving surface contacts approaching from the south-west. In due course they heard the new contacts' sonar transmissions and propeller noises and independently identified the sound signatures as those of *Kashin* class destroyers. It was cold comfort to the submarines' captains to recall that these Soviet guided-missile destroyers were equipped with anti-submarine homing rockets and VLR search sonar. There was no real danger that Soviet units would attack NATO submarines at sea in international waters in peacetime. But the consciences of *Bluewhale* and *Rockfish*'s captains—and certain of their passengers—were by no means clear and this tended to blur the truth: that it was not unusual for anti-submarine units of either side to hound each others' submarines and use them as "targets for exercise" whenever they found them. On the contrary, what was in the captains' minds was the old and recurrent fear of NATO submariners: that Soviet surface vessels might fire A/S homing rockets "for exercise" and protest ignorance of submarines in the area if called to account.

Before long, however, tension was relieved by the appearance on the submarines' sonar screens of more fast-moving contacts. These proved by their sound signatures to be three of the US Navy's *Belknap* guided-missile frigates. From their behaviour it was evident they intended to remain in close company with the *Kashin* destroyers for whom they were more than a match. The submarine captains knew that the *Belknaps* would already have *Bluewhale* and *Rockfish* on their sonar screens and have identified them as NATO units.

It became evident shortly afterwards that helicopters from both sides had joined in the fun for the submarines picked up dunked sonar buoy transmissions and found by computer comparison that they were those of both the United States and Soviet Navies.

At daylight the Soviet destroyers had evidently had enough for they disappeared in a south-westerly direction, accompanied by their helicopters.

## Twenty-Three

At noon course was altered to the south-west.

A light wind from the north had dispersed the fog. The day was fine, the sky an abstract of blues and whites, the sea calm above the undulations of a long swell.

*Bluewhale*, still submerged, had travelled a hundred and twenty miles to the north-west since picking up Krasnov and the Liang Huis. By mid-afternoon, in company with *Belligerent* and *Aries*, she had arrived in area GVF. Soon afterwards *Belligerent* made the executive signal for Phase Two of Kilo Zulu. Outward signs of the exercise were the constantly-changing dispositions of the surface ships, a surge in the volume of radio traffic, and increased activity by helicopters which executed complicated search patterns, often hovering close to the surface, tell-tale cables leading down like umbilical cords to dunked sonar buoys. The centre of all this, the target for the ASW scientists in *Aries*, was understood to be *Bluewhale*.

What was happening in *Aries'* laundry in the stern of the ship was known only to her captain and the Portland boffins. Like them, he knew a number of other things the ship's company didn't know. For example, that McGhee, the chief scientist, was the same Superintendent McGhee of the Special Branch who'd been at the *Zhukov* briefing in the Surrey farmhouse, and that Krasnov had been given the cover name of NORTON for the purposes of *Daisy Chain*.

When darkness fell, weather still fine, sea calm, the submarine and its consorts were two hundred and fifty miles south-west of Vrakoy.

At eight o'clock *Bluewhale* surfaced. *Belligerent* was in sight but *Aries*, twenty miles to the south, was well below the horizon. A few minutes later the approach of *Belligerent*'s helicopter was reported to the submarine's bridge. Bill Boyd ordered the first-lieutenant to stand by to transfer survivors. Krasnov, recovering from heavy sedation but able to walk with assistance, eyes still covered by the head bandage beneath which his ears were plugged, was taken up to the casing with the Liang Huis, Hamsov and Brough. All wore orange life-jackets. The first-lieutenant, a petty officer and two seamen accompanied them.

It was cold and dark under a clouded sky as the submarine, running at slow speed on main diesels, rolled gently to the swell, all that remained of the recent north-westerly gale. They heard the jet engines before the winking lights showed up in the distance and there was a stir amongst the little party on the casing when the first-lieutenant called out, "There she is. Fine on the port quarter." As it approached, the helicopter's landing lights came on, illuminating a moving circle of sea beneath it.

The first-lieutenant signalled with neon-lit orange wands and the helicopter closed in, its rotor blades shimmering in reflected light, the noise of the jets and the beat of the rotors transcending all other sounds as it stationed itself on the port quarter. The neon wands waved again and the Wessex V crabbed in sideways, hovering above the casing. A line was lowered, helping hands slipped Tanya Liang Hui into the harness and she was winched up; Krasnov, Li Liang Hui, Brough and Hamsov followed in quick succession. The wands were waved once more and the helicopter lifted to swing away in a sharp turn to port.

The little blip on *Bluewhale*'s radar screen moved purposefully towards the bigger blip which was *Belligerent* where it was finally swallowed. The radar operator watching the screen then knew that the Wessex V had landed on the assault ship. Soon afterwards another small blip broke away from *Belligerent* and travelled southwards until it, too, merged with a larger blip and disappeared. He knew then that it had reached *Aries*. What he didn't know was that in the course of its brief visit to *Belligerent* no one had left the helicopter. It had crouched on the flight deck, rotors turning, lights flashing, until it took off a few minutes later and made for *Aries*.

In the frigate the upper deck had once again been cleared for a nuclear fall-out exercise—"We ought to be bloody dead by now," remarked a disgruntled seaman—and only the flight deck officer saw the helicopter's arrival over the flight deck. It hovered there winching down its passengers. They were greeted by the ASW scientists from Portland who'd transferred to the frigate the day before. They helped Krasnov, Brough and the others from the winching harness, led them aft, down the ladder to the mortar well and along into the laundry, now innocent of any signs of its function. Broadcast speakers aft of the hangar had been switched off, screen doors shut and all other necessary steps taken to suppress the sounds of the ship. This, the captain explained by broadcast, had been done at the request of the scientists whose acutely sensitive equipment required a minimum of "on board" noise during testing.

In the laundry all lights had been switched off but for one red globe. On arrival there, Krasnov was placed in a chair, the bandages and ear plugs were removed, a black hood slipped over his head and secured with a light chain under his chin. His wrists were secured by metal straps to the arms of the chair, his ankles to its legs. The only people who spoke were the Liang Huis: to each other in Chinese, to Krasnov in Russian. From time to time he heard other Chinese voices. He could not know that they came from a high fidelity speaker behind a screen at the after end of the laundry.

Soon after they had strapped the Soviet lieutenant into the chair the Liang Huis were startled by his sudden cry, "Oh God, what's going to happen to me?" It was the first time he'd spoken since they'd given him the Sodium Pentothal tablets back in the *rorbu* in Kolfjord.

Instinctively Tanya put her hand over his. "Don't worry," she said. "Everything's going to be all right."

Her brother quickly remonstrated.

"I had to," she said. "I hate what we're doing to him."

Liang Hui said, "Do it again and you'll be in trouble."

She knew from the hardness of his voice that it was a threat, that he meant it.

It was understood by the frigate's crew that the latest arrivals were more ASW scientists from Portland come to take part in the secret equipment trials.

The first-lieutenant came up the starboard ladder on to the bridge two steps at a time. Seeing nothing but the glow of instrument dials he made for the dark shape on the pedestal seat. "They're all on board, sir."

"Everything all right, Number One?"

"One of them, Norton, has some sort of injury. Head's bandaged. McGhee says it's okay. Slipped down a ladder in *Belligerent* yesterday. Otherwise everything seems go. The accommodation problem's a bit dodgy. Got nine of them now, one a woman."

"What's her name?" The captain, usually a silent man, seemed to perk up.

"*Miss* Tanya Liang Hui, sir."

"Chinese. What's she like?"

"Rather a dish. Cantonese actually. Their secretary bird, note-taker and general what not."

"I want none of that in this ship," said the captain severely. "We're Mary Whitehouse fans, we are. What about accommodation?"

"With the two spare cabins—and getting the midshipmen to give up their cabin and sleep in the wardroom—we've managed to look after yesterday's party. This lot's more difficult. The girl's a problem."

"My day cabin perhaps?" suggested the captain.

"Sir!" mocked the first-lieutenant. Then more hopefully, "I thought the settee in mine might do."

"I'm sure you did, Number One. Think up something else."

"I'll get one of our subs to give up his cabin. He can join the midshipmen in the wardroom when he's not on watch and wants to get his head down."

"Sounds reasonable. Thank God we've only got them for the duration of the exercise. About twenty-four hours."

"Yes. That helps. Another thing is that McGhee, the boss boffin, says the latest arrivals will stay in the laundry, fiddling with their nuts and bolts. If they need kip, he says, they'll take it on stretchers and blankets we've put down there."

"You've let him know they can use the wardroom if they wish to?"

"Yes. I've done that, sir. And made arrangements for coffee, sandwiches, whatever, to be taken aft when needed."

"By whom?"

"One of their own party, sir."

"Splendid."

"Anything else, sir?"

"Yes. You might let McGhee know that I'd like him to take a glass of sherry with me at noon tomorrow."

"Aye, aye, sir. I'll see to that." The first-lieutenant made for the ladder.

"One other thing, Number One. Tell McGhee that if he cares to bring Miss Liang Hui I shall be delighted."

The first-lieutenant said, "Aye, aye, sir," and smiled in the darkness.


As the effect of the Sodium Pentothal wore off and increasing awareness returned, Krasnov tried to put together the bits and pieces. The motion, the vibration, told him he was in a ship. From beneath the chair came the feel and sound of churning propellers, so he knew he was in the stern. He was aware of other things: the hood over his head, the chain round his neck, the steel straps fastening his wrists and ankles to the chair, the sound of voices. Some near, some far, speaking an Oriental language. At first he took it to be Japanese, but later knew it was Chinese. The man and woman had talked to him briefly in Russian when they took him down ladders, led him into this place and put him in the chair. Otherwise they spoke Chinese.

Where was he? Why was he here? What would they do to him? Were they about to torture him? These questions kept repeating themselves.

He groped in his memory for familiar things. His parents. His brothers and sisters. Nasha Simeonov, the girl he hoped to marry. The small apartment in Kuslaya overlooking the Neva. The local primary school. The Leonin Govorov secondary school. Then on to Leningrad State University. Leningrad Naval Academy, Frunze Naval College. The training cruiser. What was its name? No. It wouldn't come. The submarine training course. That was it! Submarines. The *Zhukov*. His ship. An explosion in the forward torpedo-compartment. The struggle to beach her. It was coming back. The little harbour town on the island. Kolhamn. What had he been doing there? Leonid Gerasov? Yes, of course. They'd been in the *kafeteria* together. That was it. He'd gone to the lavatory.

Gerasov should have come too, but there was the English girl and he'd not insisted. The lights had gone out.

Two men had grabbed him. He remembered the terror of that moment. They'd poked guns into his back and neck. Frog-marched him along a dark passage. Out by a door at the back. Handed him over to two other men. He could remember them. Faces seen dimly in reflected light. Peaked caps, drooping black moustaches, white teeth, menacing eyes. Funny what you could remember from just a glimpse. They had pistol-marched him down to the harbour. What happened after that? A dark damp place, sitting in a corner. Vomiting. A man and woman speaking Chinese? How had he got there?

It didn't make sense. There were too many vague, uncertain, unrelated recollections. Like a half-remembered dream. The noise of an engine. Bumping along, a violent repetitive motion. Pushed and pulled by strong hands. An odd feeling in his head: thick, muzzy. Touching it to find a bandage over his eyes. Hitting out with a flat hand against a cold metallic wall. Realizing with a shock that he couldn't hear the sound of the slap. Thinking he had a head injury. Had he?

Later he'd been in an aircraft. Then, aware of the excessive vibration, he'd realized it was a helicopter. They'd landed. Once or twice? There'd been some interruption? He'd known for sure it was a helicopter when they'd winched him down on to the deck of a ship. That was something he'd done many times before.

What was the ship? Chinese? China was Russia's enemy. But what was a Chinese warship doing in the Arctic? Was it a warship? Submarine perhaps? The helicopter? There'd been no Chinese in the *kafeteria*. It didn't make sense. The more questions he posed the more nightmarish it became. How could he draw the line between reality and fantasy?

Then, with sudden and frightening clarity the truth dawned upon him. They'd found out that the submarine on the rocks was the *Zhukov*. They would try to force him to talk. To tell them all he knew. But he wouldn't co-operate. Nothing would make him do that. So they would . . . ? Reason gave way to terror and he cried out in Russian. "Oh God, what's going to happen to me?"

It was then that the woman had touched him. Her warm hand on his. "Don't worry," she'd said in a low voice. "Everything's going to be all right."

A number of surprising developments were being discussed in the *Ordforer*'s office the morning after Krasnov's disappearance.

"Who found the body?" Hjalmar Nordsen ran the back of his hand across tired eyes.

Odd Dahl said, "Inga Bodde and Gunnar Olufsen. They left her house at eight-fifteen this morning. Walking down the footpath they saw a foot sticking out from behind some rocks."

"What was Olufsen doing there at that time?" The *Ordforer*'s lifted eyebrows underlined the question.

"He spent the night in the Bodde house. After leaving the *kafeteria* at eleven-thirty last night."

"Of course. I was forgetting. They are engaged."

Odd Dahl took up the story again. "They didn't touch the body. Came straight to my house. I was still asleep." He looked at the *Ordforer* apologetically. "Didn't get to bed until four o'clock this morning."

"I know. Neither did I. All this business." He waved a disapproving hand. "Why should Vrakoy be troubled with such things? And now murder."

"I went at once," continued Odd Dahl. "Examined the body. He was stabbed in the throat. A fierce wound. The carotid artery severed. I looked around but couldn't find a knife. A few blood-stained tissues, a trail of blood from the path. Nothing more. I searched him—the body I mean. There were the usual things. And this unopened letter, addressed to you."

Odd Dahl passed the sealed envelope to the *Ordforer*. Hjalmar Nordsen opened it and they saw that his hands were trembling. He took out several sheets of paper, spread them on the desk. There was no sender's address, no signature. Just the date, *October 1974*, and the heading, TO WHOM IT MAY CONCERN. Impeccably typed, electric IBM, a three-page summary of the career of Gustav

206

Kroll, alias Charlsen, alias Rodsand, alias Sorensen, alias Lillevik . . .

The *Ordforer* read in silence his face hardening as the story unfolded. When he'd finished he passed the summary to Lars Martinsen. "Such a man has many enemies," he said.

They discussed Kroll's death at length, finally agreeing on three possibilities: that Kroll had been killed by the KGB, or by the CIA, or by a Norwegian patriot with a long memory. The KGB or CIA seemed the more likely.

Martinsen was strangely silent during this part of the discussion. "It is no use speculating," he said. "One must have facts before drawing worthwhile conclusions." He was thinking of Karen and Joe. Nothing about Kroll had come from the CIA through that source. So it was probably the KGB. Why now? Was it because, with the *Zhukov* stranded on Vrakoy, the KGB had dispatched an agent to the island? That he'd chanced upon Kroll? It was guesswork and unrewarding. He gave up. At the *Ordforer*'s request he took the anonymous report, undertook to pass it without delay to Norwegian Intelligence.

Then, choosing his moment, he lifted the canvas grip from the floor and put it on the table. From it he took a faded blue denim jacket and trousers, a pair of well-worn plimsolls, and the uniform jacket of a lieutenant of the Soviet Navy. "They were found this morning by two of our soldiers on the rocks in Nordvag Bay," he said. "Members of the search party sent out to look for Krasnov."

He took a worn plastic wallet from the bag. "This was found in the denim jacket. It has in it some Chinese money and a number of personal items including the papers of a Chinese seaman. Ho Lu Kwang. The denims, the plimsolls and the wallet were made in China." Martinsen picked up the naval uniform jacket. On it were traces of sand and sea water stains. "This is Ivan Krasnov's jacket. It has his name tag. Presumably the one he was wearing in the *kafeteria* last night. I say that because of these." He held up three slips of paper, print-outs from a cash register. "They are imprinted with yesterday's date.

Haakon Jern has examined them. He says they were issued last night."

"My God," said the *Ordforer*, forsaking his customary calm. "Why did you not tell us this at once?"

Martinsen shrugged his shoulders. "Odd Dahl got in first—the finding of Kroll's body. That seemed important enough."

"Is there any connection between the two events?"

"There may be. I don't see it at present."

"My goodness." The *Ordforer* looked both shocked and baffled. "What's your theory?"

Martinsen thought about that. "I don't know that I have one. Superficially it looks as if Krasnov was abducted by the Chinese. The Liang Huis are missing. These garments were found close to the sea in Nordvag Bay. There are signs of a scuffle having taken place. Krasnov may have been taken off in a small boat. Perhaps to a ship or submarine."

"Why does a Chinese seaman leave his clothes and wallet on the rocks?" Odd Dahl's rubbery weatherbeaten face creased with doubt.

"That's why I said 'superficially'," said Martinsen. "It's difficult to answer your question."

"Unless," the *Ordforer* hesitated. "Unless it was done deliberately. To create the impression that it *was* a Chinese act."

Martinsen nodded. "Of course. But there are other possibilities. They may have been about to dress Krasnov in the clothes of a Chinese seaman when they were disturbed. Or a Chinese seaman may have taken his clothes off to swim to a boat anchored off-shore—again they were disturbed. How can we say what happened?"

"I wonder," said the *Ordforer* pressing the tips of his fingers together. "It is an extraordinary business."

Martinsen was thinking of Karen and the feed-back to Joe . . . of Freddie Lewis's tip-off . . . "a great power is laying on something special by way of intelligence gathering." Roald Lund's "Is it a NATO power?" Freddie Lewis's reply "The words used were a *great power*. That's all I know."

China was a great power, not a member of NATO.

Martinsen thought, too, of Plotz and Ferret, the American ornithologists, and the United States Oceanographic Service's Sikorsky helicopter. Plotz and Ferret were still on Vrakoy. He'd checked that. Due to leave on the Wideroe's midday flight to Bodo, en route to Rost. The USOS helicopter and its survey crew were scheduled to fly to Bodo that afternoon. He'd checked that too. And the *Kestrel* manned by the English party? She'd sailed at two o'clock in the morning. That had looked suspicious. But she'd been searched before and after sailing, and the captain of the gunboat said she was absolutely clean. No one but the English tourists aboard. And they *had* arrived in Andenes at a quarter-to-eight that morning. That also he'd checked. There were so many unrelated, odd-shaped pieces in the jig-saw puzzle. It was time, he decided, to report to Roald Lund. "I must go to Oslo this afternoon, *Ordforer*," he said. "To report to my superiors."

Before the meeting broke up other items were discussed. There was still no sign of the Frenchmen who'd set out to climb Bodvag. A representative of the Sûreté Nationale was arriving in Kolhamn at midday to inquire into their disappearance. The Liang Huis had not returned to the *hospits* the night before though their hand luggage had been left in their room. There was no trace of them in Kolhamn.

"I have spent most of my life on this island," said the *Ordforer*. "It has always been a peaceful law-abiding place, except when the Germans came. Now, since that Soviet submarine ran ashore on the Dragetennene, we have these extraordinary happenings." He shook his shaggy white head. "We live in bad times."

## Twenty-Four

Extract from Top Secret file BMS/USSR Delta/Two/
2713b . . . Planning memo, Operation *Daisy Chain*.
Appendix 111, p. 7, para. 4:

*Interrogation Team:*

| | | |
|---|---|---|
| In Charge: Chief Superintendent | R. McGhee | |
| Russian language interpreters | E. F. Brough<br>G. L. Hamsov | } Special Branch |

| | | |
|---|---|---|
| *Neurologist* | G. B. Smithers | |

*Scientific Team:*

| | | |
|---|---|---|
| Sonar, radar, electronics | W. E. Wilson | } Admiralty Research Establish-ments |
| Missiles, underwater and surface weaponry | G. W. A. Curtis | |
| BMS design and operation | P. L. Grogan | |

*Assistants:*

| | |
|---|---|
| Background intelligence, simultaneous translation, Chinese conversation | Li and Tanya Liang Hui – Secret Intelligence Service |

The laundry had been divided into two parts by means of
a temporary screen erected by the ship's staff. One third
of the compartment was forward of the screen, two thirds
aft. The forward portion contained a table and chairs for

the interrogators, facing it the chair into which Krasnov was strapped. Brough was already at the interpreters' table. The rest of the party were behind the screen in the after end where a quantity of electronic equipment had been set up. A small storeroom led off it on the port side aft.

McGhee was explaining: "Krasnov is wearing headphones and a strobe light mask in place of the hood. He can see and hear nothing except the audio and visual material we feed him. As far as he's concerned he's alone. Got it?"

"Brough and Hamsov explained the technical side to us when we were in *Bluewhale*," said Liang Hui, rather in the manner of a schoolboy saying, "We've already done that, sir."

"That's right." McGhee was not to be put off. "And I explained it to you scientific gentlemen while we were in *Belligerent*. All I propose now is a quick run-through to make sure we all know what's happening."

There were murmurs of assent.

"It's essential to this technique to impose nervous stress on the brain of the interrogatee in order to introduce the hypnoid and ultra-paradoxical phases. This is scientific jargon for what we call inducing a compliant state of mind. In other words making the interrogatee willing to talk and changing his mental attitude in such a way that he wants to co-operate. It used to take a long time—weeks perhaps. Now, with the aid of electronics and drugs, it can be done in a few hours. We've come a long way since Pavlov."

"What drugs?" asked Li Liang Hui.

"We only use them if we run into difficulties, like a high level of resistance. Then mostly LSD—sometimes Nembutal."

McGhee pointed to the console at which Smithers was sitting wearing headphones. "Smithers is working on Krasnov now. He'll keep it up until midnight. After that the interrogation begins. That console contains audio mixers, selectors, input, output, volume controls and gauges and a lot more I won't bother you with." He pointed to the equipment around them: the battery of tape recorders and players, the stroboscopic light projectors and diffusers, the video projectors, the microphones, loud-speakers, earpieces and other listening devices, the multiplicity of leads feeding into and out of the console.

"Smithers controls everything," continued McGhee. "Speech, sound effects, video, light effects, whatever he wants to feed to his—patient." He looked at the scientists. "You'll be linked up with the interrogators and the simultaneous translators. The first questions to go to Krasnov will be taped ones prepared in the Admiralty research establishments. You'll get the English version simultaneously on tape. Then, as we go along, you'll ask supplementary questions on the basis of Krasnov's answers. The interrogators will hear your supplementaries, put them to him in Russian. And so it goes."

McGhee paused, thought of something. "From time to time Smithers will feed Krasnov with Chinese chat about the interrogation—some of it taped—some of it extempore by the Liang Huis. Although Krasnov can't speak Chinese we must maintain the impression that he's in a Chinese ship."

"How is the severe nervous stress you talk of imposed?" The question was Tanya's. Her brother realized that she already knew the answer but her question was an indication of her state of mind. She was deeply disturbed.

"Smithers is working on Krasnov's audio and visual reflexes now. Feeding him strange sounds. Weirdie noises. You know. Alternating these with pleasant sounds. Bit of Beethoven. Girl singing. Lambs bleating. Bird song. Stuff like that."

"Horrible," whispered Tanya. "It's calculated cruelty."

"Not really," said McGhee quite happily. "Not a patch on what they used to do. Remember the Spanish Inquisition. Now where was I? Ah, yes. With those sound effects, Smithers is feeding in light effects." He leant over the console, examined the instruments. "He's pushing in stroboscopic light now. Krasnov is picking it up through the mask. It confuses the nervous system even when there's a high level of resistance."

212

"Perhaps he closes his eyes?" suggested Curtis.

"He certainly does. But it makes very little difference. That's what the mask is for. It amplifies the light impulses. The intensity is too great. Now these lights. Very interesting. They're ultra high frequency. Varying rhythms, variety of colours and patterns. Get the right frequency, rhythm and colour changes and you destroy reality. Fantasy takes over. Very clever."

"Fiendishly," said Curtis. He was suffering from a painful dichotomy. There was a great deal he wanted to learn from the Soviet lieutenant about the *Zhukov*'s missile systems but, compassionate and gentle, he was revolted by the methods used.

"I suppose you could say," continued McGhee, "that Krasnov's nervous system, his audio and visual perceptions, are now under attack—being broken down. Smithers judges the patient's reflexes by feeding in straightforward questions at odd intervals. If the strains to which the patient is subjected become too severe, Smithers eases up."

"Very considerate of him," said Curtis dryly.

"The object is to induce a state of nervous breakdown in order to obtain co-operation—or compliance if you like. At the same time the technique induces partial hypnosis. When these objectives have been achieved the interrogatee is usually ready to assist. Got the idea?"

"Yes—and I think it's perfectly bloody," said Tanya. "Cruel. Barbaric."

McGhee smiled indulgently. "Don't worry your head about that, Tanya. It's no more cruel than the shock treatment given regularly in psychiatric therapy. And we permit that for people we love." McGhee spoke with more feeling than his audience appreciated. He had a schizophrenic daughter undergoing treatment in an institution in the south of England.

"How do you know if his answers are truthful?" asked Grogan.

"Smithers has a lie-detector feed into the console. He alerts the interrogators if necessary. It helps. In this instance the scientists will probably know if he's lying on technical subjects. No system is perfect. Ours is based on the latest neurological and psychiatric techniques. The desire to lie is removed. It doesn't often fail."

"Is there any permanent damage? I mean to Krasnov." It was evident that Tanya was not likely to be counted among McGhee's admirers.

"No," said McGhee. "Nothing permanent. Unless it's damage to his conscience. We can't do anything about that."

"I'm sure you can't." Her eyes flashed.

"Look," said McGhee, with a trace of irritation. "I'm not pretending interrogation is humane. Of course it's not. This isn't a vicar's tea party. You know that. You've done the resistance course. You may be subject to interrogation yourself. It's an occupational hazard."

"The course convinced me I wouldn't be a very good resister."

McGhee saw her quick glance at the ring she was wearing, a stainless steel hexagon. "What's in that?" he asked.

"Something," she smiled sadly. "Better than betrayal."

McGhee looked at her curiously. Only his wife would have recognized the slight twitching at the corners of his mouth as sympathy. "It's a way out." He shrugged his shoulders, seemed about to say something, looked embarrassed, then went back to his subject. "Yes. Interrogation *is* unpleasant. Certainly humiliating. But the end justifies the means. We live in a tooth and claw jungle this end of the twentieth century. Krasnov possesses knowledge which can help us survive. We intend to get it." His steely grey eyes outstared hers and she realized for the first time that he was not only a strong man but a very frightening one.

"Well, he was a tougher proposition than we thought." McGhee, wheezing from a climb up several companion-ladders, wiped his face with a large silk handkerchief, leant back in the easy chair, unbuttoned his waistcoat and lit a cigarette. "Doesn't do himself badly for accommodation, does he?" He looked with approval round the captain's day cabin.

214

"For how long have we got it?" asked Wilson.

"He'll be on the bridge for the next couple of hours. We're okay until noon."

Wilson yawned, shook his head, looked at his watch. "Good heavens! Nearly ten hours of it. Exhausted me. Goodness knows what it's done to Krasnov."

"He's sleeping. On a stretcher in that small storeroom at the after end of the laundry. They've locked him in," said McGhee. "He'll need time to sleep off the LSD and a bit of shock."

"The Liang Huis still down there?" said Wilson.

"Yes. Until we land him tonight they're the only people he'll see or hear."

"Have they discussed the landing with him?"

"Not yet. They will. When he's had a good sleep and his mind is clear."

Curtis was on the settee, feet stretched out, ample stomach bulging over his belt line, pink flesh peeping through a taut shirt. "I hated every minute of it. Absolutely loathsome. Glad I'm a scientist and not ..." He stopped short, pulled up by McGhee's stare. "Sorry," he went on. "I know it's your job."

"Somebody has to do it," said McGhee. "Warm in here, isn't it?"

"It's the heater," said Grogan. "Shouldn't have thought it necessary with air-conditioning."

"Nice and homely," said McGhee. "Nothing like the glow of artificial coal."

"He's a tough young man." Wilson clasped his hands behind his head. "Took Smithers a long time to introduce ... what was it you called it, McGhee?"

"State of compliance?" suggested McGhee, sticking his thumbs in his belt.

"Yes, that's it. He was anything but compliant at the start."

"Interesting," said Grogan. "Did you notice when the break came?"

"The threats?" Curtis shivered. "Ugh!"

"No. It was after that. When Brough put in that bit about the futility of war. How the only way to avoid it was to share technological progress. Don't let one side become dominant because that's an invitation to armed conflict. Maintain the balance. He used the joint space programme rather well, I thought. After that Krasnov began to co-operate."

"There were a lot of other things at work," said McGhee dryly. "He was going to co-operate anyway."

"Incredibly slow start," Wilson yawned. "I thought we'd never get going."

"Smithers, Brough and Hamsov are a good team." McGhee said it with the pride of a parent.

"It's not pleasant to watch," said Grogan. "But I must say it works."

He went on, "I suppose the price in moral terms *is* high. But that interrogation may have saved the West five years of research. Even then we might not have got on to the drone."

"Fortunate for us the *Zhukov* got on to those rocks," parodied Wilson. "We knew the USSR had moved ahead in submarine missilry but we were thinking in terms of MARV, range, megatonnage. That sort of thing."

"You mean you hadn't thought up anything like the secondary missile system?" suggested McGhee.

Curtis said, "We'd thought of it. But we haven't got very far with it. Too many snags. They've got it. A remarkable achievement. That and the drone give their BM and fleet submarines an offensive capacity well in advance of anything in the West. When their construction programme is completed they'll not only have the edge in terms of nuclear exchange but superiority in conventional naval warfare."

Wilson said, "They must have got a long way with AC super-conductors."

"In marine application—yes," Grogan agreed with some reluctance. "But the Japanese are already operating a test locomotive on super-conductors at 400 m.p.h. We know the technology of course, but there are problems of application, particularly with marine motors. They've overcome them. We haven't."

"What's the big advantage of the super-conductivity motor?" asked McGhee.

"A power-weight ratio ten times better than anything else around. It's as simple as that."

McGhee leant back in the chair puffing happily at his pipe, hands clasped behind his head. "So the Krasnov interrogation *was* worthwhile?"

Grogan regarded him thoughtfully. "As a scientist I don't care much for purple passages, but I think it would be no exaggeration to say that this has been one of the most important intelligence operations conducted by the West since the nuclear arms race began."

"Yes. And at what a price," Curtis grimaced. "Reduces us to the moral level of thugs, child rapists, Gestapo sadists, anything foul you care to think of. God! To think I've been involved in that."

"It would do you good to be in on an interrogation session in Lubianka Prison." McGhee stared at Curtis through a haze of cigarette smoke, shook his head sadly and changed the subject. "We've got the whole thing on tapes but I won't be releasing them in their present form. Anyway I doubt if you'd be able to use them as they are. A lot of editing is involved. We'll do that at Special Branch. Cut out the interrogation by-play. But you'll get the essential detailed questions and answers." He took a miniaturized transistor recorder from a coat pocket, put it on the table in front of Wilson. "You'd better get on with the summary. The principal facts. That's what we're here for."

Wilson said, "I hadn't forgotten. Just taking a breather."

There was a knock on the cabin door.

"Come in," called McGhee. It was the captain's steward with coffee and sandwiches.

"Marvellous," said Curtis. "Best thing we've seen for a long time."

The steward put the tray on the table, began to arrange the cups. "Don't worry," said McGhee. "We'll manage."

When the steward had gone McGhee locked the door.

Wilson picked up the recorder, slid the control to

"speak", counted aloud to ten, played it back and adjusted for volume. "Put me right as I go, if you don't agree."

He began to dictate.

*Ref: BMS/USSR/Delta Two*          *13 October 1974*
Summary of information given by Lieutenant Ivan Krasnov, sonar and torpedo officer, BMS *Zhukov*, Soviet Navy.

1. Main armament comprises sixteen SSM-SSN9 (MK II) ballistic missiles, first in service in any unit of the Soviet Navy. Range 4600 miles as against the 2250 of its *Sawfly* predecessors, and 2880 of US Navy's *Poseidon.*

2. The SSN9 (MK II) is armed with MARV nuclear warheads, each containing twelve units capable of independent targeting and manoeuvring.

3. The prominent extension abaft *Zhukov*'s fin, approximately twelve metres in length, houses two lineal batteries of defensive missiles. This armament is known in the ship as the "secondary missile system." It comprises twenty solid fuel Mach 4 cruise missiles, each of which can be used against surface-to-air and subsurface-to-surface targets at range of up to 250 miles.

All missiles are fitted with heat, sound seeking and radar homing devices.

The Delta Twos—known in the Soviet Navy as the Marshall Class—are the first BMS afloat to be equipped with defensive missile systems.

4. The twin blisters which extend over the last fifteen metres of *Zhukov*'s length and terminate either side of the tail stabilizer fin and upper rudder comprise two launching tubes. These contain a new weapon, known in the Soviet Navy as a Nuclear Sonar Drone.

I. Two drones are carried, one in each tube. Approximate dimensions are, length 12.5 metres, diameter 2.75 metres. The drones are unmanned. Propulsion is by super-conductivity motors driving hydrojets. Maximum underwater speed 35 knots. Expulsion from the launching tubes is by compressed air.

II. Once launched they are controlled by the mothership by sonar signals up to a range of 35 miles. Alternatively, if both mother-ship and drone use surface antennae, they can be radio-controlled up to ranges of 150 miles. Finally, their onboard computer can be programmed to operate the drone independently up to ranges of a high order. Lieutenant Krasnov believes that 500 miles has been achieved experimentally. The Soviet Navy apparently does not regard the drone as having a sound tactical application at such long ranges. It has been designed primarily for use under direct control of the mother-ship.

III. On completion of its mission a drone can be recovered by the mother-ship while submerged. This is accomplished by means of hydraulically-operated tail-grabs in conjunction with closed circuit television. Fouling of the propeller and the upper rudder unit is precluded by built-in propeller guards and by locking the upper rudder unit during launching and recovering. At such times the lower rudder unit works independently.

5. A drone has three tactical applications:

I. The bow contains a radome, immediately abaft it a conventional scaled down sonar system. By means of sonar re-diffusion the drone is able to relay signals to and from the mother-ship, extending the latter's sonar range from 45 to 70 miles.

II. Abaft the sonar compartment there is a tactical nuclear warhead. The drone can be directed on to a surface or subsurface target by the mother-ship, or home on to such targets by means of heat and sound seeking devices.

III. The drone can be used as a sonar decoy and as a decoy for heat and sound seeking devices.

## Comment

The above summary suggests that the Soviet Navy's *Marshall* class submarines are considerably in advance of their United States counterparts. The detailed technological information obtained from Lieutenant Krasnov—necessarily not given in this summary but now in possession of the undersigned—should ensure that the time lag involved before parity is achieved will be reduced substantially.

W. E. Wilson
Signed: G. W. A. Curtis
P. L. Grogan

## *Twenty-Five*

"Marvellous." Tanya leant back in the chair holding the mug of coffee with both hands. "I need this."

Liang Hui finished a sandwich, looked at his watch. "It's ten to six. He's had seven hours of sleep."

"Shouldn't we wake him? Give him something to eat? He can rest again later. He's got a bad twenty-four hours ahead. Hasn't had anything since he came on board."

"Don't suppose we'd have much appetite in his shoes."

"No, we wouldn't." She said it with fierce conviction.

"I'll see how he's getting on." He switched off the white

deckhead light leaving the solitary red light to bathe the laundry in semi-darkness. He picked up the black hood, patted his shoulder-holster, went to the after end of the laundry and unlocked the storeroom door. Once inside he switched on the light, shutting the door behind him.

Krasnov lay under a blanket on the stretcher. As the door clanged to, he stirred uneasily, muttered something, then propped himself up on his elbows.

Liang Hui said, "Feeling all right?"

The Russian yawned, rubbed his eyes, ran his fingers through his hair. "Don't know. Just woken up."

He got to his feet clumsily, stretched and yawned again. He was wearing the blue denim trousers, but had taken off the sweater and plimsolls.

"Like something to eat? Sandwiches and coffee?"

Krasnov stared at his questioner. "No. Only water."

"Of course. Put your things on and we'll get some."

The Russian pulled on a jersey, leant awkwardly against the bulkhead, standing first on one foot then the other as he put on the plimsolls.

Liang Hui said, "Sorry. We'll have to hood you again."

"Not more interrogation?" The Russian's eyes and voice combined in an urgent plea.

"No. That's finished." Liang Hui slipped the hood over the Soviet lieutenant's head, secured the chain girdle under his chin and locked it. Taking his hand he led the Russian to the fore part of the laundry and settled him in the interrogation chair.

"We're not binding your feet or ankles," he said. "But don't leave the chair without permission."

Krasnov drank the water Tanya gave him.

"Sure you wouldn't like a sandwich? Some hot coffee?" she said.

"No." He was abrupt. "Water is enough."

In the dim red gloom she shook her head, looked anxiously at her brother. He nodded and said, "We've good news for you, Krasnov. We're putting you ashore tonight."

"Where?" The Russian was at once suspicious.

"On a Norwegian island, Rebbensoy. Within a hundred

221

miles of Vrakoy. You'll be landed in a small cove. At daylight you can walk to the nearby fishing village. About three kilometres. Within a short time you'll be with your comrades. Back in your ship."

Krasnov's only response was to intersperse deep breathing with sighs and shakings of the head. "I don't want to be landed on Norwegian soil," he said at last.

"Why?"

"It's not safe. Too close to my country. The Norwegians fear the Soviet Union. They will hand me over."

"I don't understand."

"You should." Krasnov spoke with sudden vehemence. "You and your *friends*. You made me betray my country's secrets." He faltered and for a moment they thought he might break down, but he recovered his composure. "It's impossible for me to go back. I'm finished."

Liang Hui looked at him in astonishment. "I think you're dramatizing the situation," he said. "Think about it calmly. Of course you must go back. Tell them the truth. You were forcibly abducted. Taken against your will to a Chinese ship. Tell them all you know. From your visit to the *kafeteria* onwards. Explain how you were interrogated. The techniques used and so on. All that will be true."

"Yes," said Krasnov bitterly. "And then?"

"You do what any normal human being would do. You protect yourself. You are not responsible for what has happened. It is not your wish. Why should you accept guilt? So you tell your people that you gave us nothing of importance. That you knew from our questions that our technology was far behind yours. That it was therefore easy to give us misleading information."

Krasnov managed a hollow laugh. "I know the truth to be different. Your technology may be behind ours in certain respects, but your questions showed you know a great deal. Don't forget, we *know* what you've got. We, too, have intelligence services."

Liang Hui ignored these remarks. "You tell them," he continued, "that after the interrogation we landed you on

222

Norwegian soil because it was not necessary or practical to take you back with us."

From under the hood there came a snort of derision. "Rubbish. I'm finished as far as my own people are concerned. If I go back they will want to know everything, down to the last detail. My country knows a great deal about interrogation. They would soon break down an untrue story." He shook his head vigorously. "They would make me confess what I told you. And then ..." He spread his arms in a gesture of helplessness.

"What do you want us to do?" asked Tanya gently.

"Land me on British soil as a defector. I can claim political asylum."

"You can do that in Norway," she said.

"Maybe. And if they grant it the KGB will find me in a few days ... a few weeks. It makes no difference. They will find me. It must be Britain if I am to have a chance."

"Why especially Britain?" she said.

"The British have a tradition of granting political asylum. It is one of their remarkable qualities. They will understand my problem. There are none so fiery as the converted."

Liang Hui said, "What do you mean by that, Krasnov?"

"Britain is like an alcoholic or a criminal reformed. Now that her empire has collapsed the attitude of her people has changed. Especially that of the younger ones. There is a new spirit of socialism abroad. The British are trying to salve their social conscience. They do this by making propaganda for the underprivileged, particularly the coloured races. Yet no country exploited these people more than Britain. Now she wishes to make amends. To be seen by the world to have reformed. So she attacks those who behave as she did. This includes my country. We, too, are building an empire. But in a different way and with different objectives. We wish to see equality and social justice for all."

Krasnov took a long breath, and Tanya patted his shoulder for no other reason than that she was sorry for him. He was to her like a child in trouble. But he didn't like the gesture and shook her hand away. "As a defector

223

from the Soviet Union I will be welcome in Britain. They will make propaganda from the defection of a Soviet naval officer. So I've no option now. It must be Britain."

Liang Hui scratched at invisible cobwebs on his forehead. "Your views are very muddled, Lieutenant, not well informed," he said. "In China we regard the Soviet Union as an imperialist power. That is why she makes détente with the other super-imperialist power, the USA. As for Britain," Liang Hui shrugged his shoulders, "she is nothing—a satellite of the United States. America's most important off-shore nuclear platform. Europe is nothing. Too fragmented. NATO is growing weaker not stronger. The French started that. The balance of power will shift slowly but surely to the East." Liang Hui's tone changed suddenly. He became impatient. "But I have no time for these discussions. It is not part of my duties to become involved in such things."

Krasnov's manner changed too. He became less challenging as if he felt he'd possibly gone too far. "So what are you going to do?" he said quietly.

Liang Hui gave the hooded head a long hard look. "Tell my superiors that you don't want to be landed on Norwegian soil. That you believe Britain is the only safe country for you. But I warn you. There'll be difficulties. Certain arrangements have already been made. It may be too late to change them." His eyes narrowed and his tone conveyed that he hadn't much liked Krasnov's attempt to change carefully-laid plans. "And remember. For all your speech making, you're in no position to lay down terms."

Krasnov was silent then, weighing what had been said. "Tell them," he said at last, "that if I am landed on Norwegian soil I'm afraid the Press there may get the whole story from me."

"What story?"

"The true story."

Liang Hui stood up, pushed his chair back. "If that's a threat forget it. It won't impress my people. What you tell the Western press is immaterial to them."

Krasnov thought about that, hesitated, then blurted out

what was in his mind. "Tell them I know this is a British warship. HMS *Aries*. I think that may help."

"I'm afraid there's been rather a serious snag with *Daisy Chain*, sir." Briggs handed the signal to the Commodore (Intelligence) as if it were a very hot plate. "Just in from *Aries*."

The commodore took it, gathering his eyebrows in a bushy frown and regarding his assistant with a mixture of suspicion and disapproval. He began to read:

*Immediate: In some way unknown to us our passenger has learnt that this is a British warship and knows her name. Stop. He insists on being landed on British soil, treated as a defector and given political asylum. Stop. He threatens that if landed in Norway he will give his story to the Norwegian press. Stop. Request immediate instructions. McGee.*

The commodore looked at Briggs as if he'd like to wring his neck. "Bloody hell," he said. "Some flaming idiot's boobed."

"It's incredible, sir." Briggs executed a series of anxious shifts from one foot to the other, like a child with a full bladder.

"Incredible be damned. It's happened, man." The commodore leant forward in his chair, head bowed in hands, elbows on desk.

"I mean, sir. If only . . ."

"If only you would keep quiet, Briggs, I might be able to think."

"Sorry, sir."

The commodore resumed his grief-like posture which the lieutenant-commander knew from experience denoted intense concentration. He'll come up with something, reflected Briggs, any moment now. Sure enough it was not long before the little man rose to his feet and began a fast quarter-deck pacing of the office. Briggs meanwhile tussled unsuccessfully with the problem. How on earth could one guess what had happened? he reflected. How could such a carefully planned operation have gone astray?

His imagination boggled and he gave up. For want of something better to do he went over his last round of golf. Finding that equally distasteful he looked out of the window and thought no more.

The commodore stopped pacing, gave his assistant's back a baleful look. "I suppose you recall that on the strength of your undertakings I gave VCNS the assurance that neither British nor Norwegian interests would be put at risk by *Daisy Chain*."

Briggs turned away from the window. "Yes, sir. I'm most awfully sorry."

"Sorry! I should damn well think so. Now listen to me, Briggs. I am at this moment extremely angry and you happen to be in the line of fire. Why? Because the queen bee planner of *Operation Daisy Chain* was none other than Lieutenant-Commander William Beresford Briggs. I should think you'll be fired, and that I may say would give me a great deal of pleasure if I weren't involved too. Someone, and I suspect it may be you, has done something extremely stupid. As a result your Chinese fantasy has become a monumental cock-up. And I am left carrying the baby." The commodore paused for breath, took a few more paces. "I really don't know," he said desperately. "I just don't know what we're going to do with this bloody Russian."

"Couldn't we have the sod shot, sir?" Briggs appeared to be dazzled by the brilliant simplicity of his proposal. The commodore, however, greeted it with a chilling stare. "You're either mad, Briggs, or trying to be funny. I dislike both."

"Sorry, sir. I can't imagine . . ."

"I'm sure you can't. So please have the good sense to keep quiet." The commodore got back to the pacing business, head forward, hands clasped behind his back. He stopped beneath the gilt-framed portrait of Nelson which hung over the blanked-off fireplace at the far end of the room. "Wonder what you'd have done, old chap?" he thought with affection. Belatedly, he recalled that Nelson was only forty-six at Trafalgar, whereas he was already fifty-three. The "old chap" seemed somehow inappropriate.

At that moment—afterwards he put it down to inspiration borrowed from the great man's portrait—he saw a glimmer of light at the end of the tunnel. "I tell you what, Briggs." He stared thoughtfully at the unhappy lieutenant-commander. "This bloody Russian wants to be treated as a defector. Well, he shall be treated as one—to the letter. Our ship found him alone—repeat alone—on a life-raft north of Vrakoy, well clear—repeat well clear—of Norwegian territorial waters. We picked him up. As soon as he realized it was a British ship he said he was a defector and claimed asylum. In accordance with British policy our captain took him into custody, told him he'd be vetted on arrival in Britain, whereafter the decision about asylum would be taken at the political level. Got it? Until then he is to be kept incommunicado."

"Oh, first rate, sir. Absolutely marvellous."

"It may not be marvellous, Briggs, but that's going to be the story and all concerned are going to stick to it."

Briggs now showed some signs of anxiety. "A problem occurs to me, sir. Once he's here—if our Press get hold of him—and they will sooner or later—they may blow the whole story."

The commodore's chin shot out aggressively. "Those bloody Fleet Street butchers can say what they damn well like. It'll be his word against ours. We've got witnesses, he hasn't. And if necessary we'll slap a D notice on the story."

"Well done, sir. I'm sure this is the answer."

"Forget the congratulations, Briggs, and get busy. Draft a signal—we'll have to get Northwood's approval for this one—an immediate—C-in-C Fleet to *Aries*, ordering her to detach, to reverse course and make for the Shetlands at twenty knots. To a position twenty-five miles due west of Muckle Flugga. What's her fuel state by the way?"

"She replenished from *Fleetwave* at midnight, sir."

"Good. Now a signal for McGhee in these general terms—Our passenger is to be told that his request is

227

granted. He'll be treated as a defector, landed on British soil. He is *not*, repeat *not*, to be told where or when, and while on board he is to remain in strict isolation but for the Liang Huis who will stay with him. Got that?"

Briggs, who'd been scribbling on the signal clipboard in his own peculiar shorthand, said, "Yes, sir."

"*Aries* and McGhee to be informed," continued the commodore, "that precise details of time and place of landing will be passed to them in due course."

"Aye, aye, sir. I'll draft those right away." The lieutenant-commander made for the door.

"One moment, Briggs." The commodore held up his hand with the peremptory authority of a point policeman. "I shall have to see VCNS about this. Put him in the picture. Not a job I relish. But before that there are certain things I have to do. In the meantime please understand that there never was an *Operation Daisy Chain* . . . what's more I don't want to hear those words again. Is that quite clear?"

"Yes, sir." Briggs made once more for the door, looking back as he went with the expression of a mouse wondering whether the cat was about to have another go.


The moment he was alone the commodore picked up a phone, dialled an MOD internal number.

"Freddie," said the commodore. "Ratters here."

"Oh. Hullo, Ratters. What's the trouble? One of your lot on the sink again?"

"Listen, Freddie. This is damned serious. I want you to go to Oslo to see Lund."

"When?"

"Now. In the fastest thing your lot's got. Get back here before we open up shop tomorrow morning."

"D'you realize the time? I'm late as it is. Supposed to be meeting Jane at the club. You're making a disaster area of my private life, Ratters."

"I thought you'd already done that. But seriously, Freddie, you must see Lund tonight. It's absolutely vital."

"Well, I suppose I'll have to. What's the problem?"

"Something's gone badly wrong. Come down and I'll tell you about it."

"I see. The first part sounds normal. Not so happy about the second. I'm on my way."

## Twenty-Six

Roald Lund was wearing a dinner jacket, black tie and red carnation. He was a handsome man and knew it.

"You're looking very grand, Roald," said Lewis. "Opera?"

Lund got up from the desk, walked across the sludge green carpet and helped himself to a cheroot. "No. Diplomats' dinner. There's nothing worse. Your message was a real shot in the arm. Left at half time. My hostess gave me a frosty look and a bare-fang smile."

"I couldn't be more sorry, old chap. But as the message said, it's frightfully urgent."

Lund spun a match into the marble ashtray flanked by a silver-framed portrait of his wife and a carriage clock. He opened the door of the mahogany corner cupboard. "Scotch, akvavit, beer, sherry?"

"Akvavit and a beer to chase it."

"You like our strange customs?"

"That one definitely."

Lund poured the drinks, put them on a table between two easy chairs, lowered himself into one and stretched his legs.

"Skol," he said, raising and lowering his glass.

"Skol," echoed Lewis.

"Now, what is it, Freddie?"

"It's a problem. Peripherally, it concerns the *Zhukov*."

"Oh God! Not her again?"

"In a sense, yes." Lewis sipped the akvavit, rolled it round his tongue. "We have it on unimpeachable authority that one of her lieutenants—Ivan Krasnov—has defected." While he swallowed the chaser of beer he watched Lund's face.

"Not difficult to guess who the unimpeachable authority is. Why the stir?"

"His hosts don't want him."

Lund's grey eyes focused on the group captain. "So that's how peripheral it is?"

"You're very perceptive, Roald."

"Was that your *great power laying on something special by way of an intelligence gathering operation*?"

Lewis managed to look shocked. "Good heavens no. There isn't the slightest connection. We don't rate as a 'great power' these days. Thought you knew that."

The Norwegian tipped the end of his cheroot against the big ashtray. "Perfidious Albion," he said. "At it again."

"You do us an injustice, Roald. One of our submarines exercising north of Vrakoy found him on a life-raft. The sort carried by small boats. There was dense fog at the time. You can check with your people. Our submarine picked him up. As soon as he realized it was British he declared himself a defector. Requested political asylum."

Lund looked doubtful. "Did he say how he got there?"

"No. He refused to discuss that. Could have been a Norwegian fishing boat. Some other small craft."

"Sounds highly improbable."

"Not as improbable as you think. There was a US submarine not far from ours. The *Rockfish*. Our captain, Bill Boyd, says that a high-powered US Navy skimmer came alongside at three o'clock this morning. Mistook Boyd's ship for his own in the fog. Boyd had a chat with the coxswain before the skimmer pushed off. Gave him the distance and bearing of *Rockfish*. Boyd says the skimmer came from the direction of Nordvag Bay, going like a bat out of hell. Three crewmen in it. They might have had

230

something to do with Krasnov and the life-raft. It was soon after that he was found."

"Did Boyd ask the coxswain what they were up to?"

"Yes. He said they were doing a radar exercise with *Rockfish*, their mother-ship."

Lund hauled himself out of the chair, crossed to a window from which he could see the lights of the harbour and the dark spread of Oslo Fjord through a curtain of rain. "What was Krasnov wearing when Boyd picked him up?"

"No uniform. Navy blue roll-neck sweater, blue denim trousers."

Lund thought of Martinsen's report made earlier that day: Krasnov's uniform jacket and the other clothing found on the rocks in Nordvag Bay. "Well, Freddie," he said. "How can we help?·We certainly don't want him. If you're trying to sell him to us you can forget it."

Lewis held up his hands in protest. "My dear Roald. Nothing could be further from our minds. It's your advice . . ." he looked round the office, playing for time while he hunted for the right words, "your channels of—what shall I say, communication—we think might help."

"I don't follow. Perhaps you could be more explicit."

"This is a funny business, Roald. We don't want Krasnov. You don't want him. Who'd you think might like him?"

Lund said, "Well, first on my list would be the KGB. I take it you don't mean them?"

"Definitely not. After all the chap's a defector. We have to honour the political tradition."

"You seem to be going to a lot of trouble not to."

"No. That's not fair. We'll not let him down. We want to put him in safe, friendly hands."

Lund moved away from the window. "If you're thinking what I'm thinking and I'm quite certain you are—then yes—I think we may be able to help."

"I thought you'd come up trumps. Splendid of you, Roald." There was sudden exuberance in Freddie Lewis's manner.

Lund said, "You must give me date, time and place.

231

Precise and exact. No margin for errors. And there is one absolute, inflexible condition."

"What's that?"

"No use to be made of Norwegian territory—and that includes our territorial waters."

Lewis followed the akvavit with another generous swallow of beer. "Don't worry about that. There's no question of using your territory." He looked at his flying boots as if there was something unusually interesting about them. "We wouldn't dream of doing a thing like that."

Lund smiled sardonically. "I'm sure you wouldn't. Not like the 'great power' which winkled him out of Vrakoy."

"Yes. I do wonder. Those US chaps. Really." Lewis at his most bland, shook his head. "Never miss a trick, do they? Of course they have fantastic resources. But one must hand it to them. They're highly professional."

"Aren't they?" said Lund. "Now. Let's have it. Date, time and place."

Lewis produced a pocket wallet, took from it a slip of paper. "This is provisional. Specific date, probable time, general locality. I'll confirm tomorrow."

Lund read it. "Mind if I keep this?"

"Wonder if you could make a copy? Now. It's no more than a dozen lines."

"You trust no one, do you? Not even me." Lund spread his hands, shook his head in despair. He was fond of Freddie Lewis. "Your glass. Akvavit?"

"Yes. Love it." He handed it over. "It's nothing to do with trust, Roald. It's training. You're subject to the same rules. Never part with a document that identifies the originator."

"Of course. I was pulling your leg." The Norwegian poured the drinks, put them on the table and went to the desk. He made a handwritten copy, returned the original to Lewis. "No guarantees," he said. "We'll do our best. It's fortunate that Martinsen flew in from Vrakoy this afternoon."

"Stirring tales to tell? How's the old *Zhukov*?"

"Likely to be towed off the rocks in a day or so. The Soviet salvage people seem pretty efficient."

"Good for them. And cheers." Lewis held up his glass.

"Skol," said Lund. "Martinsen told me a few other things. Like Krasnov's disappearance. The murder of the *Vise-Ordforer*, Kroll. The disappearance of a Chinese couple with Hong Kong passports." He stopped to see how Lewis was taking that one but the group captain was imperturbable, examining a broken fingernail. "Caught it on my car door yesterday," he explained. "Sorry. You were saying?"

"Non-return from mountain climbing of two Frenchmen from Bordeaux."

"Tell me. Who killed Kroll? And why?"

Lund shook his head. "We don't know who. We think we know why."

"Can I be told?"

"Yes. But not for publication. He was a double agent. CIA—KGB. Probably no longer active. And rather a nasty sort of Quisling in '39-'45. That's enough to get yourself killed."

"Yes." Freddie Lewis nodded. "There's a good deal of mortality around currently. Our SIS lost a couple of operatives last week. One an old friend of mine. Used to be in the same squadron. Their cover was blown. Shot as they tried to get away."

Lund was sympathetic, asked where it had happened. Lewis said, sorry he couldn't remember. Lund apologized. Shouldn't have asked, he said. They returned to the subject of Martinsen's report.

"Strange happenings for a small island," said Lewis. "No knowing these days, is there?"

"Small islands have their uses." Lund looked up from refilling the glasses but Lewis was not reacting. "Skol." The Norwegian raised and lowered his glass. "Here's to a happy ending for Krasnov."

"Skol," echoed Lewis. "We did London-Oslo in thirty-eight minutes."

"Not bad," said Lund. "What in?"

"The new job. Sepecat Jaguar B. The training version. We've a couple for familiarization. Not in service yet."

"You still fit enough to be a passenger in one of those?"

233

"Just about. Nice young pilot. Did everything gently for me."

"Lucky you." Lund looked at his watch. "You'll have to excuse me, Freddie. I've got to see Martinsen about this. Then back to dinner. Make amends with my hostess and my wife."

"Give Anita a big hug for me. Put all the blame on Freddie. Not that they'll believe you with your track record." He took Lund's hand. "Can't tell you how grateful we are. Any time you think we can help let us know. We'll do our best."

Lund shook his head. "I'm sure you will, Freddie."

It was not until well after midnight that Martinsen succeeded in getting a reply from Karen's flat.

"Been on the town, have you, Karen?"

"Lars! How marvellous! Yes. Dinner."

"Dinner and what?"

"Talk. Lots of talk."

"Who with?"

"Listen to him! The dishy Major Lars Martinsen is jealous. Isn't it marvellous."

"Not jealous. Curious."

"You brute. You would spoil it. Joe Kalmeyer. He has beautiful manners."

"Big number in your life?"

"Not really, Lars. You're my big number."

"Say that again, Karen. I like it."

"I love you, Lars, you wretch. You're never here. It's like being in love with a shadow."

"Got in this afternoon. Off again tomorrow morning. Can I see you?"

"Now? You must be crazy."

"I am. Can I come?"

"Of course, darling."

"Lovely. I'm on my way." He hung up the phone and for a moment stood frowning, worrying about the relationship which had developed, the emotional involvement, never intended yet desperately real. And it was Joe who'd introduced them. With what motive was hurtfully evident.

The greatest problems of life, reflected Martinsen, are those with which we confront ourselves. Shrugging away his thoughts, he put on an overcoat and went out, locking the door behind him.

It was cold and misty in the street and pools of rainwater reflected the lights of the city in abstract nocturnes.

# THE EIGHTH DAY

## Twenty-Seven

The ship's clock on the wall of the office in Whitehall showed ten-thirty. Beyond the windows the Mall basked in the gentle sunshine of autumn morning.

"Who did you deal with at SB?" asked the commodore.

"Haydon, sir." Briggs shifted his weight from one foot to the other. "He's McGhee's boss. Fully briefed on *Daisy Chain*."

The commodore managed a low-key short. "Pity a few other people weren't. Might have avoided this monumental clanger. Anyway what did you find out about the dropping point?"

Briggs laid Admiralty chart 245, Scotland to Iceland, in front of the commodore much as a waiter would a tablecloth before a hungry diner. "Round about Esha Ness. Here, sir. The general area you suggested." Briggs's pencil poised over the Shetlands. "On the north-west coast. Just above St. Magnus Bay. It's a remote, isolated spot. Nothing there but the lighthouse, a broch and a few scattered crofts. Open moorland, no trees. The crofters run Shetland sheep, fish and dig peat."

"Where did you get this scenario from?" The commodore regarded him dubiously.

"McLelland, sir. In the Hydrographer's office. He was up there recently on a survey. Told him we wanted the local scene for an offshore oil project we have to vet."

"How far from Lerwick?"

"About forty miles."

"Accessible by road?"

"Yes. McLelland says about an hour and a half's drive from Lerwick. Fairly slow road."

The commodore found his fingers beating time to Haydn's Fifth Symphony. He at once stopped when he realized why.

"Of course," he heard Briggs saying. "They'll have to walk the last mile. I've allowed twenty-five minutes for that."

"H'm. Well let's get back to Haydon. What have you arranged with him?"

"I told him that a Soviet naval officer claiming to be a defector would be landed somewhere between Muckle Roe and Ronas Voe. That until debriefing had taken place we wouldn't know whether he was the genuine article or a plant."

"You used the word 'landed'?"

"Yes, sir. They'll think in terms of a boat bringing him ashore."

"That, Briggs, was a bright idea."

"Thank you, sir."

"Now remind me . . . at what time precisely and where do we put him down?"

Watch it, thought Briggs, the old boy's up to his usual tricks. After all it was he who'd decided the time, and the place in general terms.

"At five o'clock tomorrow morning. It'll be dark. One mile north-east of Esha Ness Lighthouse. There's an ancient deserted broch there overlooking the inlet. He is to wait in front of the broch."

"All brochs are ancient, Briggs. Tell me, did Haydon raise any difficulties?"

"He was a bit querulous about what he called the awfu' vagueness of it all. Who was going to land the man? Why could we not say exactly where and when? He thought we were leaving an awfu' lot to the police at Lerwick. Wanted to know if we'd cleared it with the ICC."

"What did you say?"

"I said we had cleared it with them, sir. That the only reason we couldn't give the details was that we didn't have them. That as soon as we did we'd pass them to him."

The commodore looked at his assistant with mild approval. "I must say you've always been an accomplished liar, Briggs."

"Thank you, sir. One does one's best."

The older man stretched his arms and yawned. "Sorry. Dinner and a theatre last night. Rather a hairy party. Now where were we? Yes. Did you make it absolutely clear to Haydon that under no circumstances are any preparations to be made at the Shetlands end, other than to ensure that Lerwick has a patrol car with two local policemen standing by from six o'clock in the morning?"

"Yes, sir. I made that very clear. Said we'd give him ample warning to get the patrol car there on time. Haydon wanted to know why we didn't pick the chap up immediately he came ashore. I said we had given certain undertakings to certain parties upon which we could not go back."

"A frightful sentence, Briggs. But I get the drift."

The commodore left the desk and began his customary quarter-deck pacing, hands clasped behind his back, head thrust forward. He stopped suddenly in front of the lieutenant-commander who was almost a head taller. "You realize that everything now depends on the Lerwick police not arriving before time. We've had one first-class balls-up with *Daisy Chain*. We can't afford another."

"I fully appreciate that, sir. I assure you the police will arrive post and not ante the event."

The commodore cocked his left eye, the angry one, at

Briggs. "I suppose you know that *post* means after and *ante* before?"

"Yes, sir. I do."

"Good. Stick to English when planning, Briggs. If this one goes wrong you'll be flogging vacuum cleaners in Upper Tooting." The commodore's manner softened. "I'm afraid I've been rather unpleasant to you since things went wrong. Pity you happen to be in my line of fire."

"Not at all, sir." Briggs set up his most reasonable smile, "I realize you've had to get it off your back somehow."

The commodore didn't much like that so he gave the young man a frosty look and went back to his desk.

"And surely, sir," Briggs was being unusually bold, "the *Aries* signal about the boffins being delighted with the results of exercise Kilo Zulu ... Well, surely one can hardly write off *Daisy Chain* as a flop after that."

"I'll let you know how surely when we've seen the last of *Daisy Chain*. And that can't be too soon for me." The commodore was shuffling papers on his desk. An infallible sign of impatience. "Let me see those signals as soon as they're drafted."

"Aye, aye, sir. Will do." Briggs hesitated. There was a question he very much wanted to ask, yet he felt pretty certain it would invite trouble. The commodore looked up. "What are you waiting for?"

That decided it. Briggs took his courage firmly in both hands. "I was wondering, sir, if you could let me know why he's being put down in the Shetlands at five o'clock when it is your intention that the police should pick him up at seven o'clock?"

The commodore shook his head. "At times, Briggs, I despair of you. I should have thought it was perfectly obvious. He will be arriving under cover of darkness because we don't want it known how he arrived or who brought him. By allowing a two-hour interval between his arrival in the Shetlands and his apprehension by the police we accomplish our purpose. Got it?"

Briggs replied with a doubtful, "I see, sir," and made for the door. He had an unpleasant feeling that the commodore was keeping something from him. It wouldn't by any means be the first time.

When his assistant had gone the commodore picked up a phone and dialled an MOD internal number.

"Lewis here," answered a cheerful voice.

"Come down to my office will you, Freddie. It's urgent."

"Be with you in a trice, Ratters."

# THE NINTH DAY

### Twenty-Eight

The pilot of the Wasp helicopter tapped the shoulder of the man next to him. "Muckle Flugga," he said, pointing to the flashing light on the port side. "Another five or six minutes to Esha Ness. See the light there? Dead ahead."

Liang Hui nodded, looked round at Krasnov. The Soviet lieutenant's head bandage covered his eyes. "We'll be landing in a few minutes," the Cantonese shouted to him in Russian. There was no response. Liang Hui remembered the ear plugs and smiled sympathetically. He looked at his watch. Five minutes to five. It was fifteen minutes since they'd taken off from *Aries*. The Royal Navy was nothing if not punctual.

The pilot switched off the navigation and dimension lights, throttled back and the Wasp began to lose height. It was dark, a night of no moon, but stars shone brightly in a clear sky.

When the light at Esha Ness was two miles ahead the pilot turned the helicopter south-east. Flying low he followed the southern shore of Ronas Voe. A mile down it he swung inland, leaving to port the flicker of light from Heyler. Soon afterwards he switched on the landing lights and put the helicopter into a slow turn. They'd almost completed a full circle when he said, "The broch is ahead. Almost under us now." The helicopter hovered. Liang Hui looked down. The stone tower was on the edge of the circle of light beneath the Wasp.

The pilot chose a patch of moorland close to the broch, lowered the Wasp on to it, switched off the landing lights. He turned to Liang Hui. "Okay. Keep your heads down and make it snappy. Sooner I get out of here the better."

Instinctively, like a woman patting her hair before entering a room, Liang Hui adjusted his shoulder-holster before opening the port door. He climbed out, crouching low, uncomfortably aware of the whirling rotor blades. Once on the ground he leant back, reached for Krasnov, told him to keep his head well down, helped him out. Bent double, the two men moved away from the helicopter. The pilot opened the throttle, the engine screamed its head off and the Wasp lifted clear. The pilot swung it to the north-west in a steep turn and made for the sea.

Liang Hui unwound the bandage from Krasnov's head, removed the ear plugs and handed the Russian a pencil torch. "Come on," he said, "You lead. We're making for that stone tower." He turned Krasnov in the direction of the broch and they set off across the heather. When they reached the tower they picked their way between fallen stones as they made through the open arch. The roof had long since gone, it was cold and damp inside but thick jerseys and duffle coats helped keep them warm. Liang Hui shone his torch round the walls. "Sit on those stones over there," he said. "Don't move until I tell you." Krasnov sat awkwardly on the pile of stones, Liang Hui leaning against the wall opposite.

A long silence followed, broken at last by the Russian. "What are we waiting for?"

"We're on British soil now," said Liang Hui. "You'll be picked up by the local police soon after daylight."

"And then?"

"They'll hand you over to the Special Branch."

"Who are they?"

"The British security police. You'll receive the usual treatment given to a defector. There are certain formalities. Debriefing, that sort of thing. When you're cleared, when they're satisfied you're not a plant, you'll enjoy the privileges of political asylum."

"What are they?" Krasnov's hoarse voice was full of doubt.

"The life of a citizen in the West. In a free society. You'll have friends. There are a good many defectors."

The Russian was silent, thinking of what had been said. "You talk of me as a defector. As if I'd done this voluntarily." He was burning with resentment. "You know it was forced on me."

"I don't know what you're talking about." Liang Hui shone his torch in Krasnov's face. "You were found on a life-raft north of Vrakoy. When they picked you up you said you were a defector, claimed political asylum."

"That's a pack of lies." The Soviet lieutenant's voice rose in a confusion of distress and anger. "You know it is. I was taken from Kolhamn by force. At gun point. Then drugged. I remember you in the *rorbu*. You and that Chinese woman."

Liang Hui drew a deep breath, eyed him severely. "Try to keep calm, Krasnov. You're suffering from hallucinations. They can be dangerous. May jeopardize your freedom. The British might think you're a spy. That wouldn't be pleasant, would it? Stick to the truth. It's safer. There's no disgrace in being a defector. Remember we have witnesses. You have none. And we're giving you the political asylum you asked for. A new life lies ahead of you."

Krasnov's voice trembled with frustration. "I've heard stories of the lies and deceptions of the imperialist capitalist powers. I had begun to believe they might be propaganda. Now I know differently."

Liang Hui ignored the remark and they relapsed into silence. Later the Cantonese said, *à propos* of nothing, "What made you think you were in a British ship?"

Krasnov didn't answer so Liang Hui repeated the question.

"It was not a matter of thinking. I knew."

"How did you know?"

"Never mind. It's not important." The Russian shook his head.

Sitting on the pile of stones waiting, cold, miserable and frightened, wondering what the future held for him, Krasnov considered Liang Hui's last question. He managed a smile in the dark because the explanation he was not prepared to give was so simple, the precautions the British had taken so elaborate. His thoughts went back to the steel cell in which he'd awakened.

After the interrogation, when he was still dazed, suffering from shock and drugs, they must have taken him there, laid him on the stretcher, covered him with the blanket. He had vague recollections of a steel door clanging, the sound of a key turning. He must have slept for hours. When he woke he remembered his surprise at finding his wrists and ankles no longer bound, his eyes no longer masked. Not that he could see for there was no light in the cell, but the mask had gone. The plugs were still in his ears, so he pulled them out and stuffed them into a trouser pocket. For some time he lay there thinking.

Later, very quietly, he got off the stretcher, stood up and tested his limbs. He found with relief that they were undamaged. Slowly, and with no plan other than a desire to satisfy curiosity, to do something rather than just sit in the dark, he explored the cell. It was small, four by three metres, with shelves along one side and across the far end. He felt along the empty shelves, found the door, the handle and the keyhole. It was a solid door, perhaps watertight because no chink of light showed through between it and the frame. Afterwards he found the light switch, turned it on. He'd been in the dark so long that it took time to accustom his eyes to the brightness of the single lamp in the deckhead. For the first time he saw the stretcher and blanket, the rows of empty steel shelves, and realized that he was in a ship's storeroom, not a cell. He was about to sit down on the stretcher when something caught his eyes. It was on the highest shelf, on the far side; the edge of something just clear of the line of the shelf. He reached up, touched it, pulled it down.

It was a cheap plastic briefcase. He unfastened the zip, took out the contents. There were a few letters in their envelopes, some writing paper and unused envelopes, a number of itemized forms—stores lists or something of that sort, he decided—a postcard and a cyclostyled sheet.

Krasnov could not speak or understand spoken English, but he had an elementary schoolboy's knowledge of the language. Enough, for example, to understand the significance of the address which appeared on each envelope:

> Laundryman Fah Ko Lin,
> HMS ARIES,
> BFPO—Ships.

All bore a London postmark and a franking date within recent weeks. The itemized lists were headed HMS ARIES, as was the blank notepaper with the ship's crest. There was a Danish postcard: a photo of Copenhagen harbour, the mermaid at Langelinie in the foreground. The writing in the body of the card was Chinese but it was addressed in English to:

> Mrs. Fah Ko Lin,
> 147 Sellaby Street,
> Soho,
> London, W.1.

Most important of all was the cyclostyled sheet headed *HMS ARIES, Visit to Copenhagen, Sept. 20—24, 1974.* Signed by the first-lieutenant, it gave the programme of events and entertainment arranged for the ship's company during the course of the five-day visit. The distribution list at its foot had an inked tick against "Ship's Laundry."

Krasnov put everything back in the briefcase, replaced it on the shelf where he'd found it, and pushed it well out of sight. He turned off the lights, lay down on the stretcher and covered himself with the blanket.

After that he lay in the darkness thinking about his discovery.

As the pale greys of morning began to show in the sky above the broch, they heard somewhere in the distance the solitary bleat of a sheep, followed by the cries of seagulls.

"It'll be daylight soon," said Liang Hui.

Sitting disconsolately, chin in hands, elbows on knees, body bent forward, weary with waiting, stiff from the damp and cold of early morning, Krasnov ignored the remark.

Not long afterwards they heard a distant rumble, low at first but growing steadily stronger.

"Helicopter," said Liang Hui. "Coming in from the sea." He stood up. "Stay here. I'll take a look." He held the revolver in front of him, prominently, in such a way that the Russian must see it.

"Don't worry." Krasnov shrugged his shoulders wearily. "I won't move."

Liang Hui went outside and looked in the direction from which the sound was coming. Before long he saw the dark blob coming in low over the moor towards the broch, the sound of its engine an enormous intrusion on the quiet landscape. When it had almost reached the broch it hovered less than fifty yards from him. There was just enough light to identify it as a Sikorsky Sea King. He looked for markings on the helicopter's fuselage but there were none. It looked curiously anonymous in its coat of dark olive.

He moved away from the stone tower while the Sikorsky, its engines and rotors reaching a crescendo, descended like some awkward bird, crunched on to the heather and rocked gently as the undercarriage spread and recoiled, the engines throttled back, the spinning rotors drooped. A door opened and two men in flying suits climbed out. Bending low they came clear of the Sea King and walked quickly through the dusk of early morning towards him.

"Morning," said the tall man. He had the brown skin and bony features of an American Indian. "I guess we'd better exchange credentials. You're Liang Hui."

"Correct," said the Cantonese. "And you are Vincent Strutt?"

"Right," said the American. From nowhere it seemed he produced a revolver, poked it into Liang Hui's ribcage. "Get your hands up, China boy," he said in a loud voice. "And keep them there."

Liang Hui raised his hands high above his head. The thick-set man frisked him while Strutt kept him covered. The frisker found the shoulder-holster, pulled the gun from it, stuck it into the pocket of his flying-suit. "Okay, Vince," he said. "He's clean now."

Strutt said, "Right, China boy. Take us to him. Make it fast. We're short on time."

Hands still above his head, Liang Hui turned towards the broch. As he did so he saw the Soviet lieutenant slip back from the entrance and knew that he'd been watching. When they got into the broch Krasnov had his back to the far wall, his arms spread. His face was drawn with fear. "What's this?" he stammered, his eyes on Liang Hui.

The Cantonese shook his head, reached higher with his hands. "I don't know." His voice was thin, reedy. "Ask them."

"That'll do, China boy," said Strutt. "We'll take over. Just watch your step. You're liable to get hurt." He turned to Krasnov and spoke to him in Russian. "Come along, Lieutenant. You're with us now."

Krasnov held back but they each took an arm and marched him out of the broch while Liang Hui stood watching helplessly. Once outside Strutt released the Russian's arm. "Put him in the chopper, Stan," he said. "I'll join you when I've dealt with our friend here."

He came back to Liang Hui who had moved outside the broch, arms still above his head. "I guess we'll be going now," said the American. "Everything okay?"

"Yes. They'll be coming for me soon."

"How's this guy Krasnov?"

"He's not a bad youngster. Treat him decently. He's had a rough time."

"Sure. We'll look after him. Have him on board in twenty minutes. In the States in a few days. He'll be okay if he's straight."

"He is." Liang Hui could see the Soviet lieutenant's face pressed to a fuselage window; very white and frightened he looked.

"Okay. Bye now." Strutt lifted his right hand and fired two shots at Liang Hui at point blank range. The Cantonese dropped his arms, clutched his stomach, bent double and wobbled absurdly before collapsing. Strutt ran towards the helicopter, climbed in through the open door. Before it was shut the jets shrieked and screamed up the sound scale and the Sea King lifted clear.

Lying on his side, Liang Hui watched it making off, flying low across the moor towards Ronas Voe until it was lost to sight in the morning twilight. Only then did he get up and dust himself. He spent the next few minutes hiding the shoulder-holster in the heather.

An hour later he saw a car stop in the distance. Two men climbed out and set off across the moor towards him. It was full daylight now. To the west he could see the tower of the lighthouse at Esha Ness and in the north, across the Voe, the black bulk of Ronas Hill.

As the men drew close he saw their uniform, the checkered bands round their peaked caps and the sergeant's stripes. When they reached him the sergeant, pink-cheeked and brown-moustached, smiled in kindly fashion. "Ye'll be expecting us, I dare say."

Liang Hui looked at him with uncomprehending eyes. "*Rada vas videt*," he muttered.

The sergeant spoke to the constable. "It's him, Andrew. But it's nae guid speaking the English. He'll nae understand."

"Looks more like a Chinaman than a Roosian to me, sergeant."

"There's many 'o them that's Mongolian, Andrew."

He turned back to Liang Hui. "Come along wi' us then laddie. We'll be lookin' after ye." He took Liang Hui gently by the arm and the three of them set off towards the car.

# EPILOGUE

Bodo, Oct. 13—A Soviet naval officer is reported missing from Russia's ballistic missile submarine 731 stranded on Vrakoy, an island of the Vesteralen Group off Norway's west coast.

The officer, Lieutenant Ivan Krasnov, was last seen in the island's only town, Kolhamn, on the night of Oct. 11. A search is proceeding.

The Soviet Embassy in Oslo has dismissed as unfounded reports that the officer may have defected.

Oslo, Oct. 16—The Soviet ballistic missile submarine 731, refloated on Oct. 12 after stranding on the Norwegian island of Vrakoy, is reported to have been lost in a gale off the North Cape while under tow to Murmansk by Soviet salvage units.

*Reuters*, quoting eye witnesses on board a Norwegian tanker in the area, said: "The submarine, supported by floating 'camels', was under tow by three tugs with an escort of Soviet naval vessels. During the gale the 'camels' broke free and the submarine sank bows first soon afterwards. Tugs were seen attempting to pick up survivors but the severity of the gale is thought to have caused heavy loss of life."

On Monday *Pravda* reported briefly the loss at sea in recent weeks of a submarine used for training. An official in the Soviet Embassy, Oslo, said: "We have no information about this."

Washington, Oct. 18—Officials of the United States Navy in the Pentagon have confirmed that a Soviet naval officer, Lieutenant Krasnov, has defected and is now in the United States.

The lieutenant was an officer on board ballistic missile submarine 731 which recently foundered in a gale off the North Cape while under tow by Soviet salvage tugs. Prior to the disaster in which many lives were lost, the submarine had been refloated after stranding on the island of Vrakoy off the Norwegian coast. She was being towed to the Soviet Naval Base at Murmansk for repairs.

The *Tass Agency* here refused to comment on Lieutenant Krasnov's reported defection.

*21st October, 1974*

254

# Take a trip to the world of
# ADVENTURE

# There is nothing like spending an evening with a good Popular Library

# Mystery